STRIKE MIDNIGHT

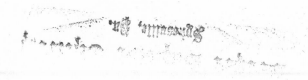

STRIKE MIDNIGHT

D.M. MATERA

VB
VINE
BOOKS

Servant Publications
Ann Arbor, Michigan

Vine Books is an imprint of Servant Publications
especially designed to serve evangelical Christians.

Published by Servant Publications
P.O. Box 8617
Ann Arbor, Michigan 48107

Cover design by Multnomah Graphics/Printing
Cover illustration by Chris Ellison
Text design by Diane Bareis

94 95 96 97 98 10 9 8 7 6 5 4 3

Printed in the United States of America

ISBN 0-89283-859-0

Acknowledgments

Special thanks for the extensive editorial assistance provided by:
>Fran Matera, Ph.D.,
>The Walter Cronkite School of Journalism and
>>Telecommunication
>Arizona State University

Thanks to my crack aeronautical advisor:
>Captain Lonnie Haney
>America West Airlines
>Phoenix, Arizona

To my biblical advisors:
>The Reverend Charles and Nina Hoblitz
>Baptist International Missions, Inc.
>P.O. Box 9215 Chattanooga, TN 37412
>(Mission fields: Mozambique, South Africa, Germany, Russia)

And to Beth Feia, Michelle M. Armbruster, and Ann Spangler at Servant Publications.

DEDICATION

To Nina, who planted a seed by a creek in North Carolina that kept me on the straight and narrow and made this all possible.

ONE

"It's coming in. You've got to intercept—immediately."

The words spun through Matt Slade's head. The ringing telephone had jarred him from a deep sleep. He was expecting an early morning call, but not this one.

"You've got to intercept. Are you awake?"

The voice on the phone belonged to Colonel Pete Hutchinson, United States Air Force, liaison to U.S. customs and other "special projects." Matt sat up in his bed and glanced at the clock. It was 4:30 A.M.

"You want me to clear out?"

"Negative. Not clear out. You've got an intercept."

"A mission? Now?"

"Affirmative."

"What about Mindy?"

There was an uneasy pause, then Colonel Hutchinson spoke again.

"She's heading in. She hit Key West a half hour ago. Leveled her down to the rock."

"Winds?"

"Two-seventy-five to three hundred."

"Three hundred!"

"She's a monster."

"You want me to lift off in *that*?" Matt ran a hand through his hair and shook his head in disbelief.

"That's their cover. They're letting the hurricane run interference."

"Great cover!" Matt muttered. "I'd be nuts to take off. Let it go. It'll probably crash."

"It's the Raven."

The code word instantly blasted the remaining cobwebs out of Matt's brain. The "Raven" was a stolen Concorde SST turned supersonic cocaine carrier. It had been hijacked from London's Heathrow Airport and was sold to a South American drug cartel. Customs, the Drug Enforcement Administration, the FBI, the CIA, Interpol, the KGB, Scotland Yard, and half the cops and spies on the planet had been trying to recapture the jet ever since. But the prospect was fading fast. According to intelligence reports, the pirated SST was painted black, armed, and had been souped up beyond its already supersonic capabilities. The one Customs jet that sniffed out its trail was blown away when the SST hit a speed of 2,500 knots—nearly double its capacity when it rolled out of the assembly plant—and soared to an altitude of 75,000 feet, a good 30,000 feet higher than the maximum operating level of the F-18 fighters sent to capture it.

For the previous two years, the Raven had been used to smuggle huge shipments of cocaine and heroin to specified locations around the world. It could outfly and outgun everything in the sky. The drug cartel's high-priced aeronautical engineers had even managed to silence the noise of the big jet's powerful engines, making clandestine landings and lift-offs that much easier.

"We have a confirmation," Colonel Hutchinson continued. "You've got to get in the air."

"The conditions aren't right," Matt argued.

Hutchinson paused—reconsidering, Matt hoped. Even without the hurricane, it was a high-risk mission. No one knew exactly what capabilities the Raven had, or what form of firepower Matt would be going up against if he could match the speed and altitude of the stolen jet. But both men knew there was no avoiding it. The order had been given.

"This goes right to the top. They want that jet bad. It's been flooding the country with drugs. How many have died? How many kids? You and Jill will be having children of your own one day."

"Don't lay that guilt trip on me."

"There's no time to argue. You can land in Orlando or Tampa afterward. You've got to get your Starling out of Miami anyway. I'll contact you after lift-off with further instructions."

Matt quickly dressed, grabbed an apple, and picked up the phone to call his fiancée. She had been holed up at the Omni in Atlanta since the day before, when Hurricane Mindy cleared Cuba and began making a beeline for Florida. Most people just moved inland away from the coast, the standard hurricane evacuation procedure, but Matt wanted Jill out of the state. He didn't want to risk losing her to a freak gust of wind. He dialed the Atlanta area code, then stopped. His call would only worry her. But if he didn't call and something happened . . .

He continued punching the numbers.

"Hello?" The voice was groggy. Matt had forgotten the time. "Matthew, is that you? What's wrong?"

"Nothing. I just wanted to tell you I love you."

"It's so early. What's wrong?" she repeated, instantly waking up.

"Nothing. Really. I've just gotta fly a jet to Orlando, that's all."

"Where? Orlando! Are you still in Miami?"

Oh no, Matt thought. He had told her the night before that he was already in Orlando.

"No, I mean Jacksonville. Jacksonville. Everything's OK."

"You're still in Miami, aren't you?"

"Are you kidding? Miami's about to get creamed. Only an idiot would be here. There. I just forgot where I was. You know how I get."

"Give me your number. Let me call you back."

"There's no time for that," Matt said, stalling. "I'm in Orlando. Near Disney World. At the Epcot Hotel. It says so, right on the key."

"There is no Epcot Hotel," Jill countered, growing more emotional by the second. "You're still..."

"Near Epcot, I mean," Matt interrupted. "Listen, I've got to go. You don't want me to get stuck, do you?"

"No. Go. Right now. When will I see you?"

"Soon. Got to run. Bye."

"I love you," Jill said. The fear in her voice was so strong it was unnerving.

"Great move," Matt mumbled to himself. "That certainly eased her mind."

Instead of being safe in Orlando, Matt had spent the night alone in the bleak barracks of a small military installation about twenty miles west of Miami. The base was surrounded by the muck swamp of the Everglades. It could be reached only by air or airboat—or by riding bareback on a bull alligator. Matt's superiors wanted him there until the last minute. They hadn't told him why. The reason was now obvious.

As he exited the barracks, a gust of wind ripped the door off its hinges and sent it flying into the dark. It happened so suddenly that Matt was left standing with his hand outstretched, his fingers shaped around the missing doorknob.

He made a sprint for the jeep and was nearly blown to the ground before stumbling into the hood. The wind whipped the rain with such force that it felt like needles piercing his skin. He crawled around to the passenger side, which was sheltered from the wind, opened the door, and climbed over the seat.

Things improved only slightly when he sealed himself inside the covered jeep. He mopped the rain from his brow and found blood on his hands. Something in the wind had sliced his temple like a razor. He glanced in the rear view mirror. The wound was survivable.

The rain was so heavy the windshield wipers were useless. He could barely see the pavement as he headed across the airfield. But driving blind wasn't a major concern because there was no chance of encountering anyone or anything in his way. He could have driven through downtown Miami that morning without running into a soul. The governor had issued an evacuation order the day before that covered all of South Florida's coast. Even the Miami Beach police department had cleared out at midnight.

Matt checked his compass and headed the green military jeep due east. Driving an automobile by instrument was absurd, but if he could land a jet that way, he certainly should be able to navigate a short jaunt across a deserted airfield. His calculations were dead on. The jeep's headlights reflected off the hangar building, the only hangar on the mini-base. Matt drove close to the cinderblock wall until he located the narrow service entrance, then pulled the jeep inside.

But the respite from the storm was temporary. Matt pushed a button to open the hangar door, climbed into the cockpit of the Starling—the single remaining jet on the outpost—and roared back out into the fury.

The Starling was one fearsome bird. It had been specially constructed to counter what the cocaine barons had done to the SST. Smaller and lighter, the one-of-a-kind XK-V fighter could reach an altitude of 80,000 feet and was capable of speeds up to 3,000 knots. For firepower, it contained a .45 caliber lightweight machine gun and five ten-inch heat-seeking "Hummingbird" missiles.

In short, it was a $200-million mechanical hitman, created and designed for one specific assassination.

Matt was surprised how easy he was able to lift off. The good feeling didn't last. He couldn't gain any altitude. The winds from the approaching hurricane had created an atmospheric force that acted like a lead blanket in the sky. Beneath this unexpected ceiling were wind shears and angry air pockets. The Starling began to drop. Clicking on the radar screen, Matt saw an even more troubling sight. The images were so foreign to his senses they took a few seconds to register. Instead of the blips and dots of distant jets and airplanes, he could see the outline of the city. It was the first time he had seen buildings from that angle on radar.

Suddenly Matt realized what was happening—he was flying twenty feet off the ground! The ominous outlines of the downtown skyscrapers were approaching fast.

Matt tried again to gain height, at least enough to carry him over the buildings. Despite the jet's powerful engines, it was hopeless. He made a quick calculation and stationed himself right over the center line of Flagler Street running through downtown

Miami. He dropped the wheels, just in case, and lowered the jet to ten feet off the ground—low enough to fly under the Interstate 95 overpass.

Then he prayed.

The Starling roared between the buildings. When he cleared the cluster, Matt jerked the throttle and just barely cleared the monorail track that stood twenty-five feet off the ground and ran perpendicular to Flagler Street. He banked sharply to the right and slid past the thirty-story Pavillion II Hotel on the bay. As he passed, the sonic boom of the jet shattered the hotel's windows.

The instant he was over Biscayne Bay, the bizarre atmospheric condition eased, and the impenetrable ceiling lifted. The Starling soared into the sky.

Matt wiped a trickle of blood out of his eye. As he did, his radio came alive.

"Slade, where are you?" Colonel Hutchinson screamed.

"Over the Atlantic."

"Already? We haven't been able to make radio contact."

"I was flying low."

"Low? That's doesn't stop the radio."

"Depends on how low."

"Don't take any unnecessary risks," the Colonel ordered.

"Risks? When I get out of this, Colonel, the first thing I'm gonna do is kick your tail," Matt threatened. "Then I'm gonna find out who's pulling your strings and kick their tails."

"The storm approached faster than we anticipated," Hutchinson explained, ignoring the threats. "We didn't know. We thought you had a good fifteen minutes."

"No excuses."

"Just get the Raven. Then you can do anything you want. Have you got it on your screen?"

Matt looked down. He was relieved to see the radar reflecting more conventional images.

"I think so. Just behind the Bahamas. About Angel 50."

"That's it."

"It wasn't difficult. He's the only other moron out here. What do you want me to do?"

"We'd like to bring it here, to Tampa. We have a force waiting."

"What if they don't cooperate?"

"Take it out."

"Has that been cleared?" Matt asked.

"All the way to the top."

"It's an expensive piece of machinery."

"It ain't ours. It's British. Tough luck. They lost it."

"OK. I'll swing around and come up its tail."

Matt swung the Starling low and wide then rocketed up to 50,000 feet—Angel 50—in a blur. Within twenty minutes, he had laid in five miles behind the Raven. Curiously, the big jet had displayed no sign of detecting him. It was cruising along at a lazy 1,500 knots, skimming the top of the hurricane. Matt switched to a radio frequency the intelligence reports said the airship was using.

"This is U.S. Customs. Please identify yourself."

In the cockpit of the Concorde, pilot Jorge Veciana jumped in his seat as if a rat had taken a bite out of his leg. He had been listening to a tape over his headphones, but had the radio rigged so any communication would interrupt the music.

"This is United States Customs," Matt repeated. "We have an interdiction escort on your tail. Please identify yourself."

Veciana gulped. He glanced at his radar screen and comfirmed what he just heard.

"This is flight 703 from Santiago," Veciana said. "We had to change course to avoid the hurricane."

"Where is your destination, Flight 703?"

"Miami."

"The Miami airport is closed. You should know that."

"We've had some communications problems. Thanks for the information. I'll divert to Merida."

"You are ordered to land in Tampa. Do you understand?"

"Tampa? No, Merida."

"Tampa. You have no choice. I'll accompany you."

"That's unnecessary. We'll be fine."

"Flight 703, you are ordered to switch over your controls to my remote. I'll fly and land your craft."

"Negative. I'm not authorized to subjugate to a foreign remote."

"If you're a commercial pilot, you sure are, buddy."

"Negative. We're not part of the treaty."

Treaty? What kind of response is that? Matt thought. A Customs remote takeover was international aviation law, not a peace agreement. The pilot was obviously lying, but was he that stupid? A light popped on in Matt's brain. The pilot's voice had sounded familiar from the moment he heard it.

"Is that you, Jorge?"

The pilot of the Raven paused. "Slade?"

"Bingo. Let's cut the games, Jorge. Lock in the remote, and I'll take you in."

"I can't. My airline doesn't allow us to do that."

"And what airline would that be, Jorge? Air Sleazeball?"

"Uh, Aero Argentina."

"Give it up, Jorge. SSTs don't fly out of Chile. They have four-digit flight numbers. There's no treaty. As usual, you didn't do your homework. That's why you flunked out of flight school."

"I learned enough. Graduation was for heroes like you."

"We all knew you'd end up doing something like flying drugs, poisoning children," Matt said. "Once a slime, always a slime."

"Spare me the preaching, Slade. I make more money in one flight that you will in ten lifetimes."

"I sure hope you've enjoyed it, because you'll never spend another dime, amigo. Convicted drug dealers now receive an automatic death sentence—thirty days' implementation, no appeal. And it'll be televised! You're finally gonna be a star."

"Stick it. I ain't going to Tampa."

"Your choice, scumbag. You can die now or die later."

Jorge kicked in his engines. Within fifteen seconds the Concorde was flying at 2,695 knots. Matt clung to his tail like a sparrow hassling a turkey buzzard.

"Not bad, Jorge. That's even faster than we were expecting. My compliments to your engineers."

Matt flicked a switch on his radio.

"Starling to base. Over," he said.

"We read."

"The Raven has refused to release control. It will not cooperate in any way. It is presently taking evasive measures, accelerating at 2600 and climbing. Over."

"You have your orders, Starling," Colonel Hutchinson said. "Please implement before land."

"Hear that?" Matt said, directing his communication back to the Raven.

"I didn't understand," Jorge choked.

"I've been given orders to turn you into a grease slick in the Atlantic. I'd rather not foul the environment like that, so maybe you should reconsider."

Jorge responded by lifting the jet up to 78,000 feet, then rolling over in a 360 loop, a bold attempt to gain the attack position. Matt rode the Raven like a cowboy on a tired bull. When the flip maneuver failed, Jorge dipped, then swerved side to side. Matt shadowed every move. Sweat was pouring in drops from Jorge's forehead. No matter what he did, he couldn't shake the Starling.

"You can't outfly me, Jorge."

A buzzer went off, and a red light flashed on Matt's console. The Heads Up Display (HUD) kicked on and projected a computer screen on the left side of the Starling's windshield. The computer showed an image of the Concorde's guns, turning rapidly.

"No way, Jorge. You move those guns another inch, and I'll blow you away. You can't outdraw me, either."

Matt checked the computer image. The guns turned back to their original position, facing forward. The red light went off.

"Good boy. You're outmatched, amigo. Hang it up."

"Listen, Matt. I've got kids. A wife. I can make you rich. I've got a billion dollars on this run alone. A billion dollars! Think of it!"

"I know better, Jorge. You dumped your wife for a showgirl. You haven't seen your kids in years. I don't want your blood money. You've got sixty seconds."

Jorge plunged the Concorde down, Matt followed, dropping so fast that the increasing G-force twisted up his features.

"We're alumni!" Jorge pleaded. "Brothers."

"You're brother to a jackass. You've got thirty seconds."

"You're not a killer, Slade. I know you," Jorge begged.

"Give me control, and we'll talk. Tampa doesn't have to be the gallows. You can hire some fancy pants lawyer. Cut a deal. Roll over on somebody. I'll testify for you."

Matt heard a hiss, then a peep. He checked the screen to confirm. The Hummingbirds had locked onto the Concorde's vapor trail.

"No deal, Slade. I'd rather die quick than rat out the cartel."

"If you head deeper into that hurricane," Matt said, "you're gonna get your wish."

"I'll take my chances."

"Don't make me do it, Jorge."

"I tried to be a hero like you, Slade. I tried to play it straight. I wasn't smart enough. The Air Force rejected me. So did the Navy. I made it this way. Now I'm flying the best jet in the world. I'm the best. You're not going to take that from me."

The buzzer sounded, and a red light flashed again on the Starling's console. Those warnings were followed by a blue light on the windshield screen. Jorge had engaged his own missiles. The blue light identified it as a Russian-made Apex, an outdated but still potent weapon. A reverse shot from the descending Raven would be little more than an act of desperation, but Matt was in no mood to play dodgeball at 50,000 feet.

Matt squeezed the trigger on his missile launcher. The tiny, dagger-like Hummingbird sprang from the underside of the Starling. He watched, expecting the Concorde to evade the missile. But Jorge didn't even try. He launched his own, then continued his descent.

The Hummingbird missile knifed into the Concorde just under its left wing. The explosion was small but effective. It sheared off the wing, leaving the fuselage intact. The impact and missing appendage sent the black jet spinning madly out of control at 1,200 knots. The centrifugal force killed Jorge before he could eject.

Matt wanted to confirm the kill, only he had his own problems. The heat-seeking Apex missile had missed, but it had circled and was heading in at 3,500 mph. Circled! Even his own Hummingbirds couldn't do that. And the Apex's velocity was a full 1,000 knots faster than the spy books said it could fly, 500 knots faster than the top speed of the Starling. The druggies had obviously jacked up the missile's performance.

Inside the Starling, Matt's alarms were going berserk.

"I get the point," he said, flipping a switch and muting the din.

The missile was closing in on three miles. Matt had only seconds to react. He plunged the Starling deeper into the clouds, flying a zigzag route at nearly five times the speed of sound.

"Come on Mindy, baby. Do your stuff."

Matt felt a heavy thud as he reached the main level of the hurricane. The Starling spun sideways and began rocking. He turned into the wind and fought to keep her steady. Thirty seconds later, the Apex entered the storm behind him. The cool, powerful winds slowed it down, jerked it around, and obliterated Matt's vapor trail, severing the missile's heat lock. Another bell sounded in the Starling to confirm the disengagement. But a second tone followed. Aside from the heat lock, the Apex apparently had a specialized tracking computer that relied upon a visual camera or a sound tracer. Whatever its tracking device, the missile was battling the storm, still coming after the Starling like some maimed psycho killer in a horror movie.

A rush of fear swept over Matt's body. The missile was riding far less steady in the hurricane than his heavier jet, but it was still gaining on him. Matt clicked a secondary HUD switch and projected his weather scope onto the right corner of the windshield. He punched the controls three times, initiating close range searches. In the third quadrant, he discovered what he was looking for. He banked the jet to the left and headed back out to sea, his eyes glued to the digital numbers at the bottom of the scope. He set the voice activator to start at ten.

Twenty seconds later, he heard the first number of the countdown. He checked the radar. The missile had closed to half a mile.

It was going to be close.

"Nine, eight, seven, six."

The missile was a quarter of a mile behind him. The water spout was an eighth of a mile in front.

"Five, four, three, two..."

Matt banked the Starling sharply to the left. For a couple seconds, he lost all control. He miscalculated a fraction and shaved the outer edge of the tremendous twister. Then he slingshotted free.

The missile plunged into the center of the salt-water tornado and was instantly swallowed up. For the next half minute it whipped around a thousand times a second, funneling down into the spout's thin leg, where it dropped softly and harmlessly into the ocean.

Inside the Starling, Matt heard a soft tone indicating the Apex had fully disengaged. But there was no time to celebrate. He had a new problem. The Starling's wild ride along the breadth of the monster water spout had caused the jet to be launched free with an awesome force. Its speed hit 3,200 knots and was increasing 100 knots per second. No one was positive how much the jet's shell could take, but Matt recalled hearing that it would begin breaking apart at 3,800.

That was six seconds away.

Matt hit the brake flaps on the wing. The speed continued to increase. He abandoned the flaps and pointed the nose at 12 o'clock. A vertical climb would take the most energy.

His speed passed 3,800. The Starling began whining as if it were in pain. He checked the altimeter. It had passed Angel 90—

90,000 feet! Matt figured he was either going to explode, or hurl himself into space.

The speed clicked past: 3,900, 3,950, 4,000... 4,200. The Starling screamed.

4,250.

4,250.

4,200!

A buzzer sounded; the speed had stabilized. Matt checked the altimeter again. He was at Angel 110. The terminology had never been more appropriate. He expected to see Gabriel at any second. Instead, an oxygen mask sprang out in front of his face and gave him a start. He strapped it on, inhaled, then eased the jet's nose back down.

"It's OK, baby. Just hold on a few seconds more."

The Starling stopped its eerie crying when its speed dropped back to 3,200 knots. At 2,800, all controls began functioning normally. Matt took off the oxygen mask and punched orders into the computer. A course setting appeared on the screen, and he programmed it in. The numbers waivered slightly. That was odd. He checked the radar. Its reading supported the navigational information. The Concorde had yet to crash!

"Base to Starling! Base to Starling!" Colonel Hutchinson's urgent voice rasped.

"I read, over."

"Matt! Are you OK? We thought we lost you."

"I'm OK."

"We lost radio communication. You blacked out on everything. Radar. Everything."

"I was flying high."

"High? That doesn't stop the scans."

"Depends on how high."

"Are you still fooling around?"

Matt just shook his head.

"Yeah, Colonel, I'm having a real blast up here. A stroll in the park. Wish you were here."

"Did you confirm the crash?"

"Negative. I show the thing still airborne."

"So do we. But moving extremely slow. Almost dead in the air. We thought our intruments had malfunctioned."

"No malfunction. It's still up. I don't know why. But I'm gonna find out. Over."

"Be careful."

As he neared the computed location, Matt was startled to see a giant red blotch in the sky. It looked like a pool of blood hovering in the clouds.

Did it bleed? Was it alive?

Matt dashed the bizarre thought. He cut his speed, gripped the control stick, and placed his finger over the trigger of his mounted gun. He had no desire to tangle with another steroid-fed missile. As he closed in, the vision came into focus. What appeared to be a huge red parachute billowed out from the Concorde's tail. A scan showed no activity in the Raven's cockpit. He released his grip on the weapon and angled closer. As he approached, he could see that some of the chute's lines had snapped from the speed and strain, but it had held. It was a strange sight. The jet was slowly drifting under the parachute like a broken toy.

Matt realized that the fact that he could see at all was just as baffling as what he was seeing. What happened to the hurricane? Visibility had gone from zero to fair. The winds were balmy. For a second, he thought the hurricane had hit its own turbos and raced up the coast. He double checked his location, then the weather scan.

He was right smack in the hurricane's eye.

"Jorge, you poor fool," he mumbled, watching the wounded jet slowly floating down to earth. "You had a chance."

Matt saw a flash of light from a small explosion as the Concorde finally splashed down in the shallow water near the beach. He circled and passed again. Because of the massive parachute, a good chunk of the Concorde survived the crash. Its battered carcass lay in the surf like some giant sea monster complete with a hooked, pointed beak.

After a second pass, the winds began increasing. Matt arched the Starling back up into the sky, above the hurricane's force.

"Starling to base."

"We read."

"Mission completed."

"Did you witness the crash?"

"Affirmative. Over water."

"Just barely, according to our radar. You cut it razor thin. Another few seconds and it would have hit a hotel."

"I created a tourist attraction," Matt cracked. "Now the kids'll have something to play on when they go swimming."

"That was a needless risk, Slade."

"I knew the pilot."

"A friend?"

"Nah, he was bad news. But I knew him. That made it personal. It's different when it's personal."

"Sorry. What slowed its descent?"

"It released this mother of a parachute and drifted down like a feather. Must have released automatically."

"Shame we couldn't save the machine."

"Maybe we did," Matt said. "I think one of the engines is intact. The water helped cushion the blow, and the wind snuffed the fire like a candle."

"The cargo may be intact?"

"Possibly. But it'll probably drain out before anyone can get to it. The fish'll be wired to the gills. That's about it."

"We'll send a recovery team as soon as the hurricane passes."

"Downing it was your order," Matt said.

"We take responsibility. We couldn't risk another Sarasota."

"Roger. That was a mess. This punk probably would have tried to do the same thing."

"Those are their orders. Bail out and destroy as much as they can," Colonel Hutchinson said. "Enrage the public. Make us look like the bad guys."

Matt didn't want to dwell on that prospect. The Sarasota disaster nearly scuttled the aggressive interdiction program. A wounded drug jet smashed into a junior high school in a ball of fire, killing 645 students and teachers. A hundred or more survived the initial crash and came running out of the building, screaming in agony, drenched head to toe with burning fuel. Some made it all the way to the street before the fire consumed them. The pilot of the Customs jet went into shock.

"That SST was unbelievable," Matt said, changing the subject. "It handled like a fighter. You know who their engineers are?"

"I'm sure the CIA knows," Colonel Hutchinson responded. "Very few people have that kind of skill."

"What's the latest on Mindy?"

"She should be right under you. Heading toward Miami Beach."

"I've got a belly full of fuel left. I think I'll take a look."

"Negative. The winds are too strong. Just come on to Tampa. Your bird's valuable itself."

"Roger. What's with all these hurricanes, anyway?" Matt asked, idly continuing the radio conversation. "This is what, the tenth this season?"

"Thirteen. Letter M. Mindy. Thirteen."

"Thirteen? What's going on?"

"The gods must be ticked off."

"Real scientific, Colonel. Thanks."

Matt cut the engine down to cruising speed and headed south for the coast. As the shore came into view, he could see buildings being eaten away like they were made of sand. The disturbing image made him loosen his grip on the control. The jet spun in the wind. Matt accelerated and struggled to regain control.

"Slade, get out of that hurricane, now! That's an order," the voice on the radio screamed.

"Roger."

Matt righted the Starling and lifted it back to safety. In seconds, he was clear again. He set a course for Tampa.

"What did you see?" Colonel Hutchinson asked over the radio.

"I don't know. I don't think my brain has accepted it."

"That bad?"

"You got any beachfront property, Colonel?"

"A condo in Delray."

"I wouldn't plan any vacations in the next decade or two."

An impatient rapping on the door woke Matt from a sound sleep. He got out of bed, groped for his pants, found them lying across a chair, and quickly slipped them on. Then he looked around and realized he had no idea where he was.

"Wait a minute," he shouted, buying time.

His eyes darted around the room, searching for anything that would shed some light on his latest bunk. Paris? Madrid? London? No, the room was too stark. The pants were military issue, not the dress slacks of his airline uniform. The sleep began clearing from his head. He was on a military base. Miami? Everglades?

Tampa.

When he opened the door, the morning sunlight was so bright he had to turn away and shade his eyes. Glancing up, he saw the silhouettes of what appeared to be two military officers.

"Mr. Slade, you are wanted at headquarters immediately," one of the uniforms said.

"What time is it?"

"O six thirty."

"Can't this wait?"

The uniforms didn't answer.

"Do you guys want to come in? It ain't much, but it's home."

No smiles. Nothing. The uniforms were stone.

"How long do I have?"

"O six-forty-five."

"Fifteen minutes? Generous of you."

He shut the door, washed up, shaved, and was out with a minute to spare. The uniforms said nothing as they drove to the base, not even to each other. He was taken to a large building and escorted into an office. Waiting inside was Colonel Hutchinson, Matt's contact.

"Sit down, Slade."

"Is this your office?"

"Temporarily."

"All your offices are temporary. Why don't you let me see the real one—the one with the pictures of the wife and kids?"

Colonel Hutchinson let the question slide.

Matt took a seat. "What's up?"

"The political winds had to blow. We didn't know how the Raven downing was going to play."

The colonel rose from his chair and walked around to the front of the desk. He sat down, looked at Matt, smiled, and slowly shook his head. The body language meant the politicians were happy. But still, Matt sensed something wrong.

"I thought it was foolhardy, crashing that plane on the beach, but it turned out to be quite a media event," Colonel Hutchinson said. "It even survived the hurricane. Nothing else did, but the Raven was anchored in the sand and protected by a tidal surge. It reappeared like magic after the hurricane passed. Clean and shiny, like it just came out of a carwash. The President and the candidate flew down and held a press conference right on the shore. The corpse of the pirate SST made a heck of a backdrop. Evil personified."

"I saw it on the news last night," Matt said. "Great video. Senator Vincent leaned down and scooped some of the soggy cocaine right out of the sand. Then he made this wave-the-flag speech about cleaning up the drug problem. Pretty dramatic."

"Playing off the hurricane was doubly effective," Colonel Hutchinson continued. "People want good news. The rest of the news down there is catastrophic. But amid all the devastation, you planted a bright beacon of hope and a testament to human courage."

"The Good Guys won one," Matt said, just a tinge of sarcasm in his voice. "The vile drug dealers were defeated."

"Exactly. And the Republicans are going to play it up. They've edited the press conference into a series of ads that'll run until the election. The polls this morning show that Senator Vincent has come back from ten points down. The election is now dead even, and the Republicans have the momentum. The President expects it to carry the party over the top."

"Nothing like some last minute TV visuals to swing an election," Matt quipped. "I'm sure this wasn't a consideration when they decided to send me out in the middle of the biggest hurricane in history..."

Colonel Hutchinson looked away. Matt continued, searching out the colonel's eyes and boring in. "... to attack a jet that was faster and better armed than I'd been warned."

"We didn't know. Honest."

That was probably true. Or at least true as far as Colonel Hutchinson was concerned. The colonel was a decent man. But someone must have known.

"You're the best, Matt. A survivor. I can't explain it, but it's true. Those missiles the Raven was carrying were unbelievable. We managed to save three and take them apart. The technology's incredible. How did you beat it?"

"Jill has an in with God."

Colonel Hutchinson laughed. "I wouldn't be surprised."

He complimented Matt on his good fortune in finding a woman like Jill. Matt brushed it off as luck, then steered the conversation back to the point.

"I didn't know you were so interested in politics, Colonel."

"I'm not. They briefed me on all this election stuff so I could talk to you."

"About what?"

"The media is screaming for the pilot. They want to make you a hero."

"No thanks."

"Why not?"

"A couple of interviews on TV? A story in *People* magazine? Not interested. I just want to get married. Have some kids. Go back to my job at the airlines. Boredom. I lust for boredom."

"I'm glad to hear that. It makes my job easier. For some reason, the powers that be don't want you to come forward."

Matt tried to suppress a laugh.

"It was never a consideration, was it?"

"No. I don't understand it," the Colonel said. "We've kept you under wraps in case anything went wrong on a mission. But now that you're a hero, I don't see the point. We need heroes. Especially after Sarasota."

"You really don't know, do you?" Matt marveled, getting up from the chair and pacing the room. "The government's good. Real good. They play a shell game with everybody."

"Meaning?"

"You thought you were the only one yanking on my chain?"

"I guess I did. It's not surprising, considering your talents. Then I guess you'll also understand why they're so hot to get you out of the country."

"It figures. Where?"

"We'll fly you to Andrews, then to London later this morning. You'll reunite with your regular TWA crew there. They've been assigned three weeks on the Europe and Asia routes."

"Oh, come on. Is that necessary? I can lay low on a domestic route. I'm getting married in a month."

"I know. Elaine and I received our invitations. Don't worry, we'll get you home in time. They're just afraid some enterprising reporter will hunt you down and splash your handsome mug all over the tabloids. Like I said, I'm in the dark on the reason. But I did sense an air of urgency. Bordering on panic."

The colonel returned to his seat behind the desk

"The idea of you becoming famous terrifies them. Whatever else you're into, Matt, it must be a lot bigger than smoking drug dealers."

Colonel Hutchinson's phone buzzed.

"Mr. Slade's escorts are here," the secretary announced.

Two starched Air Force captains appeared through the door. Matt met them at the entrance and proceeded to leave. He turned just before exiting the room.

"You wouldn't believe how big, Pete."

TWO

Jill Coette caught the first jet back to Miami the day after the hurricane passed. She rushed to the terminal as soon as she heard on the radio that Governor Gallager had given the OK.

The trip home was unnerving. She could almost feel the hushed sense of dread hanging in the dry air inside the airliner. Only the paranoid and super panicky had fled as far as Georgia. Jill wasn't in that class, but Matt had insisted that she join the trembling in Atlanta. Now she was trapped in an airliner packed with borderline psychotics. Fortunately, few were brave enough to share their thoughts with the strangers beside them. Nobody had any idea what kind of "home" they were returning to. Most appeared afraid to even speculate.

The signals out of South Florida were conflicting. The news reports were horrific, yet the Miami airport had reopened almost immediately to a full schedule of flights.

At the airport, the only noticeable difference was a strange silence. As usual, there were lots of people, people from all over the world. The Miami airport was always a maddening blend of the world's many races, and this afternoon was no exception. Thousands of foreigners owned some stake in Miami, and most were eager to see how much of it was left.

In the taxi on the way to her apartment in West Kendall, Jill was confused to see how normal things appeared. There was a tree down here and there, a palm frond or two in the road, and some telephone wires hanging dangerously low from the poles; but she had seen that many times before. This storm appeared no worse than milder tropical disturbances that had struck almost every summer from the time she was a child.

Still, it was unbelievably humid, even more unbelievably humid than normal. The air was thick with an oppressive wetness that was unlike anything she had experienced before. Her skin, face, hair, even her clothes felt like a soggy sponge. She could all but reach out and wring the water from the air. The ground had been soaked two feet deep by the hurricane's pounding rain, and now the ninety degree summer sun was extracting it back into the sky.

"Where's all the damage?" she asked herself out loud, mopping the water from her forehead.

"East," he said. "Near the water. Much damage there. Bad floods in the south lowlands."

Jill wondered what exactly he meant. His accent was so heavy that it muffled the simplicity of his words.

"Excuse me. Did you say something?"

"It is very bad east, the coast, madam. Hurricanes, they do not go too far, but where they go, very bad."

"Have you seen it?"

"No. Soldiers not allow. No closer than 12th Street. You cannot get to Miami Beach or the islands."

It took Jill a few seconds to realize he must be referring to the National Guard. They had probably cordoned off the most damaged areas to keep out looters.

"Did you lose a lot?"

The driver smiled.

"I did not have a lot."

Jill was embarrassed by her lack of sensitivity, but she sensed the driver knew she meant no harm.

"How long have you been here?"

"Six months."

"Was it difficult?"

"Yes. Four die on my boat. The sun. Terrible. Terrible. Little water. No food. Three others, they drown. Most of us, we cannot swim. We come from an island, but cannot swim. But we come anyway. My brother not make it."

Jill had heard similar stories many times before. Each one touched her deeply. So many desperate people trying to escape to America. They came by any means they could, risking their lives for a chance to work and live with dignity in the paradise they all dreamed about. Over and over she had exhausted herself doing volunteer work in the blistering hot tent cities that would spring up each time a new wave of immigrants arrived. She did her best to care for and assist the frightened newcomers from Cuba, Central and South America, the Caribbean islands, Russia, and a dozen other countries.

The Haitians had it the worst. They were colored so deeply black that even the lighter-skinned American blacks felt superior. Although no one would publicly admit it, the Haitians weren't welcomed like the others. They were the poorest of the poor. Thousands had died making what should have been an easy seven hundred mile trip from Haiti. Just loop around Cuba, bank off the Bahamas, and sail the smooth, clean waters into Miami.

Tourists had made the journey ten thousand times, sipping frozen Rum Runners while sunbathing on the decks of cruise liners and clipper ships. But it was no party for the Haitians. They came packed like sardines in death-trap boats piloted by cruel, greedy captains. They suffered from paralyzing seasickness, dehydration, and lack of food.

For those who survived, their first introduction to the United States frequently turned into the worst sort of psychological devastation. Their exhausted bodies would fill with hope as they saw the American shore for the first time. Then a sleek Coast Guard cutter with a red, white, and blue flag would stream over to welcome them to their new home. Only instead of a welcome, the powerful ship would turn them around and order them back to the nightmarish poverty of Haiti, dashing their dreams forever.

Jill leaned forward and put her hand on the driver's shoulder. "I'm sorry," she said. "I'm sorry we've made it so hard for your people. I'm sorry you had to come now. And face this."

"Oh no," he said. "I prefer face one hundred hurricanes in Miami than one sunny day in Haiti."

Jill would have liked to talk to the driver further, but they had arrived at her apartment and she had so much to do. She thanked him, gave him a far-too-generous tip, and touched his hand as she said good-bye.

The next morning, Jill rose early and immediately began tying into her volunteer network. She was a comparative religion professor at the University of Miami, but classes had been suspended for at least a week, even though the university itself, tucked safely inland in Coral Gables, had suffered little damage.

Jill figured her expertise in various volunteer fields would be especially in demand now. She had been a Licensed Practical Nurse before her advanced studies carried her in a different direction. She guessed that the hospitals would have the most pressing needs, but to her surprise, few people had been injured by the great storm. Florida Governor Estella Gallager had been diligent in enforcing the mandatory evacuation. It was an election year, and voters would be going to the polls in a few weeks. A botched evacuation resulting in scenes of twisted and broken bodies would have doomed her reelection hopes. Thus, Governor Gallager made sure she got everyone out, going so far as ordering the National Guard to comb the beachfront condominiums to roust the stubborn and the stupid. The governor was determined that this time there would be no television movies-of-the-week forthcoming about a tragic bunch of drunken fools having a hurricane party and being blown into oblivion.

Thanks to the governor's iron hand, the evacuation had gone smoothly. Even the big traffic jams everyone had feared failed to materialize. People left at a leisurely pace, by land, sea, and air, for various inland destinations. This was merely another summer. Another hurricane scare. Another quick trek to summer homes, friends, relatives, hotels, or makeshift shelters. The Floridians were getting used to it.

Actually, the whole planet was getting used to it.

As the century had turned, nature began doing more damage than the fifteen border wars that had broken out. Earthquakes, typhoons, hurricanes, hailstorms—after a while it got to be old news. Honolulu burned to the ground when a pair of volcanoes erupted within days of each other, turning the island paradise into a lake of liquid fire. The Philippines and Okinawa were blasted by a thunderous typhoon. An earthquake crumbled Bangkok and Singapore the following year. Jill had taken her volunteer efforts international and signed on with the Red Cross, spending a month in each of the two Asian countries.

Earlier in the year, the long-awaited doomsday earthquake rocked Los Angeles and much of Southern California. The unheard of 9.1 quake produced a monster tidal wave that pulverized San Diego. Jill spent three months on the West Coast, bandaging bodies, giving morphine and tetanus shots, and fielding calls from anxious relatives.

The preacher Jill watched on cable television kept a running scorecard detailing all of nature's rumblings. He was a dynamic fellow, and Jill was fascinated by his weekly descriptions of what it all meant. The televangelist called it a forewarning of things to come and zipped through his Bible quoting verses and prophecies that appeared to make sense. She tried to get Matt to watch, but he waved it off as another fast-buck charlatan with a great toupee and an even better gimmick.

Whatever the cause, at least the Floridians had advance warning. And this hurricane, this Mindy monster, had given far more notice than those that had preceded her.

Hurricane Mindy was the thirteenth hurricane-force storm of the fertile season, an ominous number whose significance wasn't lost on the unusually jittery populace. Had Lance, the hurricane that preceded Mindy, been half as determined, tens of thousands of lives would have been lost. The diehards ignored Lance and refused to evacuate. Even Governor Gallager didn't get overly concerned. Hurricane Lance fizzled out near Cuba, and the natives patted themselves on the back for not uprooting their lives for another false-alarm evacuation.

Mindy, however, was storm number thirteen, and everyone knew she was going to be *The One*—the long-feared killer cane.

The old-timers were the first to sense it. From the moment Mindy sprang from the womb of some angry sea demon down in the Cape Verde Islands off Africa, Seminole Indians, dogs, and the more psychically attuned began twitching nervously. Even the old Conchs in the Keys, who had sat out a score of storm warnings in their lifetimes, got out before Mindy arrived.

And the old-timers called it right. Mindy moved up the Florida coast in a fury, grinding magnificent hotels and luxury condominiums into fine dust. The great storm finally succumbed, as all hurricanes do, to its suicide gene. She landed on the upper peninsula and made a final run—ironically for Atlanta, the place where the most terrified had huddled. Mindy made it all the way to Macon before the land mass stripped her of her power.

Then the hurricane turned savior. She floated across America, drenching the drought-stricken Midwestern farm lands with a nourishing rain.

And yet, for all Mindy's awesome power and destruction, Jill couldn't find a single hospital hallway overflowing with the sick and injured. The handful of coastal residents who had escaped the governor's troops and held their ground were no doubt dead, their bodies never to be found. Everybody else had literally weathered the storm.

Jill ended up signing on with the huge tent city shelter at Miami's Orange Bowl Stadium. She dished out food, organized sleeping arrangements, took care of aches and pains, and comforted those who had lost property or businesses. It was the least traumatic of her past disaster area efforts. Comforting a depressed businessman who rented out beachfront condos was not exactly the sort of labor that had earned Mother Teresa her sainthood. And the folks who lived in million-dollar beach-front condos weren't the type to bake in an aging football stadium for long. The Orange Bowl began clearing out after the first few days. By the second week, it emptied further as sons, daughters, and grandchildren flew in to rescue Grandma and Grandpa. Other relatives came for brothers, sisters, uncles, aunts, and cousins.

Like most Floridians, Jill found her life returning to normal far sooner than she believed possible. The routine began replacing the emergency. For her, the biggest routine centered around thinking, missing, and mostly worrying about Matt Slade.

That was her real full-time job, one she could do anywhere. Matt was always getting into one scrape or another. And those mysterious secret missions for the government troubled her more than she liked to admit.

"Just flying some supplies," he'd lie, but Jill knew better. "I'll be back soon." He would grab her in his strong arms, dramatically kiss her good-bye, give her a tight hug, then vanish out the door to who knows where, leaving her to worry some more.

Jill also had their upcoming wedding to fret over. She had intended to delay it for a few months because of the hurricane, but that decision was meeting with resistance from her friends and family.

"You're out of your mind!" her childhood friend Sylvia admonished, waving her arms wildly and all but hyperventilating. "If I had a hunk like Matt on the line, I'd marry him right in the middle of a hurricane. Don't be a fool!"

Even an old Jamaican woman she worked with at the Orange Bowl First Aid Center offered similar advice.

"Child, you let the mon slip away dis time, you don't know if he be back de next. Big wind and de rain be temporary. A good mon be forever."

Jill laughed at the sage wisdom, but she knew she could count on Matt even if she changed the date. That is, if he stayed alive long enough.

Her father, normally a conservative type, added his vote to the majority.

"That blasted hurricane is the past," he growled, still smarting from the loss of the condo he rented to Canadian tourists for a tidy profit. "We need to move forward."

By the third week after the storm, Jill was all but convinced not to delay the wedding. The west side and suburbs had been wiped clean of all traces of the disaster. People went back to work. Cars clogged the roads during rush hour. Life was going on. But Jill knew it was an illusion. The governor still hadn't opened up the east side or the beaches.

When Matt called from Hong Kong, he left it up to her.

"It's your decision, J," he said. "You're the brains of this outfit."

Trans American Airlines co-pilot Danny Simpson was daydreaming about the lady he had met the night before in Madrid when his thoughts were interrupted by the data on his navigation screen. He quickly double-checked the instruments. Everything was functioning properly. The mechanical confirmation twisted the growing knot in his gut. There was no mistake. The airliner was three miles outside its designated airway and heading in the wrong direction.

He glanced over to make sure that Matt Slade wasn't dozing. Nudging a catnapping pilot was the first step on a co-pilot's checklist in such situations. It was a solution that corrected the problem more often than the passengers in the back needed to know. Danny was disturbed but not surprised to find Matt Slade alert at the controls. Danny had known Matt since childhood, and although his friend was something of an enigma among the fraternity of commercial pilots, he was Mr. Conscientious when it came to flying.

It would have been better if Matt had been nodding off. The discovery of an exhausted but wide-eyed pilot at the controls of a runaway airliner was high on the list of worst possible scenarios. Obviously, Matt had *purposely* swung the blue and white 787 in the wrong direction, yanking it off its strictly-regulated course.

Danny wasn't sure he wanted to know the reason.

The TAA crew was heading home from Asia, Madrid, and Paris via New York after spending most of the previous three weeks in the clouds over half the planet. Ever since management had crushed the pilots' union, workloads had steadily increased. They had crossed so many international datelines and time zones that trying to match body time with Miami time would have taken the skill of a mathematician.

This particular work overload wasn't entirely the result of the loss in collective clout. It was a gift from their team leader, the ever mysterious Mr. Slade—a man the government wanted hidden overseas for as long as possible. Matt, of course, wasn't allowed to let his crew in on the secret. He wouldn't have even if he could. The flight attendants would have lynched him.

"You're drifting. Better steady up," Danny said, barely betraying the edge of fear in his voice.

"I'm gonna take a look," Matt answered. "I'm taking her down early."

Despite the disquieting words, Matt's calm, easy tone of voice immediately relieved the tension in the co-pilot's neck.

"Miami Center will jump all over you."

"We'll see."

"TAA 107, we show you coming in east of your lane," the voice on the radio barked. "Are you experiencing any difficulties?"

Matt looked at Danny and smiled.

"Is that you, Jerry?"

"Affirmative. You OK, Matt?"

"Tired, but fine. I just want to take a look."

"They don't want anybody to see it yet. Besides, it's against regulations."

There was an uneasy pause on the radio.

"You'll get a reprimand," Jerry finally said.

"It won't be my first."

"Or your last," Jerry radioed. "OK, everybody wants to rubberneck. We might as well change the route. Just don't get too low. It scares the wits out of the passengers."

"How bad is it?" Matt asked.

For a moment, there was no response from the ground.

"You guys won't believe it," Jerry said at last.

Danny cut in over his headset.

"Jerry, this is Danny. What about my condo?"

The controller avoided a direct answer.

"Great place, Dan. I love the color schemes."

Matt stifled a laugh.

"So do I," Danny said, growing testy. "I'd like to sleep there tonight. What are my chances?"

"Haven't you guys been reading the newspapers?"

"You can't believe the papers. What about my building?" Danny repeated.

"The lady showed no mercy. Over."

"Roger," Matt said, winding down the communication before further upsetting his emotional first officer. Danny had nearly jumped ship in Frankfurt when he read the first detailed reports of the hurricane.

"Keep an eye on us," Matt requested. "We'll be about ten minutes late. Can you clear with approach and tower?"

"No way. You're on your own."

"Come on, Jerry, be a pal."

There was silence for a moment. "OK, Slade," Jerry finally said, giving in. "But you owe me one."

Matt reached over and gave Danny a tap on the arm.

"You can stay at my place for as long as you want."

"What about my 'vette?"

"It can stay, too."

That wasn't what Danny meant, and Matt knew it. Danny's beloved Corvette had no doubt gone the way of his condo.

He was about to respond when the coastline came into view. It was a bright afternoon. Visibility was nearly perfect.

Too perfect.

"What the—?" Danny muttered. "We should be over West Palm Beach."

Below them stretched miles of virgin white sand and blue and green water. Nothing else. Danny kept looking at his intruments, charting the expected row of beachfront buildings, and peering dumbstruck out the window.

They had read that the property damage was in the billions. But in London, Frankfurt, Prague, Hong Kong, and everywhere else, the rage of Mindy was just another sensational newspaper story, like Los Angeles, Bangkok, and Hawaii had been to those in Miami. But those disturbing foreign news reports said Florida was even worse than California. And this one, as the cliché went, hit Matt and Danny where they lived.

"Where are we now?" Matt asked, looking down at the coastline.

"Downtown Fort Lauderdale, according to the scope. Where's my condo?"

"Probably in Idaho."

By the time Danny's instruments reported that they were over Hollywood and Hallandale, the men knew that everything they had read was true. The forbidden east zone they could see from the air was far more revealing than the relatively undisturbed western areas Jill had been allowed to see by car. As he stared at the barren beaches, Matt couldn't shake the feeling that he was responsible. The hurricane had saved him from the drug jet's attack; without it, he would be dead.

"All this destruction just to rescue me?" he mumbled.

"What?"

"Nothing," Matt dodged. "I'm just numb, I guess."

He tried to convince himself that his guilt was self-indulgent. The world didn't revolve around him. He had just taken advantage of the situation. But if he had faced the Concorde under any other conditions, the custom-made Apex missile would have nailed him dead. No question.

Matt pushed the thought out of his mind and started to head the jet inland toward the airport. He paused, then decided instead to veer further left over Miami Beach. Whatever emotion it stirred—curiosity, shock, suppressed grief, guilt—the coastline was pulling him like a magnet.

"This reminds me of an old *Twilight Zone* episode I once saw," Matt said, trying to divert his racing thoughts. "A commercial airliner was caught in a strange cloud. When it emerged and the pilot tried to land, the airport was a forest full of dinosaurs."

"And then they tried it again," Danny finished, "and they came back to the 1920 World's Fair or something. I saw the episode, too. So what do we do—head out over the Bermuda Triangle and look for a mysterious cloud?"

"If I thought it would work, I would."

Matt lowered the 787 closer to earth.

"Unbelievable," he said, glancing down over Miami Beach. "The Fontainebleau Hilton, the old Eden Roc, the Diplomat, all history."

"Do you know what I lost?" Danny wailed. "My waterbed. The art. The big-screen, quadraphonic television. The octaphonic CC sound system. My white llama rug. The gold and white Corvette Stingray XKJ, special limited edition. All gone! Why go on living?"

"Hey, you've still got your health," Matt cracked, trying to cheer him up.

As the jet made its final approach, Matt was surprised to see how little the hurricane had affected the cities and suburbs beyond the immediate coast. The airport appeared to be totally intact. He could see rows of small houses and apartment buildings unaffected by the storm.

The passengers on Flight 107 didn't appear to be cheered by the intact inland. These latecomers were the types who had put off the inevitable for as long as possible. Some thanked Matt for giving them the unscheduled tour, but most just walked zombie-like into the tunnel and disappeared.

"Snowbirds," Matt told a weary flight attendant, referring to South Florida's bulging population of winter-only, seaside condominium residents. "Coming to curse their fate."

THREE

Matt shot Danny a smile as they pulled into the apartment complex. There wasn't so much as an overturned malaleuka tree in the parking lot. Inside, not a single lamp had toppled onto Matt's rust-colored rug. The irony was hard to miss. While most of his friends preferred bachelor pads with the requisite balconies overlooking the moonlit Atlantic, Matt had chosen to live deep in drained wetlands of the western Miami suburbs. His friends ribbed him about the bird-sized mosquitoes, palmetto bugs, and giant bufo frogs they envisioned wandering in from the nearby Everglades. The truth was, real estate was more reasonably priced the further one ventured from the ocean. Matt's modest upbringing ingrained him with a respect for money that his more affluent friends didn't share.

Besides, Matt couldn't handle a steady diet of the heavy salt air, as beautiful as those balcony views were. And that was fine with Jill. She was a confirmed inlander. She viewed the ocean as little more than a haven for sharks, a spawning ground for hurricanes, the coast a target for floods and tidal waves. The beach was a nice place to toss a Frisbee on a bright Sunday afternoon, but she didn't want to sleep there.

After calling Jill and settling in, Matt found that he was too jet-lagged to nap. Danny paced the room, rambling on about his missing toys.

"Let's go see the beach," Matt said, picking up his keys and heading for the door. "Or what's left of it."

Matt pulled his black Viper out of the parking lot and headed down José Canseco Avenue to pick up Jill. Danny's mood took a sudden turn for the better the moment he entered Jill's home. The place was overflowing with young women in various stages of dress, packed together in the small, well-decorated condominium. They were everywhere—the living room, bedroom, kitchen, even out on the small porch. Jill couldn't say no, and thus had taken in every stray friend and acquaintance who called begging for a bunk.

"Uh, why don't you go on alone," Danny volunteered, eyeing a striking young Nicaraguan woman with thick black curls and a neon-blue halter top. "You two need to spend some time alone together."

"That's real sweet of you, Dano," Matt said. "It's amazing how you're always thinking of others."

"We'll be back in an hour or so," Jill announced.

"Judy, you're in charge. And watch this guy; he's a heartbreaker."

The Viper swirled up the ramp and shot out into the eastbound lane of the Dolphin Expressway. Matt drove as far as he was allowed. A policeman flagged them down near a blockaded area near the bay.

"See, I told you they wouldn't let us get to the beach," Jill said. "No one's been able to even get close."

Matt ignored her and flashed a badge of some kind. Jill strained to see it but caught only a glimpse. Whatever it was, the officer began giving Matt instructions, explaining that there was only one road left that led to Miami Beach from the mainland. The larger bridges had blown away, but the smaller ones dotting the Venetian Causeway had been sheltered by the barrier islands. Department of Transportation inspectors found no structural damage on the Venetian bridges and had certified them for restricted traffic the day before.

"What was that you showed him?" Jill asked as they passed through the checkpoint. "Let me see."

She reached for his pocket. Matt caught her hand and playfully pushed it away.

"Just something I picked up at a gun shop. A pseudo cop's badge. They cost about fifteen bucks. Worked pretty well," he said, giving her that devilish smile he always did when he knew she knew he was lying.

"Don't hand me that," Jill said. "They treated you like you were the President. Let me see."

Jill made a second stab at snatching his wallet. Instead of blocking her attempt, Matt pointed at something ahead through the windshield. They had crossed the last connecting island and arrived on the sliver of land that had once been Miami Beach. The familiar landscape had changed dramatically. All the roads were gone. Driving, however, wasn't a problem. The storm had flattened the land and blown away the loose sand until there was nothing left but hard-packed coral rock.

"What's that?" Matt said, rolling down the window. "That noise?"

They could hear the ocean before they saw it—a loud, deep roar that warned of immense power. Matt slowed the car to a crawl, wary of what was ahead but too curious to turn back.

"Maybe it's a tidal wave!" Jill gripped her hands on the dashboard. "Turn around!"

Matt remained calm. "It's not a tidal wave. The buildings aren't around to muffle the sound."

Jill pondered the explanation for a minute, then rejected it with a burst of emotion.

"It was never this loud, not even on the surf. I think you'd better turn around!"

"We'll be all right. Trust me. I think."

When the ocean came into view, Jill was only slightly less terrified. Matt pressed forward, refusing to give in to his own fear. He didn't stop until he was about twenty-five yards from the crashing waves.

He was right. The waves were responsible for the frightening noise. But hearing them was nothing like seeing them up close... seeing them, and remembering what had been. Florida had friendly ripples that would be hard pressed to up-end a small child playing in the wet sand. Now huge twenty-footers were rolling in from far off shore and exploding onto the beach, spitting foam and mist in every direction.

"Where are we?" Matt wondered aloud. "This isn't Miami Beach. This isn't even Florida!"

Matt and Jill sat stunned, watching one monster wave after another violently assault the shoreline.

"The reef," Jill said. The hurricane must have destroyed it. That's what broke the waves here."

"How do you know that?" Matt asked. Jill knew everything about everything. Her brain was like a computerized encyclopedia.

"I saw something or read about it somewhere. You know, things just stick in my head. Lots of useless information piling up in there. I think I saw it on the Weather Channel. A feature on the ecological impact of weather-related natural disasters."

"Remind me to yank the cable," Matt said. "Between the Weather Channel and that checkbook preacher, I'm beginning to worry about you."

Jill laughed, then quickly grew serious.

"It took centuries to make those reefs. They'll never be replaced."

"Do you think God did this, Jill?"

"I've heard people say that God destroyed everything because the developers blighted the beach. But I don't see God as a destroyer. Sometimes he just lets nature take its course." Jill sighed.

Their fears eased as the sun began to set. The waves were no more dangerous than any other beach with large, rolling whitecaps. Matt and Jill exited the car and began walking near the water.

"Once you get used to the prehistoric waves, this is really beautiful," Jill said. "The way God made it."

"It's too desolate," Matt countered, shivering from the thought. "It feels like we're the last people left on the earth. I wouldn't be surprised to see the head of the Statue of Liberty around the next bend."

"It's as if nature has reclaimed the land," Jill continued, ignoring Matt's more cynical view. "This is the way it must have looked 200 years ago, before the developers took over. Just sand and the ocean. Maybe we're better off."

"Easy for you to say. Your apartment's still standing. Tell that to Danny and Consuela back there."

"Marisol," Jill said.

"What?"

"The girl in the blue halter. Her name is Marisol."

They turned and walked back toward the car.

"I'm sure you were expecting something more like Los Angeles," Jill said. "So was I. That's a mess. Broken buildings. Twisted highways. A sea of rubble. You have to admit, this is better. This, this is so, so clean."

"And so final," Matt said. "At least in Los Angeles, you have something left to remember the way it once was. The ruins have become a tourist attraction. We have nothing here. Zipola."

Matt looked out over the ocean in the dying light. The deepening darkness veiled some of the anger of the waves. The ocean at dusk was magical. It always had a calming effect upon him. He had sought its cure many times during his life. He squeezed Jill's hand, brought her close to him, and kissed her deeply.

"I love you, J," he whispered. "I'm so glad I found you. I don't know what would have happened to me if we hadn't met "

"You'd have met someone else."

"No. I had given up."

He kissed her again.

"I feel you with me all the time," Matt said. "No matter where I am. You're like a boat in the water and I'm the diver below. As long as I know you're up there, I can swim and explore. If you were gone, if your love was gone, I'd surface and then just drown."

"I'll always be there for you, Matt. I promise."

"Don't ever leave," he said, hugging her so tightly she could hardly breathe. "Don't ever leave, Sarah."

Jill's body tensed up. She hadn't wanted to; she wanted to let the mistake slide right by so she could continue to enjoy the moment. But her body betrayed her. Matt sensed it instantly. What he said hadn't registered, but he suspected. It wasn't the first time.

"Did I do it again?" he said with utter dejection, loosening his hug.

Jill rushed back into his embrace, squeezing him for dear life.

"No. No. Really. I just, I just thought I saw a fin. A shark. Over there," she fibbed, pointing out into the water. Matt turned and looked out over the ocean. It was far too dark to make out any such image.

"It was probably just a porpoise," Jill continued. "One of Flipper's cousins. I'm sorry; you know how I am."

"I know," Matt said, hugging her. "That's why I love you."

They began walking again in silence, holding hands. They continued along the beach for a hundred yards before either spoke again.

"Did Danny cancel the bachelor party?" Jill asked.

"No, I did. I figured that after the hurricane no one would be in the mood. We're just going to have some of the guys come over and watch the football game. Nothing special."

After the sun set, the beach became pitch black. The lights of the inland city were too far away to give a sparkle of life to the water. Matt couldn't tell where the sand ended and the water began. He had never seen it so black. Without the visual stimuli to disperse the senses, the pounding sound of the giant waves seemed louder and more menacing than ever. A beautiful dusk had turned into a mean, harsh night. Jill began dropping hints about returning to the car. Matt wanted to hang on to the moment. But the mood, like the reef, had been destroyed.

"Let's get out of here," he said.

Matt grew bored with the football game and quietly slipped into the kitchen to collect his thoughts. He had drifted apart from the old gang since Jill came into his life. Some of his friends were drinking, and their rowdiness was beginning to bother him. He had never participated in that kind of thing to begin with. He was too much of a fitness freak to inflict his body with that poison. Not even a hurricane wake and a low-key bachelor party could change his stance.

As with his government missions, Matt kept his personal preferences, and his emotional weakness, to himself. Most of his jet-set image was nothing more than a shield to hide the awful, un-macho truth. He didn't need to publicize the dark secret of his slow recovery from a crash-and-burn love affair. And he also had no reason to come down on his friends. They battled their own demons. There wasn't a pilot, co-pilot, or flight engineer alive who didn't have some sob story to spill while locked in a small, humming cockpit over a black ocean. Constant travel eroded marriages, ate away at relationships, encouraged infidelity, and distanced the crews from their children.

But there were no CD players in the cockpit. Pilots didn't have Willie Nelson to comfort them during the long, lonely flights with misery-loves-company tales of bad lovers and good dogs. That medicine was reserved for their blue-collar counterparts on the ground, the long-haul truckers.

Enough of this nonsense, Matt thought, snapping out of his philosophical fog. He didn't need to keep the guard up anymore. He had found the cure. He was in love again. Maybe the ache wouldn't return.

Isn't that what he kept telling himself?

"Score's tied. You OK?" Danny said, wandering into the kitchen to seek out his friend.

"Yeah, I was just sitting here thinking. I can't concentrate on football."

"That's no surprise. You should be in the Guinness Book of Records under the heading, 'Most bizarre personal makeover in history, Matthew Slade.'"

"Yeah, it's a sledgehammer," Matt had admitted. "But I'm ready."

Matt was, indeed, going through some serious changes. Not only was he getting married the next day, he was going to commit himself to the Christian faith and be baptized prior to the wedding. Before agreeing to marry him, Jill had insisted that he make a decision about Christ. In a move that stunned his friends, the tough-guy pilot agreed. And his promised moral and religious transformation would not be a phony display of insincerity. Whatever his faults, Matt Slade wasn't a hypocrite. He had promised to become a born-again Christian, and he would do it.

"Are you sure about this?" Danny asked.

"Absolutely. Love is a powerful force. You'll find out one day."

Matt motioned Danny to sit down. He closed the door to block out the play-by-play from the television.

"There's something more involved here than just my own decision," he said. "I can't explain it. Jill. Her being a Christian. The Israel project. The earthquakes. The hurricane. There's a thread."

"Thread? As in, `You don't believe we're on the eve of destruction?'"

Danny sung the last half of the sentence, mouthing the lyrics of an old protest song. Matt barely noticed.

"What went on in Israel?" Danny asked, growing serious. "We've been friends for twenty-five years, since we were kids. We've shared everything. But you haven't said one word about those six months in Israel."

"You know I can't. You wouldn't believe it, anyway. You think what we saw on the beach is bizarre? Man, that's nothing compared to what's going on in Israel. It's science fiction stuff. Star Wars. Doomsday. Unlimited power. World domination. Right out of the comic books."

"Are you ever going to tell me?"

"I hope I don't ever have to. I hope no one ever knows."

"If it's so bad, why get involved? Why keep going on those government treks?" Danny asked.

"You rich boys never understand. Uncle Sam paid for my education. He paid for flight school. I wasn't born with a silver spoon like you. In return, I have to give them time."

"You mean like the National Guard?"

"Similar."

"How much time?"

"Staggered. It started with those four years. Then two months a year, then a month. Now it's down to just two weeks. But they keep adding to it because of special assignments."

"Who do you work for?"

"Everybody. All branches. Military and civilian. Overt. Covert. You name it."

"What do you do?"

"All their dirty work. All the stuff they don't want to get caught doing with their own pristine Air Force pilots."

"Sounds dreadful."

Matt looked away.

"Sometimes it is."

Matt could see Danny wasn't satisfied with his clipped answers. His friend had probed him about his assignments for years. Most of the answers were classified.

"Anyway, it's almost over. Two more months. After that, I'm free. My bill is paid. From then on, it's nothing but big, slow commercial jets full of tourists. The good life."

"But what did you... "

"Enough of the past," Matt cut in. "I'll tell you anything else you want to know. The important stuff."

Danny cringed.

"I knew it was coming sometime. The 'important stuff' like why you're becoming a Christian?"

"Yeah. You should take the jump with me!" Matt said, suddenly becoming animated. "We've done everything else together, from summer camp to college football to flight school. Blood brothers. The Prince and the Pauper."

"You haven't told me much about this Christian thing."

"You haven't asked. Besides, I'm hardly the one to start proselytizing. I'm still learning. You should talk to Jill. She'll explain it."

"I'll bet."

Matt smiled and took a deep breath.

"I don't know. Maybe I am nuts. It sounds strange, doesn't it? But it's not just Jill. I'm not doing this just for her. It's not some line, like the ones you use when you're trying to impress a woman. I've seen your moves. You tell them anything they want to hear. If they're liberal Democrats, you're almost a member of the Kennedy family. If they're environmentalists, you're practically Tarzan. If they're vegetarians, you're Mr. Granola Bar. You're a classic, Dano."

"Hey, the object is not to get into arguments. You know the dance. And what are you talking about? I've never changed my religion for anybody."

"What religion? And how about the time you wanted us to join that cult in Sarasota? A few girls in bikinis approached us on the beach, and you were ready to give up your career, spirit, soul, first-born child, and everything to start worshiping a sand crab."

"Starfish. They were wearing some kind of starfish symbol. And anyway, I wasn't serious."

"Yes, you were! When those girls told you there were fifty more just like them back at the cult house, I had to drag you away."

"I just wanted to visit."

"If you had seen fifty young women in bikinis kneeling in front of a sand crab, I'd never have gotten you out of there. You'd have joined, staged a mutiny, and the next time I went to the beach I'd have seen all these glassy-eyed beach bunnies wearing tattoos of your profile."

"What a life that could have been! I'm still mad at you for stopping me."

"It was for your own good. And theirs."

"So what's the difference in that and what you're doing now?"

"I was about to tell you," Matt said, growing serious again. "This isn't about placating Jill. She tapped something inside me that was there all along. I've always felt this... I don't know, this closeness to God. And because of it, there's been a gnawing inside me to do something about it. It's haunted me most of my life. I also sense that the message involves more than saving my soul, or whatever. There's a greater plan at work, and everything I've done up until now is part of it.

"So what it boils down to is, Jill isn't forcing anything on me; she's helping me find my way. I think that after tomorrow, everything will start getting clearer."

"Or crazier."

"Go on," Matt said, shooing Danny away with a smile. "Go back to the game. You don't need to babysit an old married man like me."

Danny stayed put. He wasn't going to desert his buddy now. "So what makes someone a born-again Christian?" Danny pressed. "Baptism?"

Matt sensed Danny knew more than he was letting on.

"No, I think Jill wants me to do that to make sure I'm sincere. It's the commitment to Christ that's the key. An acceptance of his will over our lives. It's important that people have a personal relationship with God. It means everything for all eternity, and it's so easy for everyone to have. At least, that's what Jill believes. And you know, the commitment is similar to something we said at Mass all those years."

"What's that?" Danny looked puzzled.

"I can't remember right now. Jill knows. One of the creeds. It's really simple. Something about believing. Confessing. And Jesus is in there somewhere. On the cross."

"I don't recall saying anything in Mass that was especially miraculous," Danny said, trying to think back.

"That's the point. When Jill explained it to me, I vaguely remembered it. It was just one of the things we used to repeat back to the priest. But we couldn't have meant it if we can't even remember what it was. According to Jill, you have to say it with intense conviction."

"My father was always telling me the same thing. If it's so great, why have you waited?"

"Now you sound like Jill. I think in the back of her mind, she doubts my sincerity. But I don't think she—or any woman, for that matter—knows what it's like for a guy to get married. It's such a dramatic step, such a drastic change in lifestyle. Doing it all at once—getting married, becoming a Christian—it seems appropriate. It's an end to one way of life and the beginning of another. A rebirth on several different levels. What better time?"

"No time."

"I'm also afraid, I guess," Matt continued, ignoring his friend's jab. "Afraid of giving up my way of life. Afraid of losing all the earthly pleasures."

"Afraid of what it would do to Sarah?"

The sound of the name flooded Matt's brain like a rush of blood from a sudden drop in altitude. He struggled to keep his thoughts from spinning off into a dark dungeon.

"You believe this stuff?" Danny asked, quickly changing the direction of the conversation and letting his friend off the hook.

"I wouldn't be afraid if I didn't."

For a few minutes neither of them spoke.

"I'm really worried," Matt said at last, cutting through the silence. "I can give everything else up. But the memories. Her. That's going to be tough."

Danny looked his friend in the eye.

"You'll get over it. You've already gotten over it. I can tell. You've been different since Jill. You've bonded. With Sarah, it wasn't like that. That was just physical attraction, chemistry. Jill's the better woman. You made the right choice."

"I know."

"So what's the problem?"

Matt paused for a long time.

"The other guys have told me it's not the same when you're married, when you have a family. You have a different perspective about the risks we're forced to take in the air. You start thinking about death. The fear comes in. That could slow your reactions... "

"Come on, Matt. You're a pro. Nothing's gonna change. And how come you didn't feel that way before?"

"You mean when I was involved with Sarah? Most of my anguish came after the break up. Same old story—I didn't realize what I had until I lost it. Even when things were going well, I didn't think about the danger. It didn't enter my mind. Then, after Sarah left, I was so miserable I didn't care if something did happen. 'Shoot me out of the sky, please! End this terrible pain, Mr. Enemy.' But now, every time I go up, especially on my government missions, I think of Jill."

"You haven't frozen up, have you?"

"No," Matt said, pausing before continuing. "Maybe you're right. I'm not going to hesitate. I fly by instinct."

"Yeah, and you're going to have God as your co-pilot now," Danny joked. "The Big Guy will protect you. Isn't that what Jill says?"

"That's what she says," Matt agreed. "She says I've been flying without a net. She says that after tomorrow, when I officially become a Christian, I'll have a whole platoon of guardian angels stretched out across the sky, from one end of the earth to the other."

"I've seen them!" Danny cracked. "But they're not angels. They're mental health workers dressed in white. And they're gonna be coming after you!"

FOUR

Matt was back in high school. He was on a field trip out in the Everglades. The whole class was camping out. A heavy metal song from someone's boom box screamed in the background. It was night—a black, moonless night—and Matt was sitting in a circle around the campfire. Everyone was roasting hot dogs and marshmallows, laughing and telling jokes. He scanned the faces and recognized a score of old friends. He glanced down and saw that he was holding someone's hand. He looked up. The warm orange light bathed her face. The reflection of the fire danced in the corner of her eyes.

Sarah.

He squeezed her hand. She smiled.

A string of molten marshmallow oozed from some unseen stick and sizzled into the back of his hand. He jerked it away and shook it in pain. When he looked up, everyone was gone. The fire was dying and he was out in the Everglades all alone.

He heard a rumble and glanced to his right. A huge black panther charged toward him, fangs bared. He could see the savage hunger in the beast's yellow eyes. Matt tried to run, but he couldn't move. The panther leaped, claws extended...

Matt's eyes popped open. His hands and arms covered his face. When his mind cleared, the sounds emanating from the clock radio grabbed his attention. It was the song from the dream. A minute before, at 9:15, the radio had clicked on. The station was playing a pre-recorded Top 40 countdown. Song thirty-two was some wretched head-banger noise that sounded vaguely familiar.

The song had penetrated his subconscious and fueled his REM return to high school. It took his conscious mind a few more choruses to identify it as a remake of "My Sharona." The pounding anthem had played endlessly during that camping trip nearly two decades before.

The new version was terrible, or maybe the song was terrible to begin with. Either way, it wasn't the right mood to kick off a Sunday morning after a difficult Saturday night. Matt groped for the dial and spun it to an easy listening station. Barry Manilow was singing about New England. It was another oldie, a sweet melody released not long before "My Sharona." In retrospect, the two songs seemed as if they came from different centuries. Whatever the case, Barry Manilow was definitely a better choice for a Sunday morning.

As he lay in bed, a few flickering images of the nightmare returned. It had started out as a pleasant dream. Those were the good old days, especially that camping trip. He would have enjoyed staying a while. But he knew precisely what had snarled the film spinning through the projector in his mind. Same as always. *Sarah.* She wasn't on that trip. She didn't belong in the circle. He didn't even know her in high school. Some other part of his brain had spliced her in. His memory track had quickly spit out the alien image, taking everything else with it and turning a great moment of nostalgia into a B-grade horror flick—"Revenge of the Rabid Black Panther."

He looked at the clock. It was 9:17, Sunday morning—his wedding day. Matt was supposed to be at Jill's aunt's house by ten. He was going to have a private meeting with Jill's pastor and commit his life to Christ. After that, they would grab a quick breakfast, then go to her church for the regular Sunday morning services. They weren't getting married there, but it was going to be a special event anyway. Matt was going to be baptized. And it wasn't going to be a quiet sprinkling on the forehead. As Jill explained it, he was going to have his entire six-foot, two-inch body immersed in a miniature wading pool behind Reverend Vanderwink's choir loft. Although he fully understood the sentiment behind this public confirmation of faith, it still made him nervous.

Three hours and a blow dryer later, they would reconvene at Vizcaya for the wedding. Unless it rained, Matt would be allowed to stay dry this time.

It was certainly going to be an interesting day, Matt thought as he dragged himself out of bed and into the shower. As he was shaving, he caught a glimpse in the mirror of a figure behind him. He stayed calm, continued shaving for a few seconds, then dropped to the floor and charged out at the intruder's legs, knocking him flat.

"What's the matter with you?" Danny screamed. "Are you crazy?"

"What are you doing here?"

"You invited me to stay," Danny shouted, lifting himself from the rug. "Remember? The big breeze. Adios condo. I've been here a week."

"Oh yeah. I forgot."

"Forgot? I'm going to sue. You broke my neck."

"You'll survive."

"I'm gonna sue!"

"I'll plead massive jet leg. You won't stand a chance."

Danny rubbed his neck and checked his limbs for serious damage. Everything seemed intact. He lifted himself off the rug and flopped onto the bed.

"So this is the big day?"

"Yeah, and I'd better get rolling. Do you have something to wear?"

"My wardrobe is scattered across the Atlantic, remember?"

"That's right. What are you going to do? Wait! I've got your tux here. I guessed at the size. I hope you haven't gotten too fat."

"I'd rather have a spare tire around my waist than have all those carrots and celery stalks fouling my belly."

"You can wear one of my jackets with the tux pants for now," Matt offered, ignoring the retort. "Or you can wait here and sit out the church part. I'll come back and get you before the wedding."

"No way. I wouldn't miss seeing you get drowned for the world."

"Baptized."

"Drowned. Like a big shaggy dog that needs a bath. And you'll probably squirm just as bad."

"I'm cool. Ice cool."

"Keep believing that, buddy."

The adjustable waist on the rental tux slacks solved Danny's cake over carrots dilemma. After slipping on his tie, Matt dialed Jill's aunt's number to tell his fiancée he was on the way. Her aunt had left town, and Jill was using the house to enjoy some much-needed privacy before the wedding. There was no answer. Matt figured she dashed out on some last-minute errand. With Danny tagging along for emotional support, he sprinted out the door, climbed into his black Viper, and drove off.

A million thoughts spun through Matt's head. Dodging missiles in a killer hurricane was one thing. Becoming a Christian, getting baptized, and saying "I do," all on the same day... that was something else. The religious commitment scared him more than the marital one. Was he sincere about turning his life over to God, as he had told Danny the night before, or had he agreed merely to accommodate Jill? Was he really getting baptized because he wanted to, or because the woman he loved expected him to do it?

He tried to dismiss the doubts as wedding-day jitters. His longing for something to believe in, for God, seemed real enough. The fear of spending eternity in hell was also real. Unlike so many people he knew, he had never had a problem with accepting the dark side of the heaven/hell dichotomy. Yet he had struggled for years over his inability, or unwillingness, to respond to God's call. This left a void in his life, an emotional hollowness he couldn't fill. He ached for a personal belief he could enthusiastically embrace. Something to redirect his life and end the emptiness.

And he certainly wasn't going through with this as revenge against Sarah, as some of his friends suggested. For a while, he wasn't sure. Marrying Jill and agreeing to give her Southern Baptist religion a chance would be like a double reprisal. That would show Sarah! The irony was too powerful to ignore.

But that wasn't it.

He had argued passionately to convince everyone else that his acceptance was neither an attempt to make Jill happy nor a ploy to make Sarah miserable, all while harboring traces of doubt in himself. As the time drew near, not only had the doubts vanished, they had been replaced by a strange sense of exhilaration. All his life he had been forced to scratch and claw to accomplish his goals. Nothing came easy. He had succeeded on his own, alone. It built character, but left him physically, emotionally, and most of all, spiritually drained.

"It's what I have to do," Matt said, breaking the silence and glancing over at Danny. "What I want to do. It's time to grow up. Time to listen to the call. And I love Jill."

"I know," Danny replied, picking up on all that was unsaid.

With that settled once and for all, Matt thought about his whirlwind relationship with Jill, and about what an unusual woman she was. She had the face and body of a fashion model, yet she regarded her beauty as relatively insignificant. She could sing like Streisand and could have easily been a pop singer, but that prospect never appealed to her. The only nightingale she wanted to emulate was Florence. And she did that with a passion, trotting around the globe with the Red Cross and demonstrating a heart as big as an aircraft carrier. After receiving her nursing degree, she continued her studies and earned a doctorate in education at the University of Miami. She stayed on as a professor.

She had been a Christian all her life. Her brother Jim had led her to Christ down by a creek one cool morning in North Carolina. She was seven then, and the words stayed with her. Jim became a missionary and took his wife and family to Mozambique, in southern Africa. After the Communists ran him out in the late 1970s, he resettled in Johannesburg.

"How did you meet Jill? You never really told me," Danny asked.

"She flew over to visit her brother in South Africa. I was dead-heading to Cape Town to fill in for a pilot who got sick. When I saw Jill walk in through the tunnel, man, she was like a goddess. Soft brown hair dancing on her shoulders, blueberry eyes embedded with flecks of gold, the smoothest skin you ever saw ... "

"Oh, give me a break," Danny said, making a gagging motion. "'Golden hash brown hair? Eyes embedded with boysenberries?' Where'd you get that, off the breakfast menu at I-HOP?"

"Hey, you asked. I'm just telling you what I felt. And it wasn't even lust. I instantly pictured her in the living room of this big house with a couple of tiny daughters that looked just like her wrapped around each leg. I'd walk in and they'd all scream 'Daddy' and come running over to give me hugs and kisses."

Danny raised his eyebrows and searched his friend's face for signs of a mental meltdown. It was obvious Matt was nervous about the upcoming events. This was the most he had talked in one stretch since they had their first beer in high school.

"I found out where she was sitting and cut a deal with this Japanese guy who had the seat next to her," Matt continued. He was a Sony salesman or something. I offered him my first-class seat, and he grabbed it. I got my bag and ducked into the bathroom to put on my uniform... "

"You changed into your uniform?"

"I didn't want to look like a sleaze. So anyway, I slink down next to her. I start giving the rap of my life, babbling like a fool."

"Kinda like now."

"Yeah, probably. But I'm in my uniform, so I'm not just some axe murderer or something. Anyway, she's terribly shy and understandably wary, but I have her penned in, so she can't bolt. By the third hour, she starts warming up. And you know, for once, she was everything I imagined her to be. Kind. Caring. Smart as a whip. Sweet. Never set foot in a bar. Church-going. Not a flaw, physically or mentally. The Perfect Woman."

"Oh no! Not 'The Perfect Woman!'"

"So you can imagine how this affected me... "

Matt began to whisper this part, as if someone was going to overhear. Danny looked around the small sports car to see who else could possibly be listening.

"My heart was a mess of cracks and craters and busted valves and shattered dreams. But all that vanished. By the time the pilot hit the seat belt light, I was in rock-solid love again, and Jill was getting there. I had dinner with her and her brother's family that night. We've been together ever since."

"Like Ozzie and Harriet. Paradise found."

"For a while it was, then the roof fell in. The following year, her brother and his wife were killed in the riots."

"I didn't know."

"They supported the black cause against apartheid and even had a black church, but a wandering mob from another province didn't understand. In the violence and confusion, all that mattered was their white skin.

"When things settled down, Jill insisted on going to Johannesburg to search for their remains. I tried to talk her out of it, but she was adamant, and I ended up going with her. No one wanted to help us. They were nice enough, and everyone seemed to know Jim, but I got the feeling he symbolized their shame over the less heroic aspects of the rebellion. The whole country wanted to forget and move forward. Jill's presence there only made it worse. We came home empty-handed. She cried for weeks.

"When she stopped crying, Jill began getting deeper and deeper into her faith. While she failed in her mission to find Jim's body, she appeared to have latched on to his spirit. She also began pressing me for a more permanent commitment."

"You should have backed away. She was obviously in shock, on her way over the edge," Danny said.

"Come on. I love her. There's no way I would've left her then even if I had wanted to. That might have pushed her over. It would've been heartless."

"That's what this whole thing is about, isn't it?" Danny said. "Going to church with her. Getting baptized. You couldn't say no if you wanted to."

Matt just stared ahead.

"You know, you're a heck of a guy, Slade. Really. Most guys would have taken off like an F-18. But still, how long can you play Mr. Nice Guy?"

"She just doesn't want anything to go wrong," Matt said, ignoring Danny's insights. "She can't handle any more personal tragedy. But that's not it. I keep telling you. We were meant to be together. It's not like before. Not that agonizing, jealous, head-scrambled kind of love that wrings you out each day. This is real, mind and body love. Adult love. When I'm with Jill, I don't think of Sa ... I don't think of anyone else. For me, that's a miracle."

Matt pulled into the driveway of Jill's aunt's house. Danny was happy there would be no more adrenaline-inspired allusions to true love. But even so, he had learned a lot about his childhood friend during the short drive.

"Listen, would you mind waiting here?"

"Hey, no problem," Danny said, spotting a familiar patch of blue nearby. "I'll wait by the pool. I could use some sun."

"Thanks."

Matt took a few steps, then turned back to the car.

"The next time you see me, I'll be a different person!"

"This I've got to see," Danny said. "But hey, your life's always been a thrill-a-minute. If you're gonna get married, you might as well make the biggest 'splash' you can."

Danny roared with laughter as Matt winced again.

"Cute."

Matt rang the bell, then impatiently knocked on the door. There was no answer. He walked around to the garage to see if Jill's blue Ford was inside. It was. He returned to the door and pounded on it again. Nothing. It was unlike Jill to change her plans without telling him. Maybe there was some mix-up.

He knew there was a key hidden under the mat, but he had avoided using it. He felt it was an invasion of her privacy. This, however, appeared to be an exception. He slipped the key into the lock and entered the beautifully decorated home. Everything appeared to be in order. No sign of a thief or anything heinous. The guest room was the same, except that the bed wasn't made. That was unusual. He looked down and saw Jill's slippers by the bed. An uneasy fear washed over him.

He looked into the closet. Nothing unusual there, but he couldn't find what he was looking for. He walked over to the bathroom. There it was, hanging from the top of the door.

Her wedding dress.

Seeing it gave him a chill, although he wasn't sure why. Aside from the slippers, there really wasn't anything to become alarmed about. Matt checked the kitchen table for a message. Finding nothing, he looked under the table in case one had blown off from the air conditioning draft.

Nothing.

He returned to the bedroom. On the dresser was a blue satin garter edged with white lace. The instant he touched it, he felt a peculiar sense of dread. He quickly put it back down. Next to the garter, he noticed a small, felt-covered box. He lifted the top. Inside was a cross made of twisted gold. An envelope lay beside the box. On top of it was a pretty card with a border of flowers and hearts. The writing on the front said, "On This, Our Very Special Day... "

Inside the card was a poem about the bond of marriage. Opposite the poem, on the blank side, Jill had written the date, and *My dearest Matthew*...

There was nothing else. Jill had yet to finish her personal note.

Matt stared down at the white space under his name. The page was as empty as he felt inside. He picked up the felt box, tucked it inside his coat pocket, then left the house. Outside, he squinted in the bright Florida sunlight and walked to the pool.

"You look like you've seen a ghost," Danny said, glancing up from a lawn chair. "I thought this was supposed to be a joyful rebirth."

"Nothing happened. Jill wasn't there."

"Not there? That's crazy... " He stopped, reading the anxiety on his friend's face. "You've probably just gotten your signals crossed. I'm sure she's at the church."

"I hope so."

"Come on," Danny said, getting up. "Everything will be fine. Don't look so worried."

The two men climbed back into the car and headed for the small Baptist church. They arrived at 10:55. The parking lot was nearly empty, which unnerved Matt even more. He looked at his watch and checked the date. Twice.

"Today's Sunday, isn't it?"

"Of course," Danny said. "What do you think, that we both slept for twenty-four hours? We didn't have that much fun last night."

"Then why is this place so empty?"

"We're early. Maybe Baptists are late arrivers."

"They have Sunday school at 9:30," Matt explained. "The place should be crawling with people. Something's not right."

Matt sprang out of the car and went to the door. It was locked.

A car pulled up in the parking lot. Inside was an older gentleman Matt recognized from when he attended church with Jill.

"There's nobody around. The place is locked," Matt told him.

"That's hard to believe," the man said. "The church is always open. The parking lot should be full. Where is everybody?"

"I don't know."

"You know, my wife was gone this morning," the man continued. "No note. Nothing. She usually comes to church without me—I'm not much of a church man. But I can always hear her rustling about before she leaves. The alarm went off at eight, and she was already gone. I got worried."

"I couldn't find my girlfriend."

"Must be some event we don't know about," the man said. "They move the services around sometimes. The preacher likes to get outside in the cooler months and do flashy things to get people's attention. He held services in a Little League baseball park once. Preached a sermon about hitting a home run for God. I went to that one, being that it was in a ballpark and all. I even listened to him instead of dozing off. He knew his baseball, I'll give him that. Another time, he held a baptismal service by the light-house at the end of Key Biscayne. Dunked people in the ocean. The sun was rising, and dolphins were jumping in the back-ground. It was really something! You could almost feel God's presence, even an old grump like me. I'm not much for snoozing in the pews, but I go to outdoor services. I like those. I'm sorry I missed this one today, wherever it is. You're not real involved in the church either, I take it?"

"I haven't been. But I was planning to be," Matt said. "You mentioned that they had a baptismal service on Key Biscayne?"

"Yeah, why?"

"There was supposed to be a baptismal service today."

"Then that explains it."

"Great! I gotta go. Thanks," Matt said, making a run for his car.

"I think they're having the service by the lighthouse on Key Biscayne," Matt said. "Let's go."

"Wait a minute," Danny cautioned. "Where?"

"The lighthouse at the end of Key Biscayne. Come on, I'm late. Jill's gonna kill me."

"Matt, get a grip. Key Biscayne was leveled, remember? The roads are all blocked."

"That's right! I wonder where they are, then. Jill's gonna mur-der me!"

"What do we do now?" Danny asked.

"I don't know. Go home. Make some phone calls. Wait! I know."

Matt turned on the ignition and they sped off.

"There's something I want to check."

He drove for five minutes, then pulled into the entrance of a nearby park. The parking lot was nearly full. People were playing softball, throwing Frisbees, having picnics.

"Is everything OK around here?" Matt asked a young man walking by.

"Sure. Why wouldn't it be?"

"Is there a lake anywhere in the park?"

"No. Why?"

"Uh, thought I'd go for a swim. Thanks."

The young man hopped into a green Camaro, gunned the engine, then pulled up beside Matt and Danny.

"Nice car. What is it?"

"A Dodge. A Viper."

"That's a Dodge? Cool. Well, I've got to go find my girlfriend. I was supposed to meet her here, but she never showed," the youth said as he sped off.

Matt and Danny looked at each other.

"Let's get out of here," Danny said. "This is starting to get creepy."

Matt was silent as he drove back to his apartment. Something inside told him this was more than poor communication regarding an outdoor church service.

"Don't worry," Danny assured. "It has to be that baptismal service thing. It would be worse if it was just Jill. Then it would be a nightmare. Some freak could have her tied up somewhere, stabbing her with electric probes like that maniac in the newspapers. You know how she's always helping strangers. Weirdos and all. But it's nothing like that. Nothing sinister or terrible. Too many people are involved. There's got to be an answer. We'll find out. Hundreds of people can't just disappear."

"They did last week."

"There was a reason for that," Danny said. "There weren't any hurricanes or earthquakes last night, as far as I know."

"Maybe it was something worse," Matt said.

A child fired a cap gun right outside Matt's window, jarring him from his fitful afternoon nap. He had dreamed so much during the hour that he didn't feel at all rested. All kinds of jumbled scenes twisted through his mind. He was flying a jet full of passengers, only the passengers turned into chickens. The chickens were flying around, squawking, losing feathers, and making a mess of everything. Then he was flying an Israeli fighter, but his co-pilot was a goat. Then he was in church. Jill was there in her wedding gown. But when he lifted her veil to kiss her after exchanging vows, it was Sarah. And he was angry it was Sarah. He wanted Jill. The subconscious revelation was exhilarating. Finally, after all the anguished years, he wanted someone else more. The dream confirmed it.

Matt bounded out of bed. It wasn't until he dialed Jill's number and heard the ringing and ringing of her phone that he realized that the bizarre events of the morning were not part of the crazy quilt of dreams.

He picked up the phone again and called Jill's parents. There was no answer. The wedding was just an hour away. Should he get dressed? Was Jill going to show, or would it be the same "Twilight Zone" scene he had gone through earlier that morning? He had to go. Whatever strange hand was being dealt, he had to play it out.

As he was dressing, he heard something about "missing people" coming from the television in the living room. He rushed in. Matt caught part of the Cable News Network report. The story centered around a California church where no one had showed up. The church normally had about three hundred members. The reporter just kind of laughed it off as a coincidence— "The day everyone was sick at the same time—even the preacher!" The undefeated Los Angeles Raiders were playing a 1 P.M. game against the previous Super Bowl champions, the Tampa Bay Bucs. With the time difference on the East Coast, that meant the televised game started at 10 A.M. out West. "Football fever" was the solution the news media came up with to explain what happened to the worshipers at the First Baptist Church of Santa Monica.

Matt knew better. As he snapped on his black bow tie, his thoughts turned to Vizcaya, the historical Miami mansion turned museum where the wedding was to be held. It was one of the few structures on the inland waters that survived the hurricane. Jill took it as another sign that the wedding should go on as scheduled. She loved the place and had dreamed about an outdoor wedding among Vizcaya's sculptured tropical gardens on the shore of Biscayne Bay. Matt told her that was fine by him. He used to ride his windsurfer right up to Vizcaya's coral dock. He'd sail it back and forth just offshore so the tourists could take "Florida-like" pictures of him sailing through the setting sun. He was doing his part for tourism, giving the Northerners and Europeans the classic sun-drenched paradise photo, complete with a bronzed, sun-streaked surfer boy, to show to their friends back home.

But now he wondered if there would be any photos—any *wed - ding*—photos, taken that afternoon.

Matt was filled with elation as he pulled into the parking lot at Vizcaya. The parking lot was half full. Well-dressed people were getting out of cars and milling about. He recognized nearly everyone he saw. The tension and anxiety of the horrendous morning drained out of him. He threw his fist in the air and bounded out of the car.

In the distance, he saw Danny talking to the crowd. Danny had caught a ride with another pilot who happened by Matt's place earlier. It appeared as if Danny was holding the crowd back, motioning them to stay near the building and not come over to greet Matt. Danny came over alone and met Matt next to a cluster of multi-colored Japanese orchids.

"Come on, we need to talk."

"But everything's all right," Matt insisted. "The people are here."

Danny took him by the arm and led him to a secluded cove on the bay next to the mansion's grounds.

"What's the matter now?" Matt asked.

"A lot of people are here, but they're mostly our friends, Matt. Jill's not here. Her family's not here. The preacher's nowhere to be found. A few of Jill's friends are here. No one knows where she is. Not even the girls at her apartment. Your father's here, but your mom's not. He said he woke up and she was gone. Same story."

"Mom? Mom, too?" Matt said, turning away in despair.

"I called home," Danny said, the tears welling up in his eyes. "My dad's gone."

"Your mom?"

"She's still here. She was crying hysterically. She said the devil grabbed him during the night."

Matt had a strange thought. It flashed through his mind so quickly he couldn't quite get a handle on it. It was something Jill had said. No, maybe it was something he had overheard that preacher say on cable television. Something the guy was talking about one night.

"Was your dad very religious?" Matt asked Danny.

"Religious? When we were young, my sister and I called him 'Father Daddy.'"

"What about your mom?"

"She just kinda went along with dad, you know. Went to Mass, but never seemed to be into it like dad."

"It was the same with my family, only in reverse," Matt explained. "My mom was going to be a nun before she met my father. He was Catholic, but she went to Mass by herself most of the time."

"What does all this mean?"

"I don't know, Danny. Something's stuck in my head, but I can't get it out."

"What are we going to do about the wedding?"

"Call it off. I'll dream up some excuse. Otherwise, the people'll panic."

"You want me to do it?" Danny offered.

"No. I'll do it."

They returned to the backyard of the mansion. Matt walked under the flowered bridal arch and took the microphone.

"Attention, please. May I have your attention."

The crowd, expecting something was amiss, quickly quieted down.

"There's been a last-minute snag in the plans. Jill had to leave town last night on a family emergency. Everything's all right. We'll reschedule the wedding for next month sometime. Since we've already paid for the food and drink, feel free to enjoy yourselves and have a good time. Consider this a practice party."

The announcement eased the tension. The crowd began sipping the champagne and nibbling on the catered finger sandwiches. Matt signaled for his father to come over. They ducked back into the cove. His father looked shaken. He spoke in controlled, measured tones.

"Danny told me that Jill's disappeared, like your mother," his father said. "And Danny's father."

"A man at the church this morning told me the same story."

"Mr. Martinez did, too. His wife and your mother used to go to church together."

"Dad, do you have any idea what happened?"

"No. Do you?"

"I can't put a finger on it. I will, though. You can bet on it. When I do, I'll let you know."

"We're never going to see them again, are we, son?"

"I don't know," Matt said, barely loud enough for his father to hear. "Listen, I'm getting out of here. I don't want to answer any questions. Not until I figure this out. I'll call."

Back at home, Matt lay on his bed staring at the ceiling. He loved Jill more at that moment than ever before. He had taken her for granted, but now that she was gone, the depth of his love began pouring out. The frustration, the feeling of powerlessness, and the strange certainty that Jill was gone forever combined to tear through his mental shield. He took the small box out of his coat, opened the top, and looked again at the gold cross. Then he broke down and cried.

They were the first tears he had shed since he was eight years old, when his cocker spaniel was run over by a car.

He had never cried for Sarah, not even when she left.

FIVE

At the Cable News Network, the phone lines had been ringing continuously since the broadcast about the Santa Monica church afflicted with "Football Fever." The news executives counted 1,500 calls in the hour following the report. That was all their staff could handle. The real number could have been ten, or a hundred times that. The callers were all saying the same thing. A lot of people—friends, family, golf and tennis partners—were missing. The urgency, fear, and desperation in the voices of the callers began unnerving the CNN operators. Many couldn't make it through the hour without taking a break.

CNN had a skeleton staff operating in its Atlanta headquarters. No one on duty knew how to handle the story. Nothing like it had ever happened in anyone's memory. They repeated the clip of the Santa Monica church again the following hour, then pulled it for the rest of the day. The irreverent tone of the reporter and the "football fever" angle apparently had missed the mark. What the real situation was, no one knew.

Ned Johnson, a tall, slender, veteran newsman with sandy hair and wire-rimmed glasses, was the on-call duty executive that weekend. The task was rotated among the top dogs at the network and was supposed to kick in only when something big happened like a political assassination. When Johnson was briefed on the missing people story, at first he ruled that it didn't warrant his on-the-scene input. As the afternoon passed, Johnson was plagued with the creeping fear all newsmen suffer—the gnawing thought that somewhere, a competitor was out working on the story of the century. After dinner, he made the decision to drop by the studio, just to check things out. Entering the strangely dark office, his mood sank. Sunday nights are the dungeon shift in any business. A half-dark newsroom is a particular downer, especially to someone used to the bustle and energy of the nine-to-five life.

Johnson arrived in time to monitor the five commercial networks' weekend reports. Nothing about missing people was mentioned on any of them. The networks worked even smaller staffs on Sunday evening, but Johnson found it hard to believe that they could miss an important story. Therefore, in the herd mentality of journalism, the missing people "must not be that important." Plus, only a few of the CNN employees appeared to be unaccounted for. Johnson retired to his office and made a round of calls. Most of his friends were home.

"So who's missing?" he said out loud to himself.

There remained the disquieting reports that continued to come in from CNN correspondents, combined with the emotional state of the phone operators earlier in the day. Still, the networks' silence made Johnson uneasy about airing an update. He needed more information.

Johnson decided to cut the weekend short and put CNN's vast network of correspondents on notice. Still, by eight that evening, he had yet to piece together a follow-up. Since the original story had been pulled, the calls slowed down to about a hundred an hour. That would be alarming in itself, but compared to earlier, it was manageable. However, the new calls were coming from people who had not even seen the Santa Monica report. They were just calling in news tips about a rash of missing people.

The CNN executive ordered a geographical breakdown of the calls and correspondents' reports. The result showed that all areas of the country were affected, but a slightly higher percentage had come from the southern and southwestern states. Still, there was nothing to pin down as a pattern. Johnson picked up the phone and dialed Mac McCoy, a friend who was an editor at the *New York Times*. When Johnson mentioned the reports he was receiving about missing people, there was a pause at the end of the line.

"You're getting calls from around the country?" McCoy asked.

"Yeah. Why?"

"We, uh, we thought it was limited to New York."

"You people think everything is limited to New York."

"Listen, Ned, let me call you back, OK? Five or ten minutes."

Mac McCoy called back exactly ninety seconds later.

"I'm in my office now. Listen, our police departments have been deluged with missing persons calls. They say nothing before this has even come close."

"It's the same everywhere," Ned added, offering the perspective of his national news force. "All across the country. Every police station you call, from Boston to San Diego."

"Do they have an explanation?"

"The police? Are you kidding? They're playing it by the book. They don't investigate missing persons until twenty-four hours pass. From what I gather, this all happened today."

"The police are doing the same here in New York. But there have been so many calls they're starting to do some preliminary paperwork."

"How are you going to play it tomorrow?"

"We don't know yet," McCoy said. "Some of the big guys have been notified, but they didn't feel it warranted coming in on a Sunday night. Only World War III would warrant that. We'll probably do a short and bury it inside. What about you guys?"

"I don't know. We've got to do something. This is hard to ignore. By the way, what about your staff?"

"What do you mean?"

"Anyone miss their shift?"

"Nothing we can't handle. The usual four or five. But we run a skeleton crew on Sunday."

"Same here," Johnson said. "Whoever's missing, it ain't us."

"Maybe whoever took them doesn't want journalists around," McCoy said, only half-kidding.

"Now that's a thought. Anyway, thanks for your help. I've got to get back to work. We're on twenty-four hours a day, you know."

At 10 P.M., CNN still hadn't aired a story, even though reporters had gathered news footage from New York, Miami, and Los Angeles. The airing was delayed because the Chicago correspondent, Jessica Gale, was having trouble keeping her sources, and herself, calm. When the blonde reporter's feed finally arrived, Johnson could see why. Hale had centered her coverage around a large, Polish family that couldn't account for two-thirds of its members. The remaining third had worked themselves into a collective frenzy. Those Gale interviewed looked wild-eyed and babbled about the devil, time warps, black holes, and space aliens lifting people into the sky.

"If I air this, it'll be like saying the Martians have landed," Johnson told deputy producer Janet Shelby as they viewed Gale's rough cut. He had barely finished talking when another reporter burst into the room.

"What's going on in Chicago? We're getting calls from people who are terrified about our report that the devil and spacemen are grabbing people off the streets and eating them alive! I didn't see that. When did we run that?"

"We haven't aired anything, yet," Shelby said, her voice climbing an octave. "What's happening?"

"People are intercepting Jessica's satellite feed," Johnson guessed. "A lot of people have home satellite dishes. They listen in on everything—probably even our phone conversations. In this case, it's a good thing. This test audience told me exactly what I need to know. We can't air the piece. Get Jessica on the phone."

Thirty seconds later, a clerk buzzed that Jessica Gale was on line three. Johnson sighed and punched the blinking button on his phone. He explained to the correspondent how the satellite pirates reacted to her report. He ordered her to interview some more sensible people.

"My parents are missing, Ned," Jessica said, choking back tears.

"Just stay calm, Jessie. Go back to work. It'll take your mind off it. Just give me a straight report. It'll be OK."

Jessica Gale took a few deep breaths to settle herself, then headed out into the night. She went to a crowded diner and filtered out a few calmer people to interview. The problem now was the edge in her own voice. It took six tries before she was able to hide it enough to produce an acceptable feed.

Johnson edited the entire four-city report down to a minute. It aired at 11:04 EST. It was the fifth story of the top-of-the-hour newscast. Johnson instructed his anchors to go immediately to an advertisement without comment. He even switched the scheduled ad from a downbeat public service spot pointing out the dangers of drug use to an upbeat General Motors ad boasting about its new line of solar-powered automobiles.

The story was downplayed to such an extent that it had little effect. The phone lines lit up again, but there were fewer operators on duty, and most of the callers couldn't get through.

Johnson slotted the story into a grade two rotation. It would air twice an hour for the next three hours, up until 3 A.M. At 3:05, when most of the country was safely asleep, a longer version covering two minutes would run. After that, the story would be dropped altogether. Before he left, shortly after 1 A.M., Johnson made a note for the morning shift to "keep a watch on the missing persons story." It was third on the list of things to watch, right below a brush fire in California.

Johnson's strategy was a slick example of corporate fanny-covering. He aired the story, so he was covered should it grow into something catastrophic. But he plugged it in late enough at night so that its chances of causing unnecessary panic among the dwindling audience of insomniacs was minimized. If the story fizzled out the next day, no damage was done.

In Miami, Matt had been watching CNN most of the afternoon, waiting for the update. He had fallen asleep on the couch before the segment aired.

At ABC News the following morning, news producer Harry Nelson made the missing people story his top priority. He had caught the 11 P.M. CNN report and felt the story was grossly underplayed. The *New York Times* had a medium-sized story on page three, and that also seemed underplayed. At the 9:30 A.M. meeting, Nelson assigned his New York, Los Angeles, and Atlanta correspondents to do full reports. He wanted to lead that evening's network broadcast with it.

But the story had changed. As the reporters canvassed big corporations and smaller companies, the figures were far less dramatic. In fact, by 1 P.M., New York correspondent Hayden Feldon called and reported there was "no story."

"We've got nothing out of the ordinary here," Feldon told his assignment editor. "The companies are reporting a one to ten percent absentee rate, which they say is normal for the flu season."

At 1:25, the California correspondent called in and reported much the same thing. Twenty minutes later, the Atlanta figures followed the trend. Nelson couldn't believe things could be back to normal after the CNN and *New York Times* reports. He almost pulled the plug on the segment until he checked with Janet Perreli, a twenty-one-year-old college intern who had been given the throwaway task of calling police stations around the country. Her report was dramatically different. The police continued to be flooded with missing persons reports, and the majority appeared to hit the magic twenty-four hour requirement in the late morning. Nelson ordered his correspondents to shift from businesses to police stations and file stories along those lines.

"You know," Perreli said as she was leaving Nelson's office, "I think I know why we can't figure this out. All the people who know what happened are gone. I mean, all the people who *would* know what happened. You know what I mean?"

"I think what you are trying to say is that it's not random. That there's some link in the people themselves," Nelson said wearily. "I thought of that. But we have nothing so far to confirm it. Still, that's the best attempt at an explanation I've heard so far. Keep thinking that way. If you can pinpoint a link, let me know immediately."

"Didn't this start with the churches?" Perreli asked.

"Yeah, but we discounted that. Some churches reported only a small number of missing people. And the figures from prisons were similar. A few lost entire cellblocks, while others reported that only one or two inmates were unaccounted for. We've kept that news under wraps. We don't want to tell people that along with everything else, thousands of rapists and murderers are on the loose. What's important is that the prison figures negate the church angle. It just showed up in churches first because they're the only place where large groups of people go on Sunday mornings. No one takes attendance figures at the beach."

"Good point," Perreli said.

Harry Nelson was beginning to feel uneasy. He didn't know how to play the story. Nobody had been able to put a finger on just who was missing. Why were the police stations swamped with calls, while the major corporations seemed relatively unaffected?

And why were so few of his own employees missing?

At CBS, NBC, TBS, and Fox, the news departments were turning up similar figures. What started as a hot story had died by early afternoon. Enormous numbers of people were apparently missing, but the effect of their disappearance appeared to be minimal. Except for frantic relatives hounding the police, the day was progressing as normal. Stores opened. People shopped. The stock market had little movement. Airline schedules were unaltered. Monday Night Football was still gearing up to air a live game that evening. Both teams' starting lineups were intact, although a few subs hadn't reported.

Nelson decided to have his anchor read a twenty-second blurb on the missing people. There was no footage, and the segment came halfway into the broadcast. CBS did the same, but NBC used two correspondents and showed film of police officers taking missing person calls. TBS and Fox didn't mention the missing people at all.

As the week progressed, the story remained like a hazy, distant light. It refused to come any clearer into focus, but it also refused to go away. In fact, by Tuesday, it began picking up steam. The missing became names. Big names. Six United States senators and thirty congressmen had vanished. That sent the secret service, FBI, and National Security Council into a flurry of activity. There were rumors that they had been kidnapped by terrorists, but those stories didn't explain the thousands of average citizens who were also missing.

Since it was the height of the NFL football season, the team rosters became a barometer of the impact of the missing persons. Sixty-five players had vanished from their teams, including all-pro New England Patriot quarterback Terry Hunter. The fans were up in arms because the betting lines were in shambles. The sports books in Vegas shut down for a day fearing some kind of mass kidnapping by a gambling syndicate. Such a kidnapping had marred the previous Super Bowl and nearly destroyed the sport. But NFL officials had survived that scandal, and this time they were prepared. The commissioner held a news conference in New York and reminded the fans that the missing people dilemma was an overall societal problem, unrelated in any way to football. After this announcement, the sports books reopened and adjusted their lines to account for the missing players. On Wednesday, the critical "injury list" sent out to the newspapers to advise betting fans on the status of each team's players included a new category. After the standard "injured, probable," "injured, doubtful," and "suspended for drugs" listings the papers added the designation, "missing."

Society was quickly adjusting to a smaller population.

But late Thursday, a bulletin that came over the Associated Press news wires poured gas into the dying flames of the missing people story. Former President James Halverson and his wife Ramona had not been seen since Sunday. The item led the Thursday newscasts on all the networks. The ex-President and First Lady's disappearance gave the broadcasters a dramatic peg to hang all their unused footage upon. They accompanied the announcement with fuller reports on the whole missing person phenomena. The newspapers similarly ran long articles and multiple sidebars in Friday's papers. For the first time, they began humanizing the story by focusing upon individual cases and the grief of split families.

With this wave of reports came an intensification of the rumors. A quick Lou Harris poll revealed that thirty-three percent of Americans believed the missing were kidnapped by UFOs. Of those, 15 percent felt the people were being used for food. The next largest percentage, twenty-one, supported a story spread by one of the supermarket tabloids that the missing people had all left the country because they had a simultaneous, extrasensory vision of a massive, continent-shattering earthquake that would occur on December 7, the anniversary of Pearl Harbor.

Twenty percent, apparently those with home satellite dishes, blamed the devil.

As CNN's Ned Johnson had feared, things were getting out of hand. The nation appeared on the verge of a collective panic.

But just as the media began zeroing in on the truth, something happened that diverted the world's attention.

An even bigger story was brewing in Russia and the Middle East.

SIX

Half a world away, Soviet Defense Minister General Georgi Kalinina was making the final telephone call that would put his murderous plot into action. Kalinina, Russia's top military leader, was a conservative, hawkish Communist fiercely determined to reestablish Communist rule and reunite the shattered Soviet empire. A short, stout man with stubby fingers and a fleshy face, Kalinina resembled a Philadelphia mayor more than a Russian general. For years he had anguished over the collapse of the U.S.S.R. and the warming relations between Russia and America. His anger festered until it grew into an insane rage. His hatred of the Soviet Union's new leaders was exceeded only by his hatred of America. And his hatred of America was exceeded by his hatred of Jews.

General Kalinina had chosen himself to be the country's savior. He had planned his ascension for months. He secretly recruited the most militant anti-American fanatics among his troops. Then he bribed, threatened, and quietly killed anybody he felt would stand in his way. Some big names were missing in Russia, but the disappearances had nothing to do with what happened everywhere else.

The general's biggest enemy inside the country was Russia President Valentin Morozov, the man elected to bring freedom and recovery to the demoralized Soviet people. Morozov was dedicated to human rights, a free market economy, and world peace. A handsome man, he had captured the affection of his people in the same manner as the more popular American presidents. With his beautiful wife, Masha, at his side, Morozov had become Russia's first celebrity president.

The Morozovs' popularity made General Kalinina rabid with rage.

Captain Sakha Nikultsev was Kalinina's most trusted follower. A ruthless soldier with a battle-scarred face, Nikultsev was a veteran of the Baltic invasion and was little more than a hired killer in a uniform. His expertise in a wide variety of weapons, and one in particular, prompted General Kalinina to select Nikultsev for the historic mission.

Morozov was scheduled to address the Russian congress—and the nation—that evening. The topic was the latest in a series of disarmament agreements he had signed with America and Western Europe. This would be the most monumental withdrawal yet, and the Russian leader was certain it would win him a Nobel Peace Prize.

As he walked to the podium, Morozov received a standing ovation unlike anything ever heard before in Russia.

In the back of the balcony, Sakha Nikultsev stood in his dress uniform. Surrounding him were six officers in full military regalia. Four carried automatic rifles. The remaining two stood opposite each other, holding huge Soviet flags. It was unusual for a drill squad to be in the back of the balcony, but it was a special evening. The lower-level party members, never ones to question the military, hardly noticed their presence.

As Morozov opened his speech, the officers began descending, in progression, from the back of the balcony. They marched down the red-carpeted stairs and fanned out into a circle near the railing. In the center of the circle was Captain Sakha Nikultsev. The flag carriers stationed themselves in front and behind the group.

Morozov looked up at the waving flags and smiled.

Spectators in the front rows noticed what appeared to be a small blue flower sprout up from the center of the President's forehead. A flood of red liquid gushed from the flower. The bewildering sight hushed the huge auditorium. Behind the Soviet

President, the faces of those on the podium began twisting in horror. Sticking out from the back of Morozov's head was a steel-tipped arrow.

The President crashed to the floor.

As pandemonium swept over the crowd, Sakha Nikultsev raised his rifle aloft and began barking commands for his five officers to secure the area.

The sixth officer was already on his way out of the building, Nikultsev's crossbow safely tucked away in his military satchel.

The mechanical sound of a voice beeper interrupted Matt's fitful sleep. "Mr. Slade. Attention. Mr. Slade." He fumbled around to locate the source. It wasn't his regular airline beeper sitting on the nightstand. He reached under the bed for a second beeper, the one that Colonel Hutchinson used. It was silent. Matt stared at it, refusing to believe what he already knew. He scrunched up his face in pain, then walked to his dresser, reached behind the mirror, and retrieved a thin black card, a device no larger than a credit card. The number on the small screen had a Washington D.C. area code. Matt punched the card into a slot in his telephone. It automatically dialed a number.

"I'm sorry to disturb you," the familiar but distant voice began. Matt recognized it instantly as Colonel Warrington. Matt never liked Colonel Warrington. He was sinister and secretive, and he twitched his upper lip like a rat. They had met briefly in Israel, but Matt didn't know exactly where the colonel worked. Some dark basement in the Pentagon, no doubt.

Whatever Colonel Warrington was calling about, it couldn't be good. It never was.

"I know you're on your honeymoon," the Colonel continued. "Sorry. You must report to Tel Aviv immediately."

"Are you kidding?"

"Immediately. There's a flight out at 10:06. Everything's been arranged."

"What's going on?"

"You'll find out soon enough."

"I, I can't. I mean. I'm in no condition," Matt mumbled.

"You have no alternative."

"I'm not on my honeymoon. I can't find Jill."

"She must be among the missing. That's not important now."

The response was like a slap in the face.

"What do you mean?" Matt said, sitting up in bed. "You know about that? Where is she? Are you behind this? What did you do with her?"

"We are not behind it. We are not sure what has happened. Only that there are many missing. You must go to Israel for enlightenment."

"Is the answer there?"

"Your flight leaves at 10:06. That's less than three hours."

"There's no flight to Tel Aviv at 10:06."

"We'll have to juggle you around a bit, but you'll get there. It will all be on your ticket."

"You want me to hopscotch around the world? Are you crazy? Isn't there a military flight?"

"Can't. Not you. Not this time."

"What does that mean?"

"You'll find out soon enough."

"I want some answers," Matt demanded. "Where's Jill? Why am I going back to Israel? Why can't I take a military jet?"

"You'll find out soon enough."

"I'm not going until I get some answers."

"This is very serious. You have your orders."

"I'm a civilian."

"You have your orders."

"I'm not going!"

Matt slammed the receiver down and instinctively turned on the television. He wanted to continue to monitor CNN for updates on the missing. The announcer's words rocked the anger out of his body.

"I repeat, Russia's President Valentin Morozov was assassinated this morning at 7:01 A.M., Eastern Standard Time."

For the seventeenth time in the last forty-five minutes, CNN rolled the tape of Morozov collapsing at the podium.

"Political experts say the assassin's use of the ancient weapon is an unmistakable signal that the days of detente are over," the correspondent said in a hushed tone. "The Soviet Union, under the seized leadership of Defense Minister Georgi Kalinina, may well be returning to the brutal and repressive ways of its past."

Matt closed his eyes and clicked off the television. He quickly showered, shaved, and began packing. A hundred scenes flashed through his mind as he prepared for his long trip. He had driven to Jill's apartment thirty-six times between Sunday and Wednesday. He followed the news reports, but they just made him increasingly angry. Like all those who had lost someone, he didn't feel the media was giving the story proper play. Jill was gone. Vanished. Her parents were gone. Most of her friends were gone. Everybody at her church was gone. It was unprecedented. And the media had treated it like a rash of chicken pox.

"Get a grip on yourself," Danny had said over the phone from Hong Kong. "The press can't figure it out yet, so they don't think it's important. It'll keep slapping them in the face until someone wakes up. There's a Pulitzer Prize in it for somebody. That'll motivate 'em."

"I'm not so sure."

"This thing is worldwide. There are people missing everywhere. Even here in Hong Kong. Not many, I'll grant you, but more than usual. And Europe appears to be just as affected as America. Someone'll crack the mystery. Hang tight, buddy," Danny had continued. "I'll be back soon."

Matt finished packing, laid down, and drifted into a light sleep. He dreamed about Jill, as usual. Only this one was different. Instead of convoluted scenes and distorted visions, the dream contained the simple image of Jill standing by his bed.

"Don't worry about me," she said. "I'm fine."

As she spoke, Jill was joined by her brother Jim and sister-in-law, Matt's mother, and a strange man. They all looked very happy.

Jill grew pensive as she approached the bed. She touched his face. He tried to reach out to her, but his body was paralyzed.

"It's going to be hard for you. So hard," she whispered. "The coming years will be difficult. Don't give up. Please don't give in."

Matt had a thousand questions, but he could not speak. Jill slowly backed away, rejoined the others, then faded.

Matt awoke with a start. The image of Jill was vivid. He jumped out of bed and searched the house—the bathrooms, closets, everywhere.

It was only a dream.

A wave of depression swept over him. The jolt of energy drained away. He crawled back into bed, hoping, praying that next time he awakened, the dreams and the reality would reverse. But he couldn't sleep. He kept thinking about the strange man in the dream. Who was he? Why was he there?

Then it came to him.

It was Danny Simpson's father.

The phone rang again, jarring Matt from his memories.

"I assume you are preparing to leave?" Warrington said.

"I'll be there."

Riding in the cab to the airport, the political upheaval of a distant communist nation was crowded out of Matt's mind. Something in Colonel Warrington's voice told him he would indeed find the answers in Israel. The answers to everything. Even why he had been sent there before.

Matt became infuriated when he punched up his plastic, computerized ticket at the airline counter. The trip was a nightmare. He was flying to New York, laying over a few hours, then catching a Concorde to Paris. From there, he would connect with a flight into Tel Aviv. Doing it that way got him there just seven hours ahead of the next regularly scheduled direct flight from Miami. What couldn't wait seven hours? He didn't even want to consider the possible answers.

As he lifted off for New York, his mind flashed back on his previous Israel experience. It began as this trip had, with a call from that robot Warrington. They needed a pilot to go through some triple top-secret joint American/Israeli program. Matt asked all the obvious questions. Why him? Why a civilian pilot? Why a civilian pilot who had never officially been in any branch of the armed forces? Why a rebellious character like him?

Colonel Warrington had been about as communicative as a saltwater clam.

"We have determined that you are the right person for the job. Your country needs you." That was the only explanation Matt ever received. And Warrington said it in such a way to make Matt feel like a traitor if he resisted the assignment. Besides, his curiosity was aroused. And a trip to Israel had benefits that Warrington knew nothing about.

The remaining mysteries of his selection were slow in coming. Matt was particularly peeved to discover, when the program began, that he was the only American involved. He had been led to believe it was a big operation. That turned out to be his own assumption based upon the royal treatment he received in Washington. When the curtain began lifting, the reasons made a measure of sense.

Israeli military scientists, with the financial assistance of the United States, had developed a fighter jet like nothing ever created before. Although the jet itself was a technological marvel, it wasn't the operational advances that made the project so secretive. It was the weapon mounted on what looked like an oversized radio antenna on the tail. The Israelis had perfected laser technology to the point of creating a mini-version of the doomsday weapon that had long sizzled in the international rumor mill.

It was "Star Trek" time—set the phasers on kill. Reality had finally caught up with science fiction. Israel's new Scorpion fighters were right out of the comic books.

With the new weapon came heated political bickering between Israel and the United States. The U.S. wanted to take over the project. Israel refused, but needed the U.S.'s financial support. Compromises were argued and reargued. When Israel finally agreed to allow a limited number of U.S. scientists, military officers, and pilots to become part of the development, a shake-up in

international business and politics forced the U.S. to back off.
New relations between the U.S. and Russia had made the two
countries practically kissing cousins. Russians were in. Russian
fashions swept America. Russian movies became the new chic art
films. A Russian actress starred in an American-made movie and
won an Oscar.

The new Russian-American kinship led to arms limitation
pacts, and troop withdrawals. Military bases were shut down on
both sides. When Fidel Castro choked on a chicken bone and
died, Russia agreed to allow the island nation to have open elections to choose between communism and capitalism. A capitalist
candidate won the first election, freeing the island nation after
decades of communist rule.

Everything in the entire world seemed perfect. American
politicians decided they couldn't offend their Soviet friends by
participating in the secret weapons experiments going on in
Israel. In fact, such participation would be a violation of the most
recent arms reduction pact.

But they didn't want America to be left out of the dramatic
experiments, either. Then, as now, the solution was simple: Matt
Slade.

Colonel Samuel Cohen met Matt at the airport in Tel Aviv.
The Israeli fighter pilot was in good spirits. Everyone else
appeared tense, which Matt had noticed in Paris as well. The
rumblings out of Russia had the whole world on edge. But not
old Sammy. Sam was as boisterous as ever.

"Welcome back, friend," Sam said, vigorously shaking Matt's
hand. The uniformed colonel flashed some identification, jab-
bered in Hebrew, and like magic, Matt was swept through
Customs like a VIP. Actually, fighter pilots *were* VIPs in Israel.
And the Scorpion fighter pilots were the cream of the crop. Even
an American civilian was treated with hushed respect.

Matt was wrung out from his wedding nightmare and global
hopscotching. He tried to be cordial to his old Israeli social
guide, but the fatigue in his voice kept cutting through.

"I've changed, Sam."

"You?" Sam chided in his thick accent. "Never. I can't believe it."

Sam's energy was lifting Matt's spirits. They had, indeed, spent some memorable nights enjoying the Tel Aviv nightlife. As the valet placed Matt's luggage into the long black limousine, the memories of those nights fused together.

"Give me the credo," Sam goaded.

"The credo? What credo?"

"How could you forget? It was your philosophy of life!"

"How crazy was I when I said it?"

"Which time?"

"The time it came out best."

"It was always the same," Sam said, relishing the opportunity to repeat it. "The motto of Matthew Slade... ahem: 'Fly fast. Live faster. Love fastest. I'd rather die in a good brawl than in a bad war."

"I said that?"

"You lived it."

"I was younger then."

"It was a year ago!"

"When you live fast, you age even faster."

Matt laughed at the silliness of his own line. He had been lonely, heartbroken, and confused during his last trip to Israel, and he had overdone the macho act to compensate.

The black limo pulled into a military base and proceeded past layer after layer of security checkposts. Matt recognized the place but asked anyway.

"Where are we going?"

"I want to show you something."

They drove to a small hangar at the far end of the installation. Matt knew what was inside, or thought he did. When he entered, his intuition proved correct. There she was, the beautiful Pocahontas. Seeing the magnificent jet always made his blood rush. The Israelis wanted the pilots to cherish the fighters, to bond to their machines, so they allowed the Scorpion pilots to choose their own colors. They were promptly painted jet black, baby blue, fiery orange, screaming yellow, blinding white, whatever the pilots desired. Pin stripes. Rally wheels. Emblems. Designs. Animals. Women. Anything. Lined up together on the tarmac, the twenty-one jets were the fulfillment of a small boy's fantasy.

Pocahontas was Matt's baby. It was the most outlandish jet in the fleet—or the most gorgeous, depending upon one's aesthetic sense. Its background was cherry red, but that was only the beginning. The nose was covered with the hybrid face of an angry bald eagle and a beautiful Indian maiden. The beak was the eagle's. The ice-blue eyes were the maiden's. White and gold feathers, interwoven with black hair, spread across the jet's wings like the span of a great mythological bird. The deadly antenna on the rear of the jet curled slightly forward and had been painted gold and black like a bumble bee's stinger. Even the wheels had been covered with fender wells painted orange and black in the design of vicious talons. Matt was surprised when the Israelis actually custom-painted the $800-million war machine exactly as he ordered. It could have looked horrendous, but it didn't. Matt thought it was the greatest looking aircraft in the world.

Whenever he took the controls, the American pilot felt as if he could destroy the whole United States Air Force all by himself. That emotional rush was closer to reality than Matt imagined. What he didn't know was that his lady had been improved.

That was the part that perplexed him. The set-up inside the hangar was weird. Forty yards in front of the jet were two thin brass rods rising up about four feet from the floor. On top of each sat what appeared to be a double-barreled shotgun.

"Shotguns?" Matt marveled out loud. "What is this? First a crossbow. Now shotguns?"

"You'll see," Sam said with a peculiar smile.

Behind Pocahontas, a large white circle extended from the floor halfway to the ceiling of the hangar. Matt walked over and touched it. It was made of thin paper, like a giant version of the ring football players burst through when they take the field during homecoming.

"You flew me all the way over here to perform some circus stunts?"

"Look at the stinger," Sam said. "I'm surprised you didn't notice."

Sam shouldn't have been surprised. Matt was more in tune with the paint and design than the frightening weapon that sat on the jet's tail. Now, instead of one rotating laser box, there were two. They were set over and under, like a shotgun his father had once given him.

"We didn't need another one. The first one could wipe out half the Earth," Matt said, unable to hide his disgust.

"The second one's the most important. It will save your pretty face. Come," Sam said, nodding toward a small control booth. "I'll show you."

"Unless that thing can shoot food and medicine, don't expect me to be impressed," Matt warned.

They climbed a small flight of stairs and entered the booth. Inside was a replica of a Scorpion's console. A working replica. Sam threw a few switches, and Pocahontas's stinger came to life.

"This new button, here to the left. This has been added," Sam explained. "It activates the defense."

"Some kind of force field?"

"Not quite."

"I suppose you're going to show me?"

Sam's eyes sparkled devilishly. "Nothing but the best for the American." Sam fiddled with another switch. "The shotguns are loaded with birdshot. There are about 125 half-centimeter pellets per shell. That equals more than 500 pellets coming out of the four barrels."

"I see you get 'American Sportsman' reruns over here, too," Matt joked.

"The guns can be fired simultaneously from here by pulling this switch."

The implications of the experiment, at least from Matt's perspective, suddenly pierced his jet-lagged brain.

"You're not going to fire that thing at her!" Matt screamed.

"You'll destroy the paint! No way. You must be losing your mind."

"Watch," Colonel Cohen said.

Before Matt could protest further, Sam threw the switch. The flash of light was so quick Matt wasn't even sure he had seen it. But there was no mistaking the staggering bang of the four shotgun shells that followed a split-second later. Matt's ears rang. He was seeing spots that confirmed the flash of light. It took nearly a minute for him to recover.

"Go on," Sam insisted. "Check her out."

Matt ran out onto the tarmac. He inspected Pocahontas, rubbing its smoothly-painted surface, searching in vain for pits and chips.

He found none.

"Look at the circle," Sam suggested.

Matt walked over. It was the same as it had been before. The deadly pellets that missed the jet should have ripped apart the circle of paper. But there wasn't a single hole.

"Okay. I'm impressed. So what happened? You said it wasn't a force field."

"When the gun went off, the computer inside the Scorpion was able to read, sort, and count the incoming pellets in a millisecond. It sent a target map to the defense stinger, the second box. That activated a multiple spray of individual lasers that locked in on each pellet and vaporized it."

"Are you saying that there was a specific beam for each individual birdshot?"

"Here," Sam continued, pointing to the console. "Check the readout on the display. It says there were 527 separate beams. That means there were 527 pellets disarmed."

"That's unbelievable," Matt said. "If we ever get attacked by redneck dove hunters, I guess we're safe."

"What's a 'redneck dove'?"

"Never mind. What's the point here?"

"The defense system was designed after the eye of a fly. It can filter the laser into more than a thousand individual beams over a

360-degree angle. And each beam is individually adjusted to the exact power needed to disarm the intruder. You could be standing out there in front of the jet and one beam, so thin you couldn't even see it, could singe a single hair off your arm without your even feeling the heat. The next beam, the same size, could bore a hole halfway through the Earth's core."

"Can't you guys keep those computer nerds under control?" Matt said. "You let 'em go unchecked, and they'll come up with all kinds of crazy stuff."

"They're the real heroes, Matt. Tough guys like me and you, we're obsolete. The pale guys in the labs, they're the new warriors. They're saving the world."

"Or destroying it. Why don't they try to cure the common cold?"

"Don't be such a spoil sport," Colonel Cohen said. "They're trying to save our lives. Can't you see the implications of this?"

"Sure. Not only can you destroy the whole world with one of those jets, you're now totally invincible. There's nothing to prevent your country from going out and destroying all its enemies. And then what? Israel takes over the world?"

"We are a benevolent people. We would not use this power aggressively."

"Let's hope so, Sammy. Tell me something. What would you do if you were ordered to take me out?"

"I would never receive such an order."

"No? What if your country wanted to do something America didn't like. Like attack America, for instance. And here I am, part of your own squad. What would you do?"

"I'd make it swift and painless."

There was an uneasy silence. Then the two men collapsed into laughter.

"You would!" Matt said, doubling over.

When the laughter subsided, Matt grew serious.

"So what is this new defensive stinger supposed to protect us from?"

"Attack."

"On Pocahontas? I'm not part of any army. That's for you guys."

"What do you think they trained you for, my friend? You're part of the Scorpion Squad. How did you say it? 'The big guys pulled my dance card.' Well that's it. Your card's been pulled. We go, you go."

"Yeah, the big guys," Matt said. The unsmiling face of Colonel Warrington flashed into his mind. "We may be VIPs at the airport and with the ladies at the clubs, but we're still just pieces on a chess board, Sammy. They can make our toys more powerful, but we remain pawns to someone else's politics and ambition."

"Come on, I'll take you to your quarters," Colonel Cohen said.

As he walked back to the limo, a shiver ran through Matt's body. He hadn't been uprooted from his bed and flown around the world just to see his fighter melt a few shotgun pellets.

"Sam, what's happening?" he softly said as he peered out the window of the limousine.

"I don't know. The whole world seems to be ripping apart."

"Are there people missing in Israel?"

"You mean like in America and Europe?"

Matt just stared out the window.

"No. Not many. Not here," Sam answered. "That's New Testament stuff."

Matt jerked his head around and grabbed Sam by the shoulders. "You know? You know what's going on?"

The Israeli Colonel pulled himself away.

"Hey, calm down."

"Jill's missing!"

"We know."

"You know?"

"We know everything about you."

"Where is she?"

"We don't know."

"But you just said… "

"I don't know, really. It hasn't impacted us here. But it will. More than anywhere else."

"What do you mean?"

"Me, you, the Scorpions. Israel. What's happened will continue here. It involves us. Personally. Not just your losing Jill. But personally. Historically. And you've been chosen to be part of it. And I don't mean by the big shots."

"By whom, then?"

Sam didn't answer.

"Nothing's ever going to be the same again, is it, Sam?"

"We're not prophets or politicians," Sam said. "We're soldiers. We play our part. That's all we can do. Obey orders and play our part."

Matt turned and began staring out the window again. His brain wasn't like a fly's eye. There was only so much he could take in at once. He was tired and angry and frustrated. From one end of the world to the other, everyone talked in riddles. Everyone seemed to have a theory on what had happened to Jill. He had lost her on his wedding day, and no one would tell him why.

What was everyone so afraid of?

SEVEN

The limousine pulled up to a tall apartment building on the Mediterranean—the building Matt had stayed in before.

"Same room?" Matt asked.

"We thought you'd find it relaxing," Sam said. "Get some sleep. No parties tonight. We have a meeting at 7 A.M. sharp."

Matt winced. "Do you know what time that is in Miami?"

"No."

"I don't either. But I'll bet it's early."

Matt dragged himself from the limo. He grinned when he saw the bellhop rushing over to carry his bags.

"Mr. Slade! Glad to have you back," the bellhop said as he unloaded Matt's luggage from the limo's huge trunk. "It's been far too quiet around here!"

Matt received warm greetings from numerous employees and residents as he walked through the lobby. Everyone offered the same sincere, welcoming smile. They treated him as if he had returned home. Israel as home? It was a strange concept, but comforting. At that point, almost anything would have been comforting. The excitement of the hangar experiment was quickly wearing off, replaced by a bone-deep weariness. Matt braced himself against the wall of the high-speed elevator shooting up to the twenty-fifth floor. The bellhop navigated the hallway and opened the apartment door as Matt followed zombielike in step. He immediately flopped onto the couch.

The two-bedroom suite was just as he remembered. It was exquisitely decorated with plush, pastel-colored furniture on a thick white rug. The refrigerator was stocked with carrots, celery, cucumbers, fresh turkey, pasta, cheese, and Greek olives—all of Matt's favorites. A complete wardrobe of fashionable clothes hung in the bedroom closet. Everything was first-class, as usual.

When the bellhop unloaded the last bag, Matt forgot and tried to hand him a five. The man refused.

"No, Mr. Slade. That's unnecessary. Not for you. Not for the pilots."

The pilots. The whole country understood that the pilots—more than the government, more than the army, more than anything—were the wall of defense that kept Israel from being driven into the sea. Without the pilots, Israel would be doomed. Matt could do no wrong in Israel.

Just as he was dozing off on the couch, a noise in the bedroom jerked him awake. He reached under the frame and grabbed the pistol that remained hidden in a holster nailed to the wooden underside. He walked slowly into the bedroom, his arms outstretched in front of him, his finger on the trigger. In an instant, the blade of a steel army knife was up against his throat. The barrel of a gun dug into his back.

"Choose your death, American pig. Knife or gun?"

"Gun," Matt said instinctively.

Both the knife and the gun were released. Laughter pierced the room.

"You always choose the gun. You're such a chicken," the female voice said. "You're still terrified of knives."

A wave of conflicting emotions swept over him. He hated, more than anything, the thought of having his throat cut. The fear was so ingrained in him that he could feel the pain just thinking of it. Whenever he went to movies, traveled as a passenger in an airplane, or did anything that involved people sitting behind him, he had to button his collar tightly around his neck to rid himself of the psychosomatic pain.

Very few people knew about his fear. Even his closest friends. But she knew.

"You know how I feel about that," he gasped. "How could you do that?"

The woman just laughed louder. She rolled on the couch and kicked her feet in the air.

Matt's anger drained as more powerful emotions took control. The giant hole Jill had left acted like a vacuum, drawing in the woman's image, scent, and dark beauty.

"Don't be angry with me," Sarah said, getting off the couch and prancing over. "I thought you'd be happy to see me."

"You shouldn't have done that. Not with a knife," Matt said weakly.

"I'm sorry."

Sarah tossed back her thick black hair and smiled. The light hit her eyes. Matt was doomed. Sarah's eyes were like emeralds, with a sparkle of white light in the corners that Matt swore radiated her energy. She had a way of opening her eyes wide every few words or so that made them look even bigger than they already were. Every time she did that, every time he saw the sparkle, he felt helpless. He had hated being that much in love. He hated being so out of control. But there was no defense. No antidote for Sarah's eyes.

She reached out and hugged him. He embraced her, then pulled away.

"Why are you here—to torment me?"

"Don't say that," she countered, the glint in her eyes softening. "You know I never wanted to hurt you."

"I know. It was *The Cause*." The words came out harsh and sarcastic.

"Let's not go over that," she said. "Not tonight. OK?"

Matt turned and faced the porch. "I've missed you."

"So much that you got married?"

"I was lonely."

"You? You're never lonely."

"When you left. I learned what it was to be lonely."

Matt had anticipated this reunion since the day she left. He had rehearsed his lines a thousand times. He wanted to be strong, feign indifference. He wanted to be faithful to Jill, or to Jill's memory, wherever or whatever she now was. But something about Sarah drained his strength and scrambled his thoughts. It had been that way five years before. If anything, her power over him had increased.

Or maybe he was just vulnerable, vulnerable and exhausted. That was a dangerous combination. He needed a diversion, something to diffuse her power until he could recover. He walked out onto the large veranda overlooking the city and the sea. Night had fallen and the breeze was cool. Sarah followed and stood next to him at the railing. Matt was emotional by nature. When he was overtired, he was even more emotional. The beautiful setting only made things worse.

"It ate at me. I tried everything to forget. Anything. And I still couldn't stop thinking about you."

"She made you forget."

It was true. Jill had made him forget. But he couldn't let Sarah know that. It might hurt her. Even though she had left him, left him a mess, he was unable to hurt her. At least not that way. Then again, it might not bother her at all. She might not care. That would be worse. Either way, he couldn't take the chance.

"Don't you love her?"

"Yes. Very much."

The words sprang out, but his hesitant tone softened the blow.

"You don't sound very convinced."

"What do you want to hear?" Matt said, growing angry. "That it wasn't like us? OK, it wasn't like us. It was better."

He turned away.

"I didn't love her so much that it hurt," he whispered. "That's why it was better. I don't want to ever love that much again."

Sarah started to come to him, but stopped.

"I hurt, too."

"You?" Matt snapped, facing her again. "You didn't hurt enough!"

"How dare you say that. You don't know."

"I know there was nothing in my life that meant more to me than you. Nothing!"

"Don't pretend to be so noble. You got married. I haven't been with anyone."

Matt was stunned by her confession. Could it be true? He had spent all those terrible nights trying not to think of her in someone else's arms. Five years had passed. There had to have been someone. There had to have been at least one pair of arms to justify his agony.

"No one?"

Sarah shook her head.

"Why?"

"Oh, Matthew," she said, turning away in frustration. "Why can't you understand? It's two different things. I can't replace what we had. And unlike you, I won't even try. When I left, I gave up everything."

"You didn't have to give up anything," Matt said, clutching her by the arms.

"It doesn't matter now. You're married."

"I'm not."

"You're not?"

An expression of elation washed over Sarah's face. She quickly shielded it. He let her go and stepped back.

"What happened?"

"She's gone."

"Gone?"

"Just gone. With all the others."

"The missing? That's right!" Sarah said. The sudden revelation lifted her voice and betrayed her feelings. She quickly regrouped.

"I'm sorry. Really. I should have suspected."

"Why?"

"The missionary's sister? Of course she's among the missing."

Matt grabbed her firmly and looked into her eyes. Their power over him had momentarily lifted. Instead, they held the answers he needed.

"How do you know about that?"

"Don't you think I know? Don't you think I kept track?"

It was Sarah's turn to look away and face the city lights in the distance.

"She was a good choice. I tried to hate her. But I couldn't. I was happy for you."

That was a different story, a different conversation for another senario. It revealed nothing aside from Sarah's sacrificial nature, which was hardly a revelation. Even in his darkest moments, in his deepest anger, part of him understood that her sacrifice took far more strength than his ability to survive without her. It was always harder for the one who makes the decision. But Matt didn't want to go into that now. Later, maybe. It would give him some satisfaction to hear how she reacted, how she felt when she thought he had married. How it tore her up inside. But not now. There were more important things to discuss.

"Do you know what happened to Jill?"

"No. Maybe. No!"

The conflicting answer made Matt furious.

"What? More riddles. Everywhere I go there are riddles. I'm tired of this. Why can't I get an answer?"

"What did Colonel Cohen say?"

"Same jibberish."

"We cannot talk of such things."

"What's this 'we'? You're an American."

"I'm an Israeli."

There was no sense arguing the point. He had lost that battle five years before.

"Why can't you talk?"

"Because it can't be true. It can't. Please, Matt, I don't want to talk about it."

Sarah was nervous and afraid, so much so it rattled Matt. Fear had no place in her well-honed range of emotions. She was alway ice. It was confusing. Why was Jill's disappearance so terrifying to Sarah? Matt had a frightening thought. Had Sarah caused it? Had she done something to Jill? No, that was ridiculous. It wasn't just Jill. There were thousands missing. Tens of thousands. Maybe millions. What was he thinking? How could Sarah, how could anybody be responsible?

"I'm sorry about Jill. I really am," she said in a calmer voice. "But she's OK. Trust me."

Matt slammed his fist on the railing. Sarah closed her eyes.

"You'll figure it out, Matthew. Don't be upset. Just think of what she told you. She must have said something. I can't. I can't and I won't. Not now. Please understand."

"How can I understand? You're not making any sense."

"Let's just be together. I need you to hold me," Sarah said, touching her head to his chest. "It's been so long. Just hold me."

Matt wrapped his arms around her. He didn't know if he should try and squeeze out the information she was holding back, or just hug her. He hugged her. He was too tired and too mixed up to press her further.

Instead, his mind drifted back. Their entire affair flashed before his eyes. They had met at Embry-Riddle Aeronautical University in Fort Lauderdale. Both had wanted to be pilots, and both disdained the militaristic Air Force/Navy route. They fell in love his senior year. She was a freshman. Life was an exhilarating blend of soaring through the blue sky, frolicking in the blue-green ocean, and caressing on the white sand. Matt's love anchored him to South Florida while he served out his full-time government scholarship obligation and waited for her to graduate. The relationship progressed through their first civilian jobs on small commuter airlines, then stayed firm during the jump to flying cargo jets and express mail carriers for the majors. They both became commerical pilots the same year.

But the times were rapidly changing. Forces more powerful than love began pulling at Sarah. The cozy relationship between Russia and America made Israel nervous. The Russian fads that swept the American public made Israel even more jittery. Whenever Israel got the jitters, it beefed up its military. More fighter jets were ordered, and additional pilots were sought to man them. Israel especially needed female pilots. Men worldwide began having heart attacks at an alarming rate, and the problem seemed worse among pilots. More than a dozen Israeli, American, and Russian fighter jets had crashed after their pilots suffered heart attacks in flight. The phenomena baffled scientists and caused alarm among the world's militaries.

While medical experts searched for answers, Israeli doctors

came up with a more practical, quicker solution. They advised their military to recruit and train more female pilots.

What pushed Israel over the edge of paranoia was the intelligence information it was getting out of Russia. The Israeli leaders not only knew of General Georgi Kalinina's growing power, they predicted his coup and Morozov's assassination almost to the month. They had dispatched their own hit squad to blot out Kalinina before he could do the same to Morozov, but the general was too insulated and could not be taken except by a suicide team. That would have, at the very least, showered a blistering rain of negative world criticism upon Israel and possibly a more cataclysmic cluster of atomic bombs.

Israel wrung its collective hands and recruited more pilots. The United States was the perfect supply line. All fly boys—and especially fly girls—with Jewish surnames were hit hard. The urgency and desperation of the search was not underplayed. Sarah's recruiters managed to tap into and redirect the burning drive that had enabled her to become a pilot in the first place. They found, nurtured, and fed the seed of patriotism she held for her soon-to-be adopted homeland.

Matt found himself playing a poor second fiddle to a distant country and culture he couldn't begin to understand. Before he could figure out how to counterattack, Sarah was gone. In rapid succession, she emigrated, became an Israeli citizen, and was swallowed up into the Israeli Air Force.

Matt was left alone, shrouded in pain and unable to understand. He leaned heavily upon his friends for support and threw himself into his work. For once, he even welcomed the intensity of his dangerous government assignments. But it was all just a temporary diversion. The minute the job was over, the ache returned.

Then Jill came along and made him forget. She not only filled the void in his heart; her religion nourished his hungering spirit and further reversed his depression. And Jill offered a sense of security that Sarah never could. He was confident that she would always be there for him, even though she, too, had strong beliefs.

The difference was, Jill's beliefs were something they could embrace together.

Now Jill was gone and Sarah was back.

But the world still wouldn't leave him alone.

Matt was emotionally wrung out, and so physically tired he could hardly keep his eyes open. He escorted Sarah to the door, returned to the bedroom, and collapsed on the bed. He knew he would never see Jill again. Her disappearance remained a mystery, and he was determined to solve it. But for some reason, the finality of her situation had become clear. For the first time, he accepted it. Sarah said Jill was all right. It didn't make sense that she knew, but she did, and Jill was. Matt was sure of it now. He also knew that his love for Sarah was not a betrayal. With anyone else it would have been. As he lay in bed, drifting off to sleep, he could feel the emptiness filling up.

General Kalinina's progressive madness was accelerated by the success of his coup. He didn't sleep the first forty-eight hours of his reign. He set in motion a blinding series of reforms aimed at undoing everything Morozov had accomplished. His most fanatical project was to inact a quick and final solution to the Refusnik problem that was weakening the fabric of Russian society. The number of Russian Jews wishing to emigrate to Israel had swelled to nearly 500,000. There weren't enough concentration camps to hold them. Although the Russian general would have liked nothing better than to rid his country of Jews, giving them their wish and letting them move to Israel was beyond consideration. He had a better plan. He cackled with glee every time he thought of it. It was the perfect solution. It would snap the resolve of the Refusniks and prompt them to cancel their emigration requests.

Even Kalinina's most fervent supporters were aghast at his mad solution, but the General was not to be denied. He didn't care about world opinion. His master plan for America's pet country went far beyond the horror of his Refusnick solution.

The order was given. The plan was reluctantly carried out.

Matt could smell English muffins browning in the toaster when he woke up. Sarah must have returned to the apartment. Like so many things, the aroma of the toasted dough reminded him of her. As with all the memories, it brought pain. Now she was back, the muffins were toasting, and despite the insanity of the world around him, he felt strangely happy. What did Bogart say? *The problems of three little people don't mean a hill of beans in this mixed-up world....*

Matt had his own twist. The problems of this mixed-up world don't mean a hill of beans when two people who were once in love are reunited.

He hopped out of bed, pulled on his clothes, then dashed into the bathroom to brush his teeth and comb his hair. He splashed on some cologne and went into the kitchen. His conflicting feelings of love for the lost Jill and found Sarah were too much to contemplate. All he wanted to do this morning was enjoy breakfast with Sarah.

When he entered the kitchen, his idyllic fantasy was shattered. The reality of what had torn them apart returned without warning. There, at the kitchen table, eating a butter-drenched English muffin, was Sarah—in complete military regalia. Her flowing hair had disappeared into a tight bun. Her face was free of all traces of make-up.

Cinderella had turned into Rambo.

Even more alarming was the uniform Sarah was wearing—a Scorpion fighter pilot's coveralls. At first, Matt thought Sarah had found his and put them on as some kind of black joke. But they fit her like a glove.

"I made you some muffins," she said without looking up. "You've got to hurry. We're due at the base in an hour."

"We?"

"I was in the second class. After you left."

Matt was angry, but he couldn't pinpoint why. It wasn't the competition, or even the defeminization. And it wasn't some stereotypical macho sexism. When they were civilian pilots in America, he had supported her career wholeheartedly. His anger came from the slowly developing realization that not only was he going to be subjected to her presence, he would be forced to see her and work with her in the one role he despised. He would experience firsthand her slavery to the "The Cause."

And Matt knew that no matter what he did and how hard he tried, he would always come in second.

Sarah read it all in his face.

"I'm sorry if this hurts you," she said. "I'm not as noble as you think. It was my way of having it all. At least for a short time."

Matt passed by the chair beside her and slumped into one directly across, taking the adversarial position.

"It's just... just... this is why you left," he mumbled, playing this scene as badly as he had the others. "I don't know. Everything's so crazy. Too much has happened. And now this. This!"

She reached over and touched his hand.

"I know."

Matt was subdued as the limousine carried them to the Israeli base. He couldn't even find it in himself to touch Sarah as she sat beside him, not while they were wearing identical uniforms. Sarah understood.

"Why did all this have to happen?" he said, not directing the question to her. "What a bizarre coincidence... You and me like this. Here. In military uniforms of a strange country."

"You think it was a coincidence? Don't you understand anything?"

"Were you behind it? Me coming here the first time, being the only American? Was that you?" he said, growing agitated. "You wouldn't even see me when I tried to find you."

He would have volunteered if he had thought it would bring her back to him. But being manipulated and then jerked around didn't sit well.

Sarah looked at him sadly and slowly shook her head. "I don't have that kind of power. Not on this project. Open your eyes, Matthew. You're so naive."

"If it wasn't you, then what? What?"

"Don't you think they knew about us? Your mysterious Colonel Warrington? My superiors? That's why you were chosen. It was their cover. If you get shot down behind the curtain, they'll write you off as some lovesick lunatic. Even the Russians would buy that."

A wall crumbled in Matt's mind, revealing another section in a maze of mysteries.

"He used me. He used us."

"You fit perfectly," Sarah explained. "Made to order. Undisciplined. Self-abusive. The wild lifestyle. Me. Colonel Warrington's computer must have spit your name out with bells ringing...."

Matt's anger was momentarily diffused by his embarrassment over Sarah's knowledge of his descent.

"I knew. I had my spies," she continued, picking up on his thoughts. "At first, I was infuriated by your lack of support and understanding. Then I realized it had happened too fast."

"Any moron could have figured that out," Matt snapped. "I had no great *Cause* to make me forget. I had nothing to ease the pain. Nothing! I had to live with it every day, every minute.... Why are we getting into this again? I knew this wasn't right. Your being here. Being part of this."

"You've got to learn to control your emotions and not let them control you," Sarah said.

"Like you, right? Walk out without a tear. The original Vulcan. Ms. Robopilot."

"That's not true and you know it," she argued. "I feel. I hurt."

"I haven't seen the first sign of it. Not then. Not now. Not last night."

"I'm not like you. I don't wear my emotions on my sleeve."

"You don't wear them anywhere. They don't exist!"

"You know better, Matthew. But you can't push your emotions on me. I could never hurt the way you want me to. You want me to start crying and screaming and clawing. That's not me. But that doesn't mean it didn't hurt. That I didn't love."

Matt looked away. He didn't want to be overwhelmed by Sarah's hypnotic eyes. Even the stupid coveralls couldn't distract him from their power. And she was right. He had wanted her to cry and scream and claw. He wanted to see some dramatic evidence that she had suffered as he had. But that wasn't like her. He couldn't change the way she was. That's why he had loved her so fiercely, why he had to love her so fiercely. He never felt secure in their relationship. He always felt he had to win her heart every day, that if he eased up one minute, her love would dissipate. Being unable to drop his guard had taken a toll on his emotions. But there were benefits. It kept the romance fresh and intensified the attraction. Each time they touched, it was like that day's assurance that she still cared.

But only that day's.

Sarah countered that he was wrong, that her steady love was far stronger than his volatile passions, that he was just overreacting to her bridled emotions. He almost began to believe her. Then she left. She left so fast and went so far away that he never had the opportunity to sort it out. Was it really *The Cause*? Or was it just Sarah? Would she have found something, anything... and left anyway?

Why did he even care any more? The world was tearing apart. Was there anything more mundane than an in-depth analysis of why an old love failed? They started the conversation with Matt learning how he'd been exploited by both governments. Then everything went right back to their little hill of beans.

As always.

"Doesn't it bother you that they used us?" Matt asked, unable to steer the conversation to anything else.

"No."

"No? That's all you can say?"

"That's the way they operate. You've got to see the larger picture. Stop being so selfish."

"Selfish?"

"Calm down, baby," Sarah cooed. "It brought you back."

The limousine stopped. Matt and Sarah exited from opposite doors and were escorted to a large operations hangar.

The scene inside was chaotic. It was nothing like Matt expected. Project Scorpion had been intensely secretive. The meetings were the height of order and efficiency. But now scores of civilians roamed around among the pilots. Matt recognized the United States ambassador and some of her staff huddled in a corner with a pack of Israeli government leaders. Several American military officers were gathered with their Israeli counterparts in another corner. Matt spotted a group of bearded orthodox rabbis clutching prayer books and chanting. The hangar was buzzing with chatter and what appeared to be sounds of wailing. The tension in the room was nearly unbearable.

"Look," Sarah said, pointing to a group of civilians across the room. "Those people are crying."

General Zaccur David, the commander-in-chief of Project Scorpion, spotted Matt and walked over. The tall, leathery-faced, Romanian-born Israeli military leader had treated Matt harshly during the early days of training. He resented the fact that he was ordered to accept an American civilian as part of his team. A United States Air Force pilot would have been bad enough, but a sissy commercial airline pilot? He didn't believe Matt had the intestinal fortitude to handle it.

But there was more to Matt Slade than the General was allowed to know. Not only had Matt succeeded, he had won over his commander with both his superior aeronautical ability and his high-spirited personality. By the end of the training, the lone American had become one of the general's favorites. The night before Matt left, in fact, the two had gone out together and ended up in a rousing fight with a rat-pack of British naval officers. Matt and the general knocked out two each, and they returned to the base intoxicated with their victory and bonded as friends.

General David was all business this morning as he grasped Matt's hand. Matt noticed a tenseness in the general's body, especially around his eyes.

"What's going on?" Matt asked. "Why have we blown our unit's cover?"

"Our cover hasn't been blown. Not yet," General David said,

greeting Sarah in a more formal fashion. "But it soon may be unimportant. Come."

Colonel Sam Cohen arrived and quickly caught up with the group.

"Why so many people?" Sam asked.

"I suspect we're about to find out," Matt replied.

General David led Matt, Sarah, and Sam through a partition and into a large, separate room. All conversation stopped when they entered. Spread out across the room were twenty-four coffins. Many were open; others were draped with what at first appeared to be standard American flags. The flag had the same colors and stripes as the American flag, but instead of fifty, five-pointed solid white stars set against the blue field in the left-hand corner, there were fifty-one, six-pointed stars—as in the Star of David.

Sam and Sarah, warned by the unusual flag, hesitantly approached the caskets. Matt sensed their fear and followed at a slower pace. Inside the first, the second, the third—inside all twenty-four—was the reality of General Kalinina's sadistic vision. Bodies of dark-haired men, women, and children were laid out in the caskets. They were embalmed and dressed in the finest clothes.

Sticking up from the center of each person's head was a rolled piece of paper. The papers were set in place so neatly that it was difficult to notice that the bottom ends of the papers were buried deep in the skull through a gaping bullet hole.

Sam and Sarah knew instantly who they were and what had happened. Matt didn't have clue. He started to ask but stopped when he saw the horrified look in Sam's eyes. Sarah's face remained expressionless. She began walking from coffin to coffin, burning the vision of each corpse into her mind. When she reached the first of the closed caskets, Sarah lifted the lid in order to view the body inside. The strange flag slid to the ground. After closing the lid, Sarah gently draped the flag back over the coffin, then moved on to the next one.

"We should stop her," Matt said, taking a step in her direction.

General David reached out and prevented him from continuing.

"All of us have to deal with this in our own way. This is her way. She is an Israeli."

"Who are they? Who did this? I don't understand," Matt said.

"They're Refusniks," Sam said, his voice thick with grief. "Russian Jews. General Kalinina has finally given them their exit visas."

"They arrived this morning," General David explained. "A captured Israeli pilot flew them here. He didn't know what he was carrying. He went into shock when he found out."

"There's something else," General David said, motioning for Matt and Sam to follow. He led them into a side room where a single coffin rested, covered like the others with the bizarre flag. General David slowly folded the flag and then lifted up the coffin lid.

It took Matt nearly a minute to recognize the beautiful woman in the casket. She was wearing a bright red sequined dress and white gloves. Her hair was frosted and perfectly set. Like the others, she had the roll of paper protruding up from the hole in her forehead. Matt's mind flashed to a news photograph he had once seen. This woman had attended some party or political function at the White House.

"Masha," Sam said softly. "Masha Morozov. But why?"

"Kalinina always hated her the most, even more than President Morozov," General David said. "He hated her expensive clothes and Western beauty. His little joke was to list her as a Jew on her exit visa."

"How could he do something like this?" Matt wondered. "The world will be outraged. Everybody loved her. This is outrageous."

"He doesn't care," General David said. "He's mad. Insane with hate. In a few days, what the world thinks won't matter anyway.

"The pilots are gathering in the next hangar," General David continued, walking briskly for the exit. "You'll learn more there."

Sam left with the General. Matt waited for Sarah. She opened and closed the final coffin, then walked silently over to him. Her face remained blank. No tears. No fear. No outrage. Just a nothingness that was chilling to observe.

"What's in the room," she said in an emotionless voice.

"Masha Morozov. Like the others."

Sarah disappeared into the room, then emerged within thirty seconds. As they left the hangar and entered the sunshine, Sarah's hand reached for Matt's. She grasped his fingers so tightly it hurt.

She continued to stare straight ahead.

"Are you OK?" he asked.

She said nothing, but Matt knew the answer. Sarah was a soldier first. There remained no lingering hope that it could ever be otherwise.

Her Cause was now even greater.

EIGHT

Matt found his specially-designed chair waiting in Hangar Fourteen. He opened a small door in the back of the chair, took out the spongy headphones, and switched on the black knob. He slipped on the headphones and adjusted the volume of the classical music. After getting everything in order, he looked around the room and nodded recognition to a number of the other pilots. His comrades were cordial, but preoccupied.

General David entered from a side door and took his place at the front of the room. All the pilots spoke English, and all the in-flight radio transmissions were carried out in English, but the meetings were held in Hebrew—a concession to Israeli culture. Matt wasn't the only pilot who had to rely upon the translation. Some of the newer Israeli citizens were weak in the language, including two Russian-born pilots who had the Hebrew translated into their own language.

Matt turned and searched the room for Sarah. He was curious to see if she also needed the translation. It didn't surprise him to see her sitting without any encumbrances. Sarah couldn't speak a word of Hebrew when she left America five years ago. She was no doubt fluent now.

The classical music ended abruptly, replaced by General David's voice. The computer instantly translated General David's Hebrew to English, Russian, or any of the Earth's other languages. Along with recreating the exact pitch and tone of the voice, the machine had been designed to pick up inflections in the speech, including the most minute traces of anger, amusement, fear, anxiety, or nervousness. Although General David's Hebrew was firm and the Israeli pilots were calmed, the sensitive computer cut through the forced strength. General David's translated comments were much more alarming in English and Russian than in Hebrew.

"I don't have the time or the desire to belabor the point, nor can I afford to underplay the graveness of our present situation," the general said. "We expect Russia to attack Israel with its full military power within a few days. Our intelligence sources say the attack will begin as early as tomorrow at dawn. Only you and your twenty-one Scorpion fighters stand in the way of the total destruction of our nation.

"Everyone is on twenty-four-hour alert from this point on. You will eat and sleep next to your jets until otherwise ordered. Our intelligence sources have pinpointed how and where they expect the attacks to come. Because of the substantial troop reductions negotiated by the Americans in the past half-decade, we will have a little more lead time to react. That could be critical.

"Each one of you has a specific defense assignment already programmed into your fighter. The course, defense posture, and targets have been computed to cover every possibility—from the simple defense of our borders resulting in a quick retreat by the Russians, to the total annihilation of the entire Russian military machine. This includes the defensive detonation of all Russian nuclear missiles before they are launched."

General David's last comment ignited a buzz in the room. The after-effects of such a massive nuclear blow-out would be felt for nearly a decade in Russia, and possibly throughout all Europe.

"I know this sounds unfathomable, but we can only guess how General Kalinina will react to the Scorpions. We don't expect him to surrender. Our operatives fear that he will take his entire country down with him if he's defeated. He'll never give in to Jews."

General David paused. "Any questions?"

Hundreds of questions, hundreds of moral dilemmas and horrible scenarios were wrapped up in the general's blunt statements, but Matt knew few would be posed. The Israeli soldiers were well trained. Since its inception in 1948, Israel had been surrounded by terrorists and hate-filled enemies. Even the Israeli people seemed resigned to the fact that a monstrous war was inevitable. Still, there were questions that had to be asked, alternatives to consider.

"Shouldn't we warn the Russians of our power? Of what we have?" Matt began.

"Expose our military secrets? For what purpose?" General David countered.

"Scare 'em. Maybe they'll back off. They'll realize they can't win."

"They'll have enough time to pull back after the initial attack. We will give them every opportunity to retreat. We don't plan to occupy Russia."

That comment drew a nervous laugh from the gathered pilots. Israel continued to be criticized throughout the world for its ceaseless process of expanding its borders into the surrounding Arab nations.

"What about America?" Sam asked.

"They're on alert, but they'll probably sit this one out. They'll be with us if we need them."

General David paused, then said what all the pilots were thinking. "We won't be needing them.

"Besides," General David went on, deadpanning a perfect set up, "we have Matthew."

The laughter was less forced this time. All the pilots accepted Matt, even the ones who had initially resented his presence. The tension in the room had started out like a taut rope ready to snap. Now the rope was slackening. What struck Matt the most, however, was the way General David had pronounced "Matthew." It made him sound almost... almost Jewish.

"There's got to be a way to prevent this," Matt said.

"Our leaders have considered everything," General David responded.

"This is all the doing of that one maniac, Kalinina, right?" Matt grew animated. "If we can stop him, we can stop the war."

"We tried that," General David explained. "We sent in some Death Angels. He was too insulated. Even the D.A.s couldn't get to him." Matt shuddered. If the "Death Angels," one of Israel's crack squads, couldn't take Kalinina out, war might be inevitable, unless...

"Couldn't we try with a Scorpion?"

"What are you suggesting?"

"Why don't you let me take Pocahontas into Moscow? I'll burn a hole through that maniac's skull and beat it out of there before they know what hit them. The way my jet looks, and with what it can do, the Russians will think it was a UFO!"

General David turned and slowly sat down at his desk. While his back was to the pilots, he smiled. Matt Slade possessed a crazy kind of blind courage that the general admired. A dangerous, out-of-control courage, but courage nevertheless.

"How do you propose to pinpoint General Kalinina out of the crowd?"

"I don't know. At a speech. At his house. In his bed. We can do extraordinary things with those stingers. One of the computer geeks said that if a man was standing on the ground, we could shave his whiskers from 20,000 feet. Killing him should be a lot easier than that!"

Matt hadn't intended the line to be funny, but the way it came out made everyone roar with laughter. The tension was beginning to work in reverse, making the pilots a bit giddy.

"If we could find him in a crowd or at an outside podium, you might be able to accomplish it," General David said. "But we don't have the time. Not any longer. Besides, it's out of the question. Can you imagine what would happen if something went wrong?"

"What could go wrong?" Matt asked.

"The Scorpions are still machines, Matthew. A gas line could break. An O-ring could come off. The computer could crash. It's remote but it's still a possibility. Then we would have the Russians capture a crazy American in an Israeli uniform flying a hideous-looking jet. They'd clamp some electrical teeth into your thigh, and you'd sing like a nightingale."

"What do you mean 'hideous'?" Matt said, standing up defiantly from his chair. "She's the most beautiful jet in the fleet!"

General David didn't try to suppress his amusement. The unusual painting allowance was intended to bond the pilots to their jets in a personal way. Obviously, it had worked with Matt.

"Let's get back to the point here. We just can't risk it."

"I'd chomp the pill," Matt said, referring to the suicide tablet the pilots were issued. "I've felt like chomping that pill anyway."

The men and women roared again. Those who knew about Matt's love life cast their eyes toward Sarah, who buried her face in embarrassment.

"In all seriousness, Matt, I respect your courage. I really believe you'd get in that thing... that lovely lady... and fly your one-man mission right now. And I believe you'd take the tablet. But then the Russians would have a Scorpion. And that would be disastrous. Besides, the Knesset would never approve it. We can't be the aggressor. If something went wrong, we would be accused of starting World War III. If something went wrong and you were part of it, the Americans would also be guilty."

"Then I'll go," Sam said.

General David was taken aback. Matthew Slade, he could understand. But an Israeli-born soldier and military veteran like Colonel Cohen volunteering for what appeared to be an insane suicide mission?

"We can't strike first. That's it. End of discussion."

"All right, I'll buy that," Matt said. "This hand seems to have been dealt. But there's one thing we don't have to do. We don't have to explode the nuclear bombs on the ground. This is the work of one insane man and his followers. We shouldn't murder millions of Russian civilians because of it."

"We've got to stop them," General David reiterated. "We can't take any risks. Israel is a small country. Only a couple of bombs would have to get through to destroy us."

"None will. There's no humane reason why we have to

explode them on the ground. We'll blow them out of the sky. There'll be some radiation damage to the environment, but we'll save millions of innocent lives. We can handle it."

General David knew exactly what Matt was saying. The ground detonations were programmed into the computer. They could accomplish that by flying one of the jets by remote control. But once the nuclear missiles were launched, the battle would return to the realm of human ability. The pilots would have to track down each missile and manually shoot it down. The prospect of exposing the existence of an entire nation to human reaction was unheard of.

"We can do it," Matt said, standing and facing his fellow pilots. "We can do it, can't we?"

There was no response.

"Come on. I don't know about all of you, but I'm not some robot pilot. I'm sick of being the least important part of the jet. We're the best pilots in the world. We can do it. Sam? Levi? Saul? Lisa? Sarah?" Matt said, looking each person in the eye. "We can save millions and millions of lives. Children. Babies."

Matt looked around.

"You people, in this room right now, are sentencing them all to death by your silence. You know what those jets can do. It'll be simple. "Are you with me?"

Again silence. Then a soft female voice came from the back of the room. Sarah's voice. It was hardly more than a whisper.

"We can do it."

"What?" General David said, looking for the owner of the voice.

"We can do it," Sarah repeated, speaking more forcefully. "Matthew's right. We can't lose our humanity. Even in time of war."

"We can do it," Sam added.

The voices of the others started slowly, then built into a crescendo.

"We can do it! We can do it! We can do it!"

The pilots chanted for a full minute.

General David sat at his desk and took it in. It had finally happened. His elite band of pilots had everything. Talent. Training. The most advanced fighter jets. An awesome new weapon. They had everything but a group intensity, a team spirit.

The fear that cold technology would turn his pilots into robots ate at the general every night as he lay in bed waiting to fall asleep. It was the first thought he had every morning when he awakened. Now his squad had a spark. As his eyes scanned the room, he could see it springing to life in each individual animated face. The aerial detonation alternative gave the pilots back their sense of pride. Pilots were arrogant beasts by nature, and Project Scorpion had all but eroded their self-esteem. Matt had tapped into something that ached inside each one. Now, at last, their pride was returning. It spread over them, melding them into a team.

General David stood slowly and raised his hands for the pilots to end their chant. They obeyed as one. Their pride had returned, but they were by no means rebellious.

"I will propose it to the military council. I'll make it plain that we expect them to follow our wishes."

"All right!" Matt said, turning and slapping hands with those around him. Throughout the room, others were doing the same.

With the Russians breathing down their necks, the Scorpion force had finally been born.

By late that evening, the waiting was already beginning to drag. There were only three jets to a hangar, so there weren't many people around to help kill the time. Although the seven hangars were side by side, the pilots were ordered to remain in their own berths. The jets had to be airborne within seconds of the first blip of the Russian MIGs or missiles on the radar.

Fortunately, both Sarah and Sam were in Hangar Seven with Matt. Sam had been there all along. But Sarah had replaced Zipporah, bumping the native-born Israeli to Hangar Five. As they sat on the floor playing the card game, Hearts, surrounded by $2.4 billion worth of fighter jets, Matt was curious how Sarah had managed to trade positions.

"I volunteered to take care of Pocahontas while you were away," she explained matter-of-factly. "Someone had to turn over the engine and take an occasional test flight. I put in for Zipporah's slot. She was transferred out, and I was transferred in. Simple as that. It was all official."

"Keeping Poci warm was Sam's job," Matt said, looking accusingly at his buddy.

Sam shrugged. "You wouldn't want Sarah camping out with two men, would you?"

Matt grinned. "No. But Zippy was a stone fox."

Sarah shoved Matt on the shoulder. Then she threw down the Queen of Spades.

"You witch. You did that on purpose."

"What? Did 'Zippy' let you win? Not me. It's too much fun beating you."

"Haven't you… " Matt stopped and looked up at Sam. Sam looked away. No need to bore the colonel with the latest rendition of Matt's sob-story about how Sarah had stomped on his heart. The game ended, and they all returned to their jets. They crawled into sleeping bags set directly under the jet's underside. General David wanted the pilots to sleep as close to the fighters as possible, since being asleep would delay their reaction time. Shortly after the overhead lights were dimmed, Matt felt a presence near him.

"Isn't this disobeying orders?" Matt whispered to Sarah, who was perched on the edge of his sleeping bag.

"Your jets are in front of mine. I have more time."

Of course, Matt thought. *Sarah had everything covered.* Even her romantic gestures were governed by her adherence to The Cause. Had her fighter been first, she'd have remained bolted to its belly.

"Besides," Sarah said. "This might be our last night."

Matt's relationship with Sarah had been marred by "last nights." But this time, she wasn't dumping him for a greater cause. This time, at least, they were in it together.

"You think it will happen tomorrow?" she whispered.

"I think so. You didn't hear the translation. I think General David knows more than he's saying."

"How did he sound?"

"Those translators are like lie detectors. He was scared."

Matt sensed Sarah's uneasiness. Even though he was by far the more emotional of the two, he was like a teapot, building up steam and then letting it blast out. Sarah just simmered, holding everything under the surface.

"They'll attack in the morning," Matt continued, "but not early like everyone thinks. Late morning. The Russians have to figure it'll be a breeze. Israel is such a tiny country. A powerful one, but small geographically."

Sarah was silent for a while. Matt began drifting off to sleep. Even with the tension and uncertainty, the lingering effect of jet lag was getting to him.

"I'm sorry I brought you into this," she whispered again.

"Don't be," Matt answered groggily. "I think it was something bigger. A destiny. I don't know. It's all so wrong. But it feels like I was meant to be here. Can you understand?"

Sarah crawled over and hugged him tightly.

"Now maybe you understand," she whispered.

Sarah was gone when Matt awakened. Matt retreated to the bathroom, quickly freshened up, then walked over to a small table. He glanced at a window high up in the hangar and saw the soft light. Obviously the Russians hadn't attacked at dawn. The instant he sat at the table, someone appeared and served an ample breakfast—soft scrambled eggs, just like he liked them. Fruit. Toast. Hash browns. As he began to eat, Sam appeared and sat beside him. The "food people" instantly placed his breakfast in front of him.

"See any Russians?" Matt cracked to his friend.

"This is not a joke, my friend. This is my country."

"I'm not worried about your country. I'm worried about theirs," Matt countered, matching Sam's seriousness.

Sam ignored the point. "They didn't attack at first light."

"I never expected them to. They'll come in broad daylight. No trick plays," Matt said.

"You really think they are that confident?"

"Russia against Israel? Are you kidding?"

"We are strong."

"You are tiny. A flea."

Sam's pride reared up for a second. Before he could say anything, he realized Matt wasn't being insulting. "You are probably right. The Russians have nothing to fear. They will come in daylight."

"Late morning," Matt said, repeating his earlier prediction. "The hour of arrogance."

"Goliath was arrogant, too. And David kicked his butt."

"And so will we, Colonel. But this ain't a boy and his rock. That's what worries me."

Sarah arrived and took her place at the table. She always looked fresh and beautiful in the morning, and this morning was no exception. Matt was even getting used to seeing her in uniform. As before, the "food people" appeared from nowhere, laid down a placemat, and positioned the food before her.

"Hey, how come you got English muffins?" Matt asked.

"I requested them. Did you?"

"No. They never give me what I want."

"What did you request?"

"Bacon."

Sarah looked at Sam. They both shook their heads and laughed.

The three continued eating, then Sam returned to the conversation that was interrupted by Sarah's arrival.

"You said you were worried about something. You didn't explain."

"The power," Matt said without looking up. "Will your country know when to stop?"

"We are a God-fearing people," Sam stressed. "We will know. We will defend ourselves and our country. No more."

"Let's hope so."

In Moscow, General Kalinina had been awake seventy-eight hours, popping mescaline and drinking pots of coffee. His eyes were so wide and bright that his aides grew fearful. But they were also afraid to confront him. And the less they challenged, the more powerful General Kalinina became.

The plan had been to wait for Israel to react to the gruesome present he had sent the night before. Israel was notorious for quick retaliation. The slaughtered Refusniks would surely sucker them into making the first move. That would allow the Russians to counterattack and level the country. By nine that morning, Kalinina's aides knew the General wasn't going to be able to wait. He was so hyped-up by speed, caffeine, and power that he was practically jumping through the roof. He demanded constant updates from his military liaisons, and was enraged each time there was no mention of tell-tale blips on the radar screen forewarning an Israeli bomber attack. He monitored the news reports all over the world from his satellite-fed media center. There had yet to be any mention of his Refusnik solution. General Kalinina was counting on Israel to "go crying like baby pigs" to the rest of the world.

"Have they no pride?" he roared. "How many do I have to kill before the Jewish sheep respond?"

There wasn't time to kill and deliver twenty-five more Refusniks. General Kalinina's chemically-fed impatience couldn't handle any more delays. At 10 A.M., Kalinina ordered his Air Force to ready fifty MIGs for a strike on all the mapped-out Israeli military bases. A second force of fifty MIGs would follow half an hour later, hammering Tel Aviv and surrounding cities, cleaning up whatever was left.

All over Moscow, the entire Russian war machine was placed on full alert in case the Americans wanted to show their grief over losing Israel. The anti-ballistic missile network was alerted to intercept any long-range incoming warheads. Behind that, General Kalinina ordered his doomsday forces to be ready. Should something go wrong, should the Americans trip him up, he was prepared to ignite a full-scale nuclear war.

"Let them come," he said to himself, squeezing his stubby hands together with insane anticipation. "Let the Americans come."

At 10:47 A.M., the first dots appeared on Israeli Lieutenant Shimon Yitzhak's radar screen. A wave of panic washed over him as he pushed back his seat and caught a glimpse of an adjacent screen. His eyes met the eyes of Lieutenant Binyamin Burg, his friend in the next stall. They each saw the other's terror. Almost as one, they rolled back into their positions and looked down at the large red button at the top left of each console. They had lived with the ramifications of those buttons for years. But as time passed, their significance waned and they hardly noticed them anymore. That had suddenly changed. The moment they dreaded dawned.

The two officers reached over and simultaneously pushed the red buttons. Yitzhak was startled to see the button light up, signaling that it had accomplished its mission. He jerked his hand back as if he had been shocked. He never realized it had a light.

Yitzhak and Burg's forefingers set off a wave of alarms from one end of Israel to the other. Bells, buzzers, and personal beepers came to life everywhere from the Prime Minister's belt to the Knesset, from the American Embassy to the individual homes of military and political leaders.

The alarms rang loudest in the seven Scorpion hangars. For an instant, the twenty-one pilots froze in place. In Hangar Seven, Matt looked at Sarah as a rush of adrenaline shot through his veins. There was no time, but he kissed her anyway. She was so surprised she didn't have time to kiss back. Before she could react, Matt had grabbed his helmet, turned and climbed into Pocahontas. Sarah, momentarily stunned by the intensity of Matt's kiss, threw on her helmet and ran to her fighter. Sam, unfettered by love or emotion, was already strapping himself into the cockpit of his blinding, sun-yellow machine.

At 10:48 A.M., the first Scorpion was airborne. By 10:52, all twenty-one had left the ground.

A gunfight at 20,000 feet, Matt thought as he raced toward the wave of blips on this radar screen. *And the world will never be the same.*

NINE

Pocahontas' radar screen told Matt everything he needed to know. Although the entire Scorpion Force could see what was coming and the battle plan was computerized to the last detail, Matt had flown solo on so many missions that he wanted to make voice contact before attacking in a force. He also liked to chatter in the heat of battle, a personality quirk that was tolerated because it helped break the tension.

"I see fifty little Miggys coming straight down the chute from Moscow between thirty and forty lat," he radioed to Colonel Cohen, tracking the invaders by latitude. "Tight pattern. Like bowling pins. Not smart, but no surprise."

"Roger," Colonel Cohen confirmed.

"Second wave should have as many or more behind them," Matt predicted, his tongue loosening further. "They'll spread out next time. That's when we'll earn our stripes."

"Roger."

"We got only fourteen up? Did the others get cold feet, or are they holding back for a broadside?" Matt asked, speculating that the remaining seven Scorpions had peeled off in case of a sneak attack from Jordan, Syria, or any other unfriendly nation.

"Roger."

Throughout the Scorpion force, the pilots were tight. Despite their superior weaponry, they were flying untested jets. Anything could go wrong. Their throats were so dry that no one but Matt felt the urge to speak. That was fine with him.

"You guys want to fall back? I can handle these fifty myself," he cracked.

Smiles cut through clenched jaws. Levi, Saul, Lisa, and Zipporah all laughed to themselves and relaxed the death grips they had on their controls.

"Negative," Colonel Cohen responded.

Matt's remark had an unnerving effect on Colonel Valery Karvoff, the leader of the incoming MIGs. Educated in America during the decade of detente, he understood English so well he could decipher accents. The size of the intercepting force had previously amused him. Only now, the cocky and strangely familiar American voice coming from the heart of the Israeli defense made him uneasy.

"Did you read that?" one of his pilots radioed in Russian.

"Yes."

"What do you think?"

"American educated."

"Sounds confident," another Russian pilot said, breaking in.

"They are seeking courage before their deaths. It's an obvious ploy. They are meeting us with no resistance. This is a suicide force. An insult!"

The two Russian immigrant pilots in the Scorpion Force, knowing what channel to use, eavesdropped on Colonel Karvoff's conversation. Both kept their thoughts to themselves.

"We're going to engage early. Should we move up to Lon 38, Turkey? Or 44, Black Sea?" Matt asked.

"Negative. Original orders in play. We hit at Lon 33 off Nahariyya. Splashdown in the Med."

"We're on course to engage early. Should we circle?"

Instead of deflecting Matt's idle chatter, Colonel Cohen now had a command decision to make. He made his own calculations and determined that the American was correct. The opposing forces, flying slower than anticipated, were set to come into range over Turkey instead of the Mediterranean Sea. Colonel Cohen radioed General David and was ordered to stick to the original plan. The Knesset was firm in its insistence that battle had to start over Israeli air space.

"Positive on the circle. Follow command lead," Colonel Cohen radioed.

"Here we go loop-de-loop," Matt quipped, swinging in behind the colonel's conservatively painted silver jet. "Sightseeing Gaza at thirty lon should bring us back to D-Day by Nahary, or however that's pronounced. Sound good?"

Colonel Cohen did some fast calculations and again determined that Matt's instincts were right on the mark. Only his geography was off.

"Negative. Swing at Barbarit and cut speed. Chip the strip. Let's stay in Israel," he directed.

"I thought Gaza was Israel," Matt said. "Sarah, didn't you want to take me to Barbarit once? Well, here we go. Point out that beach you were talking about as we pass."

Sarah, flying her first combat mission, tried to respond to Matt's nonsense, but the words wouldn't come.

"Negative on the beach," she finally said after a few false starts. "Positive on Slade clamming up!"

"Thanks sweetie," he said, much to the amusement of the other twelve.

Colonel Karvoff was relieved to see the Scorpions retreat.

"We have no resistance now," he announced to his pilots as they passed over the Black Sea and headed into Turkey. "The Jewish cowards have withdrawn."

"Check again," another pilot said.

The fourteen dots on the Russian's radar screens hooked around Barbarit, fanned out for fifty miles, and were heading north toward the Russians.

"What is this insanity?" Colonel Karvoff mumbled. "They come. They go. An American makes jokes?" He switched back to the Israeli channel.

"I'm heading down to Beer Sheva for a six pack," Colonel

Karvoff heard Matt quip. "This WW Thrice stuff could work up a thirst."

"Negative," Colonel Cohen said.

Something struck Colonel Karvoff about the voice he was hearing. He opened the channel.

"Matt Slade?"

"Who wants to know?"

"It is you?"

"It's always been me. Who are you?"

"Colonel Valery Karvoff, U.S.S.R."

Matt was staggered by the ID. He had served with Colonel Karvoff on half a dozen missions for the joint United States/Russia international anti-drug task force. They socialized together and had become friends. Karvoff had even saved his life once, knocking out a surprise ground missile launched by a heavily-armed drug lord in Istanbul. Now, for the second time, Matt found himself in a dogfight that had suddenly turned personal.

"Karv, are you leading this invasion force?"

"That's confidential."

"Hey, the secret's out, buddy. You've got two minutes to live. This isn't the time for the cloak and dagger stuff."

"Pocahontas, break off communication," Colonel David ordered.

"Colonel, there's some history here. I may be able to stop this."

"Negative. Orders from below are to break."

"But... "

"No buts; break off."

"Sorry Karv, I'd love to chat with an old eighty-eight snow bird, but I've been silenced."

"Roger."

Matt punched some numbers into his communication net. His last message was a code for Colonel Karvoff to switch to a specific short wave band they used on their previous mission.

"Karv, you got ears?"

"I'm here."

"We've got less than a minute. Pull off your team. You're over-matched. Believe me."

"You're bluffing."

"No bluff. Listen, why do you think we've only sent fourteen jets to intercept? We have a new weapon. You can't compete. You're going to die in forty-five seconds. Your entire squad is going to die. Every pilot that comes after us today is going to die. Every soldier in the U.S.S.R. is going to die. You can stop it. Trust me. You saved my life once. I owe you. Pull off."

"I'm under orders."

"Forget your orders. You're serving a raving lunatic! His orders don't count. You've got thirty seconds, Karv. Please, in the name of God, pull off!"

"We will be victorious."

"You'll die a fool! And you won't even know what hit you."

Matt had a sudden thought. He pulled out of formation, eased back the throttle, hit a booster and accelerated to 3,500 knots, faster than any jet had ever flown in history. In five seconds, he hit 90,000 feet, higher than any fighter was known to fly. He targeted the last ten MIGs in the Soviet formation, pushed a red button on his joystick, and unleashed a beam of deadly light that destroyed the entire rear guard of the Soviet attack force.

"I could have taken out all fifty, Karv. You've seen it now. Back off!"

Colonel Karvoff couldn't believe what he had just witnessed. However, his men did. They filled another channel with fearful cries of desperation.

"The American is right. We're overmatched. Let's abort," a voice said.

"Remain on course," Colonel Karvoff ordered.

"Thank you, Matt," the Russian colonel said, his voice etched in pain as he awaited death. "It's just as well. Kalinina is quite insane. I hated being recalled. Let's hope, when the last Russian is dead, whoever emerges as your leader won't be equally insane."

"Karv! No! Pull out! Please. You can fly your jet to America, and they'll welcome you. I'll get your family out. I promise."

"Too late. Did you get married?"

"No. Jill vanished. With the rest. Please pull out!"

"She was among the taken?"

"You know about that?" Matt asked, the tense anticipation of battle dissolving. "Tell me!"

"Didn't she?"

"No. Tell me!"

"She was... "

The voice cut off. Matt frantically switched the dials, saw a flash of light, then looked on his radar screen. There were millions of small fragments fading away like a Fourth of July fireworks display.

"NO!" he screamed.

Composing himself, he fell back into his position with the Scorpion Force and switched to the command channel.

"S-1 back on."

"Matt, you really did it this time," Colonel Cohen said.

"I know. It was a judgment call. I thought I could stop the slaughter."

"You can't. It's bigger than you and me."

"The guy saved my life. I owed him. He was a human being. I thought he might listen."

"He didn't."

"No. But he knew what happened to Jill."

"Did he say?"

"You killed him before he could. Him and everybody else. What did that take, two seconds?"

"I'm sorry, Matt. For a lot of things. They picked up your shortwave broadcast below. They view it as an act of treason, warning the Russians."

"That's garbage. It's what we should have done all along."

"That's not the way they see it. They want you down."

"What? To stand trial for treason? Isn't that an automatic death penalty in Israel?"

There was no response.

"And I'm supposed to just land and give up?"

"Affirmative."

"I'm operating one of the most powerful weapons of destruction in existence, and I'm supposed to just touch down and put up my hands."

"It's the honorable thing to do."

"I'm not doing it. Let me fight this battle. I'd rather die in combat. If I survive, we'll sort it out afterward."

"Negative. The orders have been given. You sit it out."

"And if I don't, what? We start fighting each other?"

In her jet, the tears were streaking down Sarah's cheeks. She found her voice.

"Do what he says, Matthew, please."

"Do you know what you're saying, Sarah? They'll execute me as a traitor."

"We'll stand up for you. All twenty-one of us. We'll change their minds."

"No, you won't. The law is clear. They won't listen. Politicians never do. I can't believe you want me to give up and die."

Matt heard a ping, then saw both his offensive and defensive systems go down.

"I'm off! Did you do that, Sam?"

"Affirmative."

"Great. That's a neat trick. Why didn't anyone tell me?"

"Emergency precaution."

"We can all do it to each other?"

"Negative."

"Only you?"

"Affirmative."

"Don't bet on that. Nice little Achilles' heel you created. So, I'm impotent and defenseless. I assume you can drop my fuel, also?"

"Affirmative."

"Wonderful," Matt said, pushing away the throttle in disgust. "You can take my controls and fly me down yourself, can't you?"

"Affirmative. It's more honorable for you to take it in."

"I'll go down," Matt relented, dropping out of formation. "By the way, you have 150 MIGs coming over the Black Sea. I saw them on my scope when I was at Angel ninety. That's 150 more pilots you're going to incinerate. Then another 150 after that, until the last officer is dead. And I guarantee you, every one of us knows at least one of them personally. They trained beside us all over the world. Yesterday, they were our best friends. Today, we kill them. Right, Viscoff? Serge?" Matt said, bitterly addressing the two Russian-born pilots on the Scorpion Force.

Neither replied, but like Sarah, both Serge and Anton Viscoff were crying.

"I'm out. Good luck, guys," Matt said. "I invite you all to my execution."

"S-7, can you continue?" Colonel Cohen asked, the emotion choking his words.

There was a long silence. A faint voice finally broke through.

"Affirmative," Sarah said, brushing away a flood of tears with her black aviator gloves.

"Of course she can, Sam. You think my pending death would rattle the Ice Princess?"

"You sure?" Colonel Cohen asked, ignoring Matt.

"Affirmative."

"Good. We're one short, and we have a long day ahead of us."

In Moscow, General Kalinina refused to believe the reports of the advanced Israeli weapon. He ordered a third wave of MIGs, 300 strong, to follow the force that was already airborne. When the second wave was destroyed with equal ease, General Kalinina issued a "Code Black" doomsday command, launching an all-out nuclear assault against Israel. A thousand more MIGs took flight, and 5,000 missiles with nuclear warheads were launched. In the confusion, thirty-five missiles struck MIGs in the crowded skies, resulting in a series of awesome explosions that took out another 50 Russian jets before they had a chance to die in battle. Chaos reigned.

Still, enough got through to strain the limits of the Scorpion Force. The seven remaining jets were launched, abandoning the Jordan and Syria watch. They were instead redirected to hit targets deep inside the Soviet Union. Although the Scorpion technology was vastly superior, the sheer size of the Soviet arsenal evened the odds. The Scorpion pilots were caught in a hellish video game that taxed their reflexes to the maximum. They couldn't afford one mistake. After an hour of non-stop fighting—during which they transformed the eastern Mediterranean Sea into a churning depository for blazing chunks of molten metal—the pilots were physically and emotionally spent.

A second problem was also emerging. The constant spate of nuclear explosions sent out violent concussions that tore at the Scorpions' outer shells. The radiation was so thick that a blanket of invisible poison hung in the sky, causing critical instruments to fail. Any pilot bailing out after a freeze-up or a hit would be immediately consumed in the super-charged atmosphere.

Matt Slade watched it all from the radar screens in his hangar. He had been placed under arrest for treason immediately upon landing and was now surrounded by ten armed soldiers.

"They're coming unglued up there," he told his captors during the second hour. "They can't take the strain. I've got to get back up!"

The commanding Sergeant refused.

Distracted by the explosions in the sky, no one noticed that one Scorpion jet had been missing for the past half hour. Anton Viscoff's black and gold war bird had disappeared over Turkey thirty minutes before. The young pilot was devastated by the massive destruction of his former homeland. As the fatigue of the battle set in, he began to visualize the tortured faces of friends, relatives, and Air Force comrades in the fiery hell above and below. His paranoia was fed by the knowledge that he, and he alone, could stop it. After a test run one night, he had entered a control room at the central hangar and found Colonel Cohen's secret codes for disarming the Scorpion fighters. He copied the material and hid it in his personal items. At the time, he didn't even know why. It was just a secret that he stumbled upon, a carrot that was too big to ignore.

Now, as his sanity faded, eaten away by stress and the effects of radiation, the only thought flashing in his brain was the code and sequence for disarming the Scorpion Force. He headed south over the Black Sea, hooked west over the Mediterranean and came up behind the area where the Scorpions had advanced their proverbial line-in-the-sand. Once again, they were engaged in battle, shooting down helpless MIGs and missiles like giant dragonflies feasting on a swarm of mosquitoes. Viscoff punched in the code, put it on lock, and flew in behind the twelve Scorpion fighters protecting Israel.

He disarmed them all.

Circling, he destroyed three of the defenseless jets before the remaining nine could comprehend what was happening and use their speed to scatter.

"We've been disarmed!" a frantic Colonel Cohen radioed to General David. "We're completely disarmed!"

In hangar seven, Matt Slade swung into action.

"Your whole country is going to be destroyed in the next ten minutes unless you let me get back up. I'm all you got. If you want to keep me here, shoot me now, because I'm not listening anymore."

With that, Matt ran to another booth and grabbed hold of one of the computer experts by the collar. The sergeant and soldiers charged after him.

"Halt," the Sergeant demanded.

"Don't 'halt' me. If you're not going to shoot, get out of my way!"

He turned to the thin man he had by the throat."

"Get my system back on line. Now!"

"Uh, I don't have to," the man choked. "When a jet's down for half an hour, it comes back on automatically."

"What's the code to block him from doing it again?"

The man didn't answer.

"There are 500 nuclear warheads heading toward us right now. WHAT'S THE BLOCK CODE?"

"677.25."

Matt ran to his jet, jumped in, and roared out into the sky.

"This is S-1 back up and on. I'll hold the fort until the others can help. What's that going to take?"

"They need to land and be reprogrammed. Five minutes down, minimum," General David said from command headquarters.

"Do it. Now! Sam, you out there?"

"I'm coming in. It's all up to you, Matt, the life of our country. Maybe even the history of the world."

"Thanks for reminding me. Did we lose, who did we... did we lose... "

"She's OK. She went inland."

Matt exhaled deeply. "Who did this?"

"Viscoff. He was either a double agent or cracked."

"He blew a fuse. Otherwise, he would have warned them about what we had. They didn't have a clue. I'll go after him when you get fixed."

"Good luck, Matthew."

There was no more time for even Matt to talk. MIGs and missiles filled the sky. He elevated to 40,000 feet, about 25,000 feet higher than the incoming enemy, then went to work. With no friendly aircraft in the sky, he put the stinger on automatic, programming it to knock out all flying objects a pound or more in weight within a mile of his jet. He used the manual controls to shoot down anything the computer missed, a problem which was increasing substantially due to the nuclear concussions and radiation fouling the instruments.

Pocahontas began firing at a blinding rate, sending pulses of fifty to a hundred separate beams with every second. Still, it wasn't enough. Fifteen minutes of intense automatic and manual shooting, combined with the blast of hundreds of nuclear explosions, frayed Matt's nerves like a rope burning through his hands.

He found himself flying in thick mushroom clouds of scalding ash, using nothing but his faulty instruments to guide him.

"I'm overloading up here. Get me some help, soon!"

"Hang on five more minutes. We'll have the first three back up."

"Mayday. Mayday," his radio screamed. "One got behind you. It's heading in to Tel Aviv. Mayday."

"MIG or missile?"

"Missile."

"It must have ridden another's shadow. I've beaten the wall back fifteen miles. That gives us about thirty seconds. The three are going to have get up here now."

"Affirmative."

Matt banked down and went after the missile like a hawk dropping on a dove. He sighted it on his windshield target scope. It was whistling through the clear southern skies eighty miles south of the battle line near Netanya. He aimed his manual control and detonated the missile with a single, hair-thin beam.

Down below, every glass window and every light bulb in the Jewish port city shattered from the tremendous nuclear explosion 5,000 feet above.

"Anything else?" Matt radioed.

"We're clean to the wall," General David said.

"Anybody up?"

"They're up. First three."

"Thank God."

Matt rocketed back to 33 Lon and continued peeling back Kalinina's relentless wall of death. After five nerve-shattering minutes, Sam, Levi, and Zipporah joined him.

"Glad you guys could make it. I'm going after Vis."

"Negative. We need you here," Colonel Cohen ordered.

"He's going to do the same thing to the seven inland. They have no place to reprogram. We can't sacrifice them to him."

"They can get back."

"They won't. He's got a lot of space to chase, and they're spread out. He can disarm and destroy each one before they know what hit them. I'm gone."

"Negative."

"I'm not feeding her to him, Sam. I've already lost one woman. I can't lose another. What can they do, charge me with treason?"

Matt hit his booster and raced north toward Moscow at 3,800 knots. He kept his stinger on, carving a mile wide path through the Soviet air attack as he traveled.

Matt switched on the Scorpion tracking system and projected it on the left windshield Heads Up Display. The computer could only pinpoint five of Pocahontas' sister jets. The others, he speculated, had already been destroyed. He focused in on the blip identified by the computer as Viscoff's black and gold aircraft. The Russian was heading west toward his next target. Matt took another read. Fear gripped him as the screen displayed the ID number of Viscoff's target—S-7. The Russian was going after Sarah.

Matt punched the boosters to the max, hitting 4,000 knots and creating a sonic boom so powerful it detonated a number of the incoming Soviet missiles. Still, there was no way he could catch Viscoff before he locked Sarah's baby blue bird in his gun sights. He'd have to stall him.

"Sarah, Vis has turned. He's coming after you!"

"Affirmative. Taking evasive measures."

"Are you disarmed?"

"Affirmative. All are."

"Hang on. I'm coming. Fly into a nuclear cloud."

"Too late. I love you."

"It's not too late! Fly into a nuclear cloud. It'll foul the instruments and buy time. Please!"

"Too late. Helpless. I love you."

"Vis, do you read?"

Silence.

"Vis, it's Matt. I've been arrested. They're going to execute me. I'm not one of them. Do you read?"

"You were right, Matthew," Viscoff said, his voice scratchy and stripped of sanity like an exposed wire. "They didn't stop. They wouldn't stop. Why wouldn't they stop? Too many dead, Matt. Too many. My family's down there. My wife and kids. My country. This has got to stop."

"It can. But this isn't the way."

"What way is there? It's already almost over."

There was no debating that. Although the war was in its second hour—embryonic by normal standards—the resurrected Soviet Union stood on the verge of total destruction.

"That isn't your country," Matt argued. "Remember why you left. The oppression. The inhumanity. You're a Jew. You can't allow them to destroy your homeland."

"They have destroyed my homeland."

"Get off S-7 and we'll talk. There must be a way."

"I'm taking them all out. I've made up my mind. It's the only way."

"Your brain is cooked. You need help. Get off S-7. You know how I feel about her."

"Millions have died today. She is just one more."

"No, she's not! She's special to me. I can't allow it. I'll come after you. You do this, and you'll never set foot on the ground again."

"I'm invincible."

"The disarm code's been rewritten. Most of the force is back up. All you did was kill some of your friends."

"I don't believe it."

Matt heard a warning buzzer as Viscoff locked on to Sarah.

"Don't do it, Vis!" Matt screamed. "Don't kill her!"

"She'll never change, Matthew. She's one of the worst ones of all. She's too fervent. You just see her beauty. You don't see the ugliness that I see. She must be exterminated."

"Don't do it!"

A sickening blip sounded in Matt's cockpit. In an instant, Sarah's dot vanished.

"Ahhhhhhhhhhhh!" Matt screamed in despair. "Dear God, No!" Matt's anguish instantly turned to rage. He zeroed in on the crazed Russian. As he closed to a mile, he hit a strange black space. An instant later, he emerged into a different world. A series of nuclear warhead explosions in the same area had sprayed so much radiation in the atmosphere that the sky had turned into a photo negative. The air was inky black. The jets and missiles were blinding white. Matt checked his instruments. They were still functioning despite the weird phenomena.

The reverse atmosphere did nothing to cool Matt's rage. Even Pocahontas herself seemed possessed. The black eyes of the Native American maiden now blazed like white-hot pokers. Her once blue-black hair fell like molten lava down the aircraft's sides. In negative, her exotic beauty had taken on the fierce appearance of an angry demon.

Matt locked on to Viscoff and fired. The Russian's defensive laser negated the shots. Viscoff returned fire. Matt's defense similarly defused the deadly lasers. The two jets passed like ancient knights in a jousting battle filmed in negative, both effectively shielding the other's blows.

They circled and repeated the attack. Nothing. Although the theory had never been tested, the Scorpion jets, operating at full capacity, were incapable of destroying one other.

Neither pilot was satisfied with the standoff. Matt, burning with anger, was bent on revenge. Viscoff, burning with insanity, was growing frustrated over his inability to continue his self-proclaimed Soviet Union rescue effort.

"Leave me alone, Matt. I'll let you go."

"No chance. Not until you're a ball of fire."

The pair circled and headed toward each other again, each hoping a computer glitch would allow a single, thread-like beam to get through. That would be enough to disable, or destroy, the other's jet.

Matt's mind raced, searching for another option. Two jets, so advanced they were unable to take each other out... but was that entirely true? *No,* Matt thought. *There is a way.*

"You want to go mano a mano, Vis, then you got it," he challenged.

Matt programmed Pocahontas for a different tactic, one far less advanced.

"Don't be a hero, Matthew," Viscoff argued, sensing Matt's new strategy. "You're not fighting for your country. You're just a mercenary under a death sentence. Go home to America."

"You already took everything I have. If this is what it takes, then I'm prepared. You think you're crazy. Well, you ain't seen nothing yet!"

Viscoff was suddenly paralyzed by fear. His plan had been seeded in the knowledge of his own indestructibility. Now that had dramatically changed.

"I don't believe you. You love life too much, Slade."

"You took everything I love. I have nothing."

"You'd kill yourself for revenge? That's stupid."

"It's my life."

"Well, I've got too much work to do. I don't want any part of this," Viscoff said, pulling out of the approach.

"You're not getting away that easy. I know where your family is. The exact house in Salekhard on the Gulf of Ob. Sam never trusted you. He kept a file. You isolated them way north, out of fire. They'll survive this. But you knew that. Well, they're not surviving any more. You run from this fight, you sentence them to die."

The thought of losing his wife and children, whom he had indeed stashed in the small, frozen Soviet city of Salekhard, seemed to push Viscoff further over the edge. He locked back into the approach.

"I thought that would get your attention," Matt said.

Both men put the attack and defense stingers on full capacity as they approached. It was computerized technology at its highest level. Millions of shots were fired and defused in seconds, all taking place in the blackness of reverse negative, radiation-soaked sky that visually swallowed each deadly shot.

As the jets approached at 3,000 knots, Matt knew he had only a tenth of a second to execute his plan. With the stress of the day and the fatigue of having to carry on the entire defense single-handedly for twenty minutes, he wasn't sure if his skills were up to it. Either way, the die had been cast.

As Viscoff roared into his face, Matt flipped his wings perpendicular to the ground. Instead of crashing head on, he rammed his nose into the end third of Viscoff's gold tipped wing, cutting through it like a knife. The impact came at such a great speed that it was barely detected by either pilot.

Matt did a 360, nearly passing out from the G-Force, and pulled in right behind the Russian. The image was now alternately flashing from negative to positive, causing a dizzying strobe effect. Focusing his eyes, he could see that in positive or negative, part of Viscoff's right wing was missing. That was the break he needed.

Viscoff's jet, flashing black and gold tipped, then blinding white and black tipped, tumbled erratically as the Russian fought the throttle to regain control. Even so, if Matt's mental calculations were correct, the Russian could probably still fly and land the innovative jet with part of the wing missing. But he would have to slow to under 1,000 knots to maintain stability. Apparently that's exactly what Viscoff was thinking. He cut his acceleration and regained a shaky control at 950 knots. Matt mirrored Viscoff's drop in speed.

"I'm wounded, but you still can't kill me," Viscoff sneered.

"Oh no? Watch."

Matt dropped back to a half mile, then accelerated to 3,000 knots. In fifteen seconds, he had closed the gap, passing over Viscoff as if the Russian was standing still. As he passed, he again used Pocahontas's nose as his weapon, this time breaking the stinger from Viscoff's tail.

Matt circled around and locked into the Russian's crippled aircraft.

"You want to crash, or you want me to take you out up here?" he said, a trace of compassion in his voice.

"Take me out."

"Roger. You shouldn't have killed Sarah," Matt whispered as he squeezed the button on the throttle. Ahead of him, Viscoff vanished into the darkness. The explosion, as with the laser beams themselves, was swallowed by the bizarre, negative sky.

Killing Viscoff dissolved the anger that had shielded Matt from his overpowering sorrow. The adrenaline-fueled exhilaration of the battle was replaced by a fatigue-laced depression. At that moment, in the middle of a cataclysmic war, he didn't know what to do or where to fly. He was shooting across the sky at 3,000 knots—with nowhere to go.

His sense of mission took over. He searched the Scorpion radar for the remaining three jets.

"This is S-1. The problem has been eliminated. You need to return to base immediately to reprogram your weapons. Relay your assignments to my computer, and I'll finish the mission here."

The three pilots acknowledged Matt's message and sent the information. When the data was relayed, another voice came over the radio.

"What about me?"

The woman's voice stunned him.

"Zipporah?"

"Zipporah! I haven't been dead five minutes, and you're already thinking of Zipporah?"

TEN

"**S**arah!" Matt exclaimed. "Where are you? Heaven?"

"You think there'd be this much static on the line if I was in heaven? Try Germany."

Matt, certain that he was losing his mind, widened the range of his radar. Sure enough, S-7 was now identified as heading northwest over Poland.

"I thought... "

"So did Viscoff, fortunately."

"What happened?"

"I'm not sure. As far as I can guess, an instant before he fired, I hit a nuclear updraft. It masked my signal and blew me to Angel 125. Up where no man or woman has gone before."

"How was the view?"

"Don't know. I blacked out. When I came to, I was nose diving Berlin."

"You OK?"

"Pulled out, obviously. I think I'm in one piece, but I'm afraid to look into the mirror. Will you still love me if I don't have any eyebrows?"

"Forever," he said, finally convinced it wasn't a dream. "Even if you're bald. I'm just glad you're still with us. Did you catch what I told the others about going on line again?"

"Part of it. Let me get close enough for a computer kiss, then I'll head in."

"OK. The front liners could use the help."

"How'd you beat Viscoff?"

"We played chicken."

"What?"

"I'll tell you about it later. When you're in my arms. Thanks," he said, sighing deeply.

"Thanks for what? You saved me."

"For ah, just for..."

"For not being dead?"

"Yeah," Matt said sheepishly. "Thanks for that."

"You're welcome. You've certainly become easy to please. I'll keep that in mind."

Matt couldn't help thinking how Sarah's sarcasm was steeped in reality. It seemed that all he really required of a woman lately was that she remain alive.

"Comes with maturity," he answered.

"What maturity? You're still not out of the woods on that stupid stunt you pulled with the Soviet commander. And let me guess, you had no authority to come out here, right?"

"Well, not exactly."

"You broke from the front line, where you were needed, to come out here and save me, right?"

"Not exactly."

"Exactly! That was stupid move number two!"

"I couldn't let you... "

"I'm expendable. You should be protecting Israel!"

"But... "

"No buts! I'm a soldier, Matt. No different than the others. I'm not some breathless little bimbo that needs a big strong man to protect her. You got that?"

"Affirmative."

"Try to remember it."

"Did you fall into that negative image stuff?" he asked, changing the subject. He couldn't deal with a further tongue-lashing for saving her life.

"Earlier. That was wild, wasn't it? We're going to have to do some serious detoxing. Our scientists have developed some new scrubbing techniques, fortunately. Otherwise, you might have thanked me too soon. I think I'm close enough now. Let me try to download my assignment. Are you receiving?"

"Got you."

"No more hero stuff, OK? I'm off."

"OK, over."

"Hey, S-1," a male voice stated over the radio. "I don't know what's eating Little Miss Soldier Girl, but I for one am glad you showed for this party. I'm sure the rest of the gang feels the same way. We were totally defenseless. Life is always the preferred option."

"Thanks, Levi. I'm sure almost everyone would have done the same for me."

"Everyone but Soldier Girl. And I don't blame you for what you tried to do earlier. You could have saved a lot of senseless destruction today."

"I thought it was worth the shot. How's the congestion where you are?"

Levi checked his screen. "They're still coming. Both MIGs and missiles, but not as thick as before. We were able to take out a lot on the ground before Vis shut us down. What got into him?"

"Humanity."

"Roger on that. We're doing a lot of damage. It's so clean up here. You know what word was chosen for our plan in the Hebrew? Sterilization. That's what they say we're doing. Sterilizing the Soviet Union."

"Sort of like the 'Final Solution.' Was this inland attack necessary?"

"Yeah, the idiot kept launching. I don't know why, but they've kept coming like lemmings. If we drew the line any farther back, the radiation would devastate Israel. It's already raining invisible fire on Turkey and many of the Arab nations, although that's a bonus. This way, we isolate most of the radiation on the Soviet Union, making them suffer from their own aggression. Seems logical."

"For generals. Not for people."

"Roger. Or pilots. It's hard to visualize what's happening below."

"Viscoff apparently did," Matt said.

"He must have," Levi agreed. "Wish I was on line. I could ease the load on the front. They must be tired."

"Try going it alone for twenty minutes. You'll be back soon enough."

"Save some MIGs for me. Over."

Matt displayed the first inland assignment from the disarmed Scorpions on his screen and began firing on the ground targets—mostly missile bases, weapons factories and tank arsenals. From this distance, he felt as if he were eradicating termites from behind the baseboard of a home instead of killing human beings.

After the hands-on excitement of the dogfight, the computerized ground cleanup was almost mundane... a chilling thought in itself. The Soviets were still launching an occasional volley of missiles, but their effort appeared hopeless. Either way, Pocahontas could handle it with Matt napping.

"This is the little wildcat, coming by you."

Sarah's voice snapped Matt from his slumber.

"What are you still doing here?"

"Change in plans. They've launched an attack from Tashkent near the Chinese border. The Bear had an arsenal there to watch China, Afghanistan, and India. We didn't know about it."

"You haven't had time to go on line!"

"I'm coasting. In fifteen minutes I can restart with full weapons."

"You're going to shut down? In the sky?"

"Pittman says I should only slow to around 500 knots before the weapons come back on line."

"That's insane. It won't work. You'll crash! And you'd be flying dead. If a stray MIG spots you... Go back in. Now!"

"Hey, I don't take orders from you. It's too late, anyway. I already switched off ten minutes ago."

Matt winced in anguish.

"Did you do this on your own?"

"I suggested it. But unlike some people, I got clearance first."

"They cleared this harebrained scheme?"

"Affirmative."

"I'm coming to shadow you."

"No! Stay on your mission. You've got seven people's jobs to do. There's no time."

"I don't care... "

"We just went over this. I volunteered. Stay away."

"But... "

"Be a solider, Slade, not a whipped wimp."

"A what?"

"You heard me. When you've finished your assignment, go to the Caspian Sea and watch my back. A lot will get by me before I'm juiced again. They also have some tanks coming in from there."

"But... "

"I'm signing off. Do your job!"

"Let me know when you restart!"

Sarah didn't answer. As Matt continued his attacks, his eyes were riveted to the Heads Up Display. He programmed it to monitor Sarah's speed, altitude, and location. The computer gave voice read outs every time her speed dropped 500 knots. Matt could see that a dozen MIGs were in range to give chase as she coasted, but none seemed to want to risk it. That lasted until her speed dropped to 700 knots over the Aral Sea. Somewhere, a Soviet command post desk jockey tracked her deceleration and calculated that she was flying dead. In an instant, ten MIGs were ordered to destroy the stalled jet. Five peeled off from the Black Sea, while the second five were meeting her head-on from Tashkent. The ten pilots, certain that they were doomed that day, went after the Scorpion with a vengeance. If it was to be their only victory of the war, they would relish it.

"You've got company, babe," Matt said, pulling out of his ground mission and heading to intercept the Black Sea five.

"I see. I should be back up before they can lock on."

"No way."

"Back off, Slade. I can handle it. That's an order!"

"I don't take orders from you, at least not in the sky," he said as he hit his booster. Matt knew he needed ten minutes before he could target the Black Sea MIGs on his long range stinger. Sarah would have to handle the Tashkent interceptors herself.

At 600 knots Sarah switched on her stinger. Nothing. At 550, she gave it another flip. Silence. The five MIGs were now a few minutes from locking on their suddenly archaic missiles. Sarah tried at 525. The stingers on her baby blue fighter refused to come to life.

Matt's screen recorded the missile launch from the Tashkent force just as he targeted the Black Sea MIGs. Each of the Tashkent jets spit out three heat-seeking missiles, sending a total of fifteen into Sarah's face. It was tremendous overkill, but overkill was what they wanted.

At 500 knots, Sarah tried again. Nothing. The missiles were twenty seconds away.

"Start up and fly out!" Matt cried.

"Negative. That'll delay the stinger another thirty."

"Forget that! Just start up and get out of there! I'll take care of Tashkent!"

She hit the switch at 480. Nothing. The lead missile was fifteen seconds away. Matt tried furiously to target them on his long-range stinger but couldn't lock on. The distance was too great.

"You've dropped to Angel 400! You're belly-rubbing rooftops! Fire up! Now!"

Sarah ignored Matt and kept her cool. Four-sixty knots. Still no weapons. The missiles were ten seconds from impact. Four-fifty and five seconds. No stinger. Four-forty five and Angel 200. Sarah hit the switch a final time...

The stingers beeped to life. Cat-quick, she programmed her defense. The missiles detonated in her face.

On his display, Matt recorded the explosions. They were so close to Sarah's jet the radar was unable to differentiate between them. Everything vanished on the screen.

"No, not again!" he cried. "Dear God, I lost her once. You brought her back. Not again! Not like this."

He stared at the display, too shocked to believe what he had just seen. Suddenly, a beep sounded. A single image reappeared. S-7!

Sarah switched on her engine and rocketed toward Tashkent.

Matt wiped the sweat from his brow.

"This has been one really bad day," he mumbled to himself as he clicked on his radio. "Sarah, I assume?"

"You're not going to start with that maudlin 'thank you for being alive' stuff again, are you? I told you I'd make it."

"Did you have to push it to the last millisecond?"

"Isn't that what you would have done?"

"You've still got five coming head on."

"Oh, thanks, I forgot about them. Silly me," she said, affecting a high-pitched voice. "I'm just too scared to push my buttons. Can you please come rescue little ol' me? These bad Russians have tied me to the railroad tracks! The train's comin', Matt! The train's comin'! Oh please Matt, please—save me!"

"Cut it out, Sarah."

"You cut it out. I can take these five, and the five on my butt if you had let me. They'll send a couple hundred more before I'm finished today. Go back to Moscow and finish your assignment! I'm so tired of your piggishness!"

"Piggishness? I thought that was forbidden in Israel. I love you too, sweetie," Matt said as he banked his jet and hung a sound-breaking U.

"What am I doing wrong?" he mumbled to himself again. "I keep trying to save her life, and she keeps hating me for it. Am I missing something?"

It took Matt forty minutes to finish off the last of the pre-programmed Soviet targets. "Just like blowing out a candle," he said to himself, still talking even though no one was around to listen. Sarah met with equal success, skillfully beating back everything they threw at her from Tashkent. She was able to disarm the surprise attack in less than thirty minutes. By then, the only thing coming up from the crushed Soviet nation was smoke from 10,000 fires—including as Matt learned later, a ravaging, radioactive blaze that roared through the capital and consumed General Kalinina and virtually all of his command staff.

Matt didn't even want to guess at the extent of the overall destruction the Scorpion Force heaped upon the once-dominant communist nation. Because of the radiation, most of those left alive were already doomed to suffer a slow, agonizing death. The land around Moscow, Tashkent, and a dozen other Soviet cities would be unlivable for decades. And because of General Kalinina's refusal to surrender in the face of the annihilation, a large part of Turkey had also been poisoned by radiation.

"You were right, Vis," Matt whispered as he destroyed the last ground target. "It was overkill. There had to be a better way."

Overwhelmed by the devastation and uneasy about his status, Matt thought of hanging a left and flying straight to Homestead Air Force Base in Miami. Despite his heroics in saving Israel, the tiny coastal country had some strange laws. It would be just like them to pin a medal on his chest shortly before signaling the firing squad.

"Forget it," he said as he banked toward the Atlantic in a final act of command defiance. "No telling what they're going to do to me down there."

Two minutes later, he turned back. He couldn't leave Sarah, even in the face of death.

Matt saw the armed soldiers sprinting out to greet him as he rolled Pocahontas into the hangar. This was one time when he wished his jet wasn't so noticeable. Rebellious to the end, he fired up the stinger and spit a short laser blast in front of the charging arrest crew, blowing a foot wide hole in the tarmac. The men and women scattered like startled quail and lunged for cover.

That gave him time to park his jet and trot over to see Sarah, who had pulled in minutes before. He spotted her checking the landing gear of her machine. Consumed by emotion and drained by fatigue, all he wanted was to embrace her.

Sarah stood her ground as he approached. She froze icily in his arms, then melted a little in the intensity of his hug.

Matt withdrew from the hug and leaned in to kiss her. Sarah

met him with roundhouse right that started from her heels. She slapped him so hard across the face the sound rang out like a shot. The approaching soldiers ducked for cover again.

A sharp pain stabbed through Matt's head. He grew dizzy and nearly fainted. Sarah was petite, but she packed a mean wallop. When his senses recovered, he looked into her blazing eyes like a puppy who had just been whacked by its master.

"You had no right to do what you did," she said fiercely, her words hitting as hard as her hand. "You disobeyed orders. You shamed Israel. You embarrassed me. We can never be together now!"

Before he could answer, the soldiers came, raised their weapons, and nervously surrounded him.

"Take him to the decontamination chamber," a sergeant barked.

Matt stood staring at Sarah, refusing to move. Even if they pierced his body with their bayonets, the approaching soldiers couldn't hurt him as much as Sarah just had. Instead of apologizing and comforting him, Sarah turned her back. A soldier gently pushed Matt to get him going.

"Come on, Captain," the soldier said. "Don't make this hard on yourself. You're lit up like a Fire Fly tree. We need to get you clean."

Matt was taken to a distant corner of the base and ordered to remove his clothing, starting with his fireproof flight coveralls. He was lead into a sealed, elevator-sized room. Inside, he was told to stand on a red circle in the center of the room. The minutes passed like hours as he stood there, naked, alone, under military arrest, crushed by the thought that he had lost Sarah. He couldn't help thinking that it was a fitting end to a terrible day.

"Jill, where are you?" he whispered. "Why did you have to leave?"

The anguished words had barely left his lips when he was hit from all sides by a burst of chemically-infused water. The burning, deep red spray blasted him with such force that a single stream could have driven him into the wall, flattening his body. As it was, the 360-degree pattern froze him in the circle.

For twenty torturous minutes, the radiation decontamination spray fanned up and down his body in a vertical motion, painting his hair and skin bright red. The crimson liquid slowly filled the room, creeping up his knees, to his waist, shoulders, and neck. The spray stopped when the water reached his chin. A plastic snorkel fell from the ceiling.

"Take the breathing device and remain submerged until the water drains," a voice said.

Matt did as ordered. Despite the harsh way in which he was treated, he knew it was for his own good. He remained under the red liquid for another twenty minutes before he heard a thunk and felt the water swirl around his ankles. Within seconds, the suction became so strong it caught hold of his right foot and tried to pull it through the tiny drain holes. Matt grabbed his leg with both hands and tapped into his last ounce of energy to yank his foot away. He fell backward into the water, causing a splash.

"Please remain standing and stay in the center of the room," a voice ordered.

When the last drop of liquid whirled away, Matt fell exhausted to the floor. As he lay there, too tired to move, he lifted his right foot and wiggled his toes, making sure he still had them all.

Two men in laboratory coats entered the room, lifted him off the floor, handed him a pair of white terrycloth shorts, and escorted him out of the chamber. Matt glanced at his arms. His body remained coated with the red liquid.

He was taken to a large steam room, where twelve similarly reddened people were sitting on tiers of benches made from square wooden slats. They all stopped and stared at him through a strange blue steam.

"Slade?" someone asked.

Matt shrugged. "It ain't Geronimo."

The people in the room all stood and applauded, many with tears in their eyes. Matt was taken aback by the bizarre scene. He was being given a standing ovation by a bunch of red people in a room full of blue haze.

After the applause subsided, the men and women of the Scorpion Force surrounded Matt, slapped his back, and thanked him for saving their country and their lives.

"This is not the welcome I received earlier," he said, taking a seat on the wooden bench.

"Don't worry about them," Levi said. "We'll take care of your army shadows. The Knesset is already working on your pardon."

"That's not what I meant."

"Don't worry about her, either. She'll come around."

"I don't think so. She's so... so stubborn! I think she really would have preferred to die than have me rescue her."

"Women and pride—an explosive combination. What can you do? Giving them a jet and a uniform doesn't change what they are."

A female figure, her blue and white eyes dancing inside a red face, glided forward and gave Matt a warm hug.

"Your problem is you never pick the the right woman, cowboy," she said.

"Zippy?" he asked, staring at the strange apparition standing before him. She nodded.

"Red suits you."

"I was thinking of keeping my hair this color," she joked, stroking her long crimson locks.

"What's this blue haze stuff?" Matt asked.

"Phase two. When the blue hits the red, it neutralizes the radiation. Or something like that."

"Then why the horror chamber?"

Zipporah shrugged. "That's the way it works. Blast and steam, like a rug. Just be glad we have it."

A third red zombie approached. The others drifted away. Matt looked up wearily.

"*Et tu, Brute?*"

Colonel Cohen sat down beside him. "That was some scrub job, wasn't it?".

"Especially when they give you no information what to expect."

"You weren't briefed?"

"Nothing. They're treating me like a Nazi war criminal. 'Matt the Marauder.' I thought it was part of my punishment. Some form of pre-execution torture. I nearly lost my foot in the drain."

"They know you've been charged with treason."

"Do they know the rest of it?"

"They know. Everyone knows. We tried to keep it hushed, but the press got hold of it. The leak had to come from one of the pilots trying to save your skin. By tomorrow, you'll be quite the hero in the newspapers."

"They have a lot to report. It was a big news day."

"You'll get your due," Colonel Cohen said with a laugh.

"So what am I, hero or traitor?"

"That's what we're trying to figure out. The fact that you saved Israel from nuclear destruction should count in your favor."

"I'd think."

"But then, after redeeming yourself, you followed the illegal chat with the Russian with that unauthorized rescue mission, which turned out to be unnecessary. So you bookended your heroics with two serious breaches of command."

"Nobody's perfect."

"It was personal, Matt. You disobeyed my orders. We've been friends a long time."

"Tell me something, Sam, imagine that your wife, your son, and daughter are drifting dead in the sky. Ten MIGs are coming after them at 2,000 miles per hour. What would you have done?"

"Followed my orders."

"No way."

"We Israelis are always prepared to make the ultimate sacrifice for our nation."

"This ain't my nation, pal."

"That wasn't your wife and children. It was another fighter pilot carrying out her mission. That's different."

"Not to me. I'm a civilian, not a soldier."

"They're going to give you a hearing," Colonel Cohen said, standing to better allow the blue steam to dissolve away the red fluid from his body. "It's your neck. Try to be a little more contrite."

"Before I go into my shell, tell me something, Colonel. Whose idea was it to give the Scorpions such a huge Achilles' heel?"

"It was a command decision, agreed upon from the inventors on down. We couldn't give so much power to a single man."

"So you built an indestructible Air Force, and then made it totally vulnerable because you couldn't trust twenty-one pilots?"

"We were right not to trust the pilots, obviously."

"Were you right to give one pilot the capability of disarming the entire unit?"

"We don't know how he came across the knowledge. Only a few knew."

"You knew. You did it to me. In the air. In combat!"

"You had the speed and maneuverability to bank out and come in."

"That didn't mean a thing after Viscoff disarmed the entire unit, did it? He had the same speed and the weapons to destroy us all."

"We're re-evaluating the safety system."

"I'd do that."

Before disappearing into the haze, Colonel Cohen turned.

"By the way, she went to bat pretty hard for you."

"Who?"

"You know."

"With whom?"

"General David. The politicians. Even tried to get to the Prime Minister. She probably would have if she wasn't glowing like the center candle in a menorah. We had to track her down and drag her kicking and screaming into the tank."

"That's not the way she came across to me," Matt said, rubbing his still sore cheek.

"She loves you. But she wants to be treated like a soldier. She's earned the respect."

"I do respect her. But letting her get blown to bits is a rotten way to show it!"

"Let's hope you're not presented with that situation again."

"What do you mean, 'let's hope?' What's left? China? That would be like shooting a herd of blind buffalo. So that leaves America. You guys gonna try to annex America?"

"We're going to annex peace."

"I wouldn't bet on it. You're a tiny country with a great big weapon. The two concepts don't add up."

"We only want to keep what we have."

"Sure."

Matt remained in the sauna until he and the other pilots turned from red to blue. Sarah wandered by, looking like a Smurf Princess, but he wasn't ready to fight World War IV just yet, so he let her pass without comment.

Steamed like rice and a blink away from passing out, Matt was barely able to make it to the shower room. The soap and hot water turned him back into something that remotely resembled a human being but depleted his energy further. By the time he reached the small dorm room that served as a military prison, he was ready to sleep for a week.

ELEVEN

Matt was awakened early the next morning by a tag team of grim-faced military police. Although still dead tired, he was forced to dress hastily and was taken outside and shoved into an awaiting vehicle. Colonel Cohen greeted him.

"I need to sleep, Colonel."

"We all do. But thanks to you, we've got to play some politics."

"Thanks to me, you still have politics to play."

Colonel Cohen tossed a newspaper into Matt's lap. The lead story was about the war, but the main sidebar was a human interest feature about how an American pilot saved the country. The story included a large photo of a roguish Matt from one of his earlier visits.

"Where'd they get the photo?"

"Someone supplied it. We thought you might be able to help us find out who."

"You think I'm gonna sell out whoever is trying to save my red and blue skin? I've never seen the photo before in my life."

"I thought you'd say that. The problem is, the government is not too happy with the fact that an American bailed us out."

"And they're not too happy with the reason, are they? Does the story explain that?"

"The sources withheld some details, thankfully. The story says only that there was a temporary problem with the other fighters. But it'll get out before the week is over. Our reporters are tenacious. It'll become a major embarrassment."

"It should. Does it mention why I was grounded?"

"Just for 'disciplinary reasons.' But that might leak also. You've created quite a dilemma for the government."

"They can't justify hanging the guy who saved their country?"

"Not easily."

"I'm sure they'll try. So where are we going?"

"Back to your apartment."

"Doesn't look good to have me in jail, does it?"

"Not very."

"House arrest?"

"For now. But we'll rectify this soon. The hearing is this afternoon."

"Open?"

"Closed."

"Figures. I see Sarah got a little ink herself," Matt said, noticing a smaller story about her.

"We'll be pushing that hard as the week progresses. We need a native hero. Got to get your ugly mug off the front page."

"She's not a native."

"She's native enough. Better than you, anyway. She'll wear the mantle of heroine well."

A large contingent of reporters was waiting when they arrived at Matt's apartment.

"This is not what we wanted," Colonel Cohen groused. "I don't know how they found you."

The colonel radioed for reinforcements. Within minutes, Israeli soldiers arrived and secured a path into the condominium. Matt was quickly escorted into the building as cameras flashed and reporters shouted questions.

"We'd appreciate it if you didn't talk to the media until we get this settled," Colonel Cohen said as they entered the elevator.

"Why not just give me an order?"

"I know how well you take orders. I want your promise."

"You've got another day. But if I start reading about that treason nonsense, then I'm going to spill."

"Fair enough. Go get some sleep," he said, motioning for a pair of guards to station themselves at Matt's door. "We'll come get you for the hearing."

Matt went right to bed, falling asleep without bothering to undress.

The media got wind of the special military hearing, and reporters attended *en masse*. They were left in the dark about why the proceeding was being staged, and they followed Matt into the courtroom, flashing cameras and shouting questions. He shrugged and feigned ignorance.

Inside, he was escorted to a table up front. Colonel Cohen was seated to his right. A female officer he had never seen before was at his left. Behind him sat a dozen of his fellow Scorpion pilots.

"Who's the lady?" Matt whispered to the Colonel.

"That's your counsel."

"My counsel!" Matt exclaimed, whispering so loud the Colonel had to shush him. "Shouldn't I at least have a conversation with her before they hang me? What kind of defense is this?"

"The best kind. Just be quiet. You probably won't have to say a word."

Matt drummed his fingers impatiently on the polished wood as he waited for something to happen. The prosecutors' table remained empty, as did the tribunal bench. After twenty minutes, a clerk appeared and motioned for Matt, Colonel Cohen, and Matt's counsel to approach the chambers behind the bench. As Matt entered the inner hallway, he spotted Sarah about twenty feet away leaving through another exit. She was flanked by four military officers and two men in suits.

"Sarah!" he called.

Colonel Cohen grabbed his arm.

"This is a courtroom, not a ballpark," he whispered firmly. "You've got to keep quiet. You can talk to her later. And don't say a word inside. That's an order!"

Sarah turned. For a second, their eyes met. She looked sad and a bit overwhelmed. One of the officers gently pushed her along.

"What does she have to do with this?"

"Later," Colonel Cohen said as they entered the tribunal chambers.

Matt was directed to an overstuffed chair in front of a large desk. Colonel Cohen sat beside him. Matt's silent attorney stood to his right. Crowded behind the desk were General David, two Israeli generals he didn't recognize, two politician types in suits, and Colonel Warrington from America.

Although he was to be judged under Israeli law, it was the presence of Colonel Warrington that most unnerved him. Warrington would sell him out in a heartbeat if it was politically expedient. He tried to read the Colonel's face but was distracted by his ever-twitching, rat-like upper lip.

"You've presented us with something of a dilemma, Matt," General David said with an odd half smile. "We've tried to work out an equitable solution for all parties. On the one hand, you valiantly saved our country from what could have been total destruction. On the other, the only reason you were in a position to do so was because you were grounded during a pivotal battle for disobeying orders and committing what many believe was a heinous act of treason."

Matt started to defend himself. Colonel Cohen gave him a swift kick to his shin.

"We've decided, after considerable debate, that the two actions cancel each other out," General David continued. "Therefore, for your heroism, you will be allowed to attend the awards parade with your fellow pilots, where you will receive the Israeli Medal of Valor. I also understand that upon your return to America, you will be awarded a U.S. Medal of Honor for your performance as an on-loan officer from the U.S. military."

So far so good, Matt thought, though he doubted whether the American award was Colonel Warrington's idea.

"Following the ceremonies here in Israel, we must insist that you retire from the Scorpion Force and return to the United States. Colonel Warrington has informed us that you will also be released from all your remaining U.S. military commitments.

"We thank you for your service to Israel and wish you luck in the future."

Before Matt had a chance to collect his thoughts, he was

whisked out of the chambers, taken through a side door, and pushed into a waiting car. Colonel Cohen hopped in beside him.

"Why didn't you let me speak?" Matt snapped.

"Because a lot of effort went into reaching this compromise. And I didn't want you to undo everything with your sharp tongue."

"So who are you, my handler? They've got you poking sticks at me as if I were a trained bear in a circus."

"I prefer the term 'friend.'"

"Why was Sarah there?"

"I don't know. I'm sure you'll find out."

"Do you support what just happened?"

"It was a fair compromise."

"It was a backroom deal. A fix. And to top it off, they invited the press, then did their dirty laundry behind closed doors. Beautiful."

"What are you complaining about? We saved your life and gave you everything you wanted."

"What about my dignity? They kicked me out!"

"They allowed you to retire with honor."

"They gave me the boot!"

"So? You never wanted to be here anyway."

That was true. The whole thing was wildly ironic. Matt hadn't volunteered to be part of the Israeli Air Force. He wasn't even Jewish. If he had served without incident, he'd now be trying to resign and return home. But the idea of being forced out stuck in his craw. He considered protesting, then realized how absurd it would be to fight for something he didn't want.

The American reaction was equally galling. Were they honoring him by letting him off the hook early, or did they consider him a loose cannon that could never be controlled?

He cared even less about solving that riddle. He had long wanted out of his increasingly dangerous United States service commitment, so whatever the military's feelings were regarding his behavior during the short foreign war, he'd take the medal and the early exit and run.

Although he now had the freedom he always desired—with two gleaming medals to boot, the events of the first post-war day depressed him. He couldn't figure out why until he was in bed that evening. He had finally achieved the "Jill scenario"—the safe, civilian life he had dreamed of sharing with her. But she was still missing, and everything from his instincts to the uncomfortable looks he saw in the faces of others led him to believe that she would not return. That left Sarah as the fly in the ointment of his newly unencumbered life. Despite the chaos of the surrounding countries and his tenuous status as a war hero, he was in no rush to leave Israel. Not until he had a final showdown with the heroic Israeli fly-girl.

Israel's military publicity machine was working overtime in its campaign to transform Sarah into a Jewish Joan of Arc. Her story helped erase the embarrassment of how easily the Scorpion's offensive and defensive weapons were neutralized—and how an American pilot had saved the country. It also helped keep everyone's mind off the suffering going on in the Soviet Union and the Arab nations as millions died slowly and painfully from flesh-eating radiation poisoning.

Sarah was so busy in her new "Sarah of Israel" role that Matt was unable to see her for five days. He was finally able to arrange a meeting with her, but only because Israel's leaders were growing increasingly uncomfortable with his continued presence. It thus became one of Sarah's new patriotic duties to rid the country of her rival in the hero sweepstakes. Initially, it was a tough order to swallow. But, as with everything else, when it was couched in the "it's vital for Israel's national interests" argument, she relented.

Sarah felt like ice in Matt's arms when he embraced her at the door. He withdrew and stared into her once fiery eyes, seeing nothing but a dull hollowness that frightened him.

"What have they done to you?"

"What do you mean?"

"This isn't you. I've seen you angry. I've seen you jumping

with excitement. I've felt your passion, your love, and your rage, but I've never seen you dead like this. What's going on?"

"You. You're going on."

"What?"

"You've got to leave, Matt."

Matt walked to the couch. She followed lifelessly.

"Is this what you want, Sarah, or is this Israel speaking?"

She said nothing.

"You've gotten out of my shadow," Matt said. "The plan worked. You're the big native hero. My 'legend' is already fading. For you, I kept quiet. No interviews. Nothing. And I don't care. You take all the limelight. Do the fashion spread I saw on television. Ride in the parade like a homecoming queen. Be 'Joan of Israel.' I don't care. As long as we're together."

"We can't be together now, Matt. Can't you see?"

"No."

"I have a new role to play. And you, you're... you know."

"I'm *persona non grata*. But only in the twisted eyes of the politicians. I'm a hero to the people. They'll accept us. That's all we 'heroes' live by, the adulation of the public. And when the people accept us, the leaders will follow."

"You make it sound so easy."

"It is. Believe me."

"I'm a soldier, Matt. I follow orders."

"They can't order you who to love and who not to love."

"I have an obligation. Things have changed. The world has changed. There are things going on you don't know about. Things I have to play a major role in. You can't be part of it."

"'Things?' Like what?"

"I can't say."

"Why not?"

"Confidential."

"Great."

Matt stood and began pacing the room.

"So you're going to do it to me again. The same as before. You're going to put this little ant of a country ahead of me."

"It was always that way. I never told you any different."

"You did in the beginning, before the recruiters brainwashed you. I just thought that maybe this would be enough. You've done your duty a thousand times over."

"That's your problem, Matt. You thought. You didn't ask."

"I'm asking now. Come back to America with me. That's your home. This is a nightmare. You and I don't belong here. We belong at a fast food joint eating french fries, or grabbing a hot dog at the ball park. Come back. Live that life. With me. As my wife."

"As your wife?" she said, unable to bridle her emotions any longer. "How can I marry you? If it wasn't for... " She paused and took a breath. "You wanted to marry someone else just last week. How can you be so fickle?"

"Last week seems like a million years ago. What were you about to say?"

"When?"

"When you stopped. You know something, don't you? What happened to Jill and all the others?"

"I don't."

"You do. Everyone around here knows. She's not coming back. You know it. You know why. But no one will say."

"We don't know. What you suspect, we don't believe."

"What I suspect? I don't suspect anything! What do you think I suspect?"

"Didn't she tell you?"

"No."

"She did. You just didn't listen. Same as always, Matt... you didn't listen to her. You didn't listen to me five years ago. You didn't listen to your commanding officers five days ago. You just don't listen. That's why we couldn't be together then. Why we can't be together now."

"I can listen. Tell me about Jill; I'll listen."

"I don't want to talk about her. Stop this! You propose to me, then start talking about her."

"You brought her up."

Sarah turned away.

"OK, then tell me about us," Matt said, forcing her to look at him. "I want you to marry me. Whatever is past, is past."

"You haven't heard me."

"That it's over? Because I tried to save a hundred million lives? Because I tried to save yours?"

"No, because I had to save yours."

Matt tried to respond, but the words wouldn't come. He sat down beside her.

"You made a deal? For me? That's why you were in court that day?"

Sarah admitted nothing.

"Of course. They needed you to play the dutiful war hero. That's not your style—all the news conferences, parties, and political functions. I couln't believe it when I saw you on television, parading around like a champion show dog. Now it makes sense. You agreed to go along with it for me. But you didn't have to. They weren't going to touch me. They made you show your hand after the game was over. It doesn't count!"

"It wasn't over. The charges were serious."

"After the newspaper stories, their hands were tied."

"Don't be so naive. Nothing is as fragile as a newspaper hero. Another story the following day could have changed everything. The reporters love nothing better than to destroy the heroes they create. And the one thing no Israeli will tolerate is treason. The people would have been calling for your head."

"I refuse to believe that."

"Matthew, this is war. You make sacrifices. You put your personal happiness aside. That's what's expected of soldiers. You did it for me. I did it for you. You were willing to accept the consequences. So am I."

"The war ended last week. We won. It's over. Remember? All deals are off."

"It's just beginning, Matthew."

Her words chilled him. At that moment, he didn't want to explore it further.

"I've got to go," she said, getting up. "There's a function tonight. I've got to get ready."

"Well, I certainly don't want to get in the way of your *functions,*" he snapped bitterly.

"Don't make this harder than it already is."

"It's supposed to be hard," he said. "That's part of the sacrifice, isn't it?"

She walked to the door, then stood on her toes to kiss him good-bye.

"I do love you, Matthew. One day you'll realize that."

"I'm not giving up on us," he said. "I'll see you again."

Sarah walked silently through the doorway, then turned.

"Don't wait five years this time," she said.

While Israel continued to bask in the glory of its great victory, the reports on the international front were harrowing. Television cameras couldn't operate in the radiation, thus sparing the world a visual image of the horror. Newspapers and magazines, however, were under no such restraints. Through stories received from contact inside Russia, they published accounts of zombies walking aimlessly through the ruins, the radiation literally eating away their flesh. The people had nowhere to go for help, nothing to do but wait to die from the radiation or starvation, whichever came first. There was no government left to respond to their needs and no way for any other nation to ease their pain. The radiation levels rendered rescue missions impossible. Air-dropped crates of food, water, and medicine became contaminated before they reached the ground. Disease quickly spread from the dead bodies to the survivors, making their final days even more miserable.

As one magazine put it, the former Soviet Union had been transformed into "The Continent of the Doomed."

Conditions were so terrible that the "nuclear plague" began to spread across Europe. The radiation moved like a death cloud in the skies, fouling food, water, and the air everyone breathed. Rampaging diseases, including mutant strains created in the radiation, attacked from the ground like an invading army. A third to half of the affected populations succumbed to the deadly one-two punch. The clouds of nuclear ash blotted out the sun and changed weather patterns, resulting in widespread crop failures from France to China.

It didn't take long for the anger of the world to rain down upon Israel. The consensus was that the Jewish nation should have anticipated the cataclysmic results of their power and taken a different tack. Some journalists and foreign leaders even began suggesting that Israel should have let the Soviets win, sacrificing their country for the "good of the world." Even if the Soviets went on to swallow up other countries, a harsh dictatorship under a brutal madman was deemed preferable to the horror of a nuclear plague.

Israel, ostracized by the surviving nations, turned further inward, intensifying the "us against the world" attitude it had developed almost from its inception in the late 1940s. The Israeli people found themselves trapped in their small country and began suffering from trade embargoes that strained a nation with few natural resources. In response, the people demanded that their leaders use the country's tremendous military advantage to conquer the surrounding nations, expand Israel's borders, and re-establish the critical trade routes. If the world was willing to accept an oppressive Soviet dictatorship, then why not give them a benevolent Israeli one?

A young member of the Israeli Knesset heard the cry of the people. It was just the opportunity he'd been waiting for.

TWELVE

Jonathan Absalom, a suave, eloquent Israeli MK (member of the Knesset) and rising political star, did everything he could to flame the rebellious passions of the people. The Harvard-educated, American-born attorney had business interests in both Israel and the United States, and for a long time he wavered upon which rock to build his ambitious political career.

His father, Elias Absalom, was a Palestinian who had moved to the Middle East twenty-five years earlier after the landmark Israeli/Palestinian peace accords. His mother was a beautiful Texan of Mexican heritage. Jonathan was ten when his family made the long-distance move from San Antonio to Israel.

Elias Absalom had been a major defense contractor in America. He used his wealth and entrepreneurial skills to bring jobs and industry to the once barren Palestinian sections of the new Israel. Because of his expertise, and his genuine desire to ease tensions and banish old hatreds through joint business ventures, he was able to secure the contract to build the Scorpion fighters.

Although the project was top secret, Jonathan Absalom used his position as president of Absalom Industries to monitor the construction of the space-age aircraft. That was the insight he needed. With Israel looming as the dominant world military force, he knew its leader would have extraordinary power.

Jonathan Absalom used his father's influence to become one of the first Palestinian representatives in the expanded Israeli Knesset. His non-threatening background as a half-Mexican, half-Palestinian immigrant who was shielded from the old cultural hatreds enabled him to quickly become a popular and well-respected political leader. In contrast to his likable public persona, his private goals were dangerously ambitious. His plan was to work his way to the Prime Minister's seat and then goad the Soviets or Chinese into an attack. Once he conquered either or both of those dominant nations, he'd use it as a stepping stone to get what he really wanted—the United States Presidency. The fact that he was willing to achieve his goal violently through the aggression of a foreign military revealed the fervent lust for power beneath the surface of his quiet, dignified personality.

General Kalinina put Absalom's plan into motion long before Absalom was ready. The attack made Absalom overwrought with fury. As the battle raged in the northern skies, he stood in front of his mansion, waved his arms in the air, and screamed "Not yet! Not now!"

After the day-long war, he sank into a deep depression. But as the months wore on and the hardships increased, he was re-energized by the people's demand for more aggressive leadership. He quickly sprang into action, using his family's vast finances to mount a campaign for a special post-war election. His thunderous rhetoric about a jealous and hateful world closing in on Israel unless they did something, and did it fast, fell upon receptive ears.

"Lest anyone forget, we won this war, this terrible war we didn't start," he said in a televised speech. "The people of Israel should be enjoying the spoils of our great victory instead of suffering because of it. The longer we wait, the more suffering we will endure as the world's anti-Semitic jealousy continues to pour down upon us. The survival of our country depends upon our willingness to seize the moment. We must re-open the trade routes—by treaty, or by force. We must expand our rule before we grow so weak and desperate that our enemies will easily consume us."

As Sarah watched his speech on television, she didn't know what to make of this man. She agreed that Israel shouldn't be punished for winning a war that was forced upon it by a larger, attacking nation. She had fought that war and come within a few seconds of dying, not only for her adopted country, but for all countries. She was naturally angry when these countries began to turn their backs on Israel.

On the other hand, she had long learned to be wary of politicians, especially demagogues who rose to power on the anger and greed of the citizens. Absalom had brilliantly melded the two emotions by railing against the embargoes and promising that the Israeli people, under his leadership, would profit from the great military victory. That, Sarah felt, was going too far.

Still, she was intrigued enough to accept when Absalom's chief aide called and said the charismatic young leader wanted to meet her.

"It should be someplace quiet, informal," the aide suggested. "We don't want it in the papers the next day."

Sarah didn't want that, either. The trouble was, she and Jonathan Absalom were probably the two most recognizable figures in Israel. Neither could go anywhere without attracting a crowd. The aide suggested a late-night encounter in a small, secluded park in a prosperous, residential neighborhood.

Absalom was waiting in a black limousine when Sarah arrived shortly after 11 P.M. It was a moonless night, and the park was dark and deserted. She could hardly see him when he emerged alone and shook her hand. The only thing she noticed from the shadowy introduction was that he was shorter and thinner than he appeared on television, and his handshake wasn't the firm, macho grip affected by her military cohorts.

"It's a lot darker out here than I expected. I apologize for that," he said in perfect English. His voice was soft and soothing, a far cry from the brash, shouting tone of his populist speeches. "There's no moon tonight. Why don't we go over to the east end, by the swing sets. The glow from the city will give us some light."

Absalom made small talk as they walked to the park's edge. The setting brightened considerably as they cleared a patch of shade trees.

"This is a beautiful country, isn't it Sarah?" he said almost whispering as he glanced out over the park. She could see him in fleeting glimpses as he moved in and out of the soft, hazy light. He was a handsome, refined man with delicate, aristocratic features under a shock of thick, wavy black hair.

"This is probably my favorite place in Israel," he continued. "We lived nearby, up on the hill over there. I used to come here when I was a little boy and missed my home in America, which was practically every day. My father dragged me here when I was ten. I was miserable at first. There was so much residual distrust and anger among the people. The peace accord couldn't erase the memories everyone held of the decades of violence and hatred. That made it tough. Plus, it took me a long time to adapt on a cultural level. You know, no hamburger places or Little League or good television shows, things like that. Instead, everyone seemed so tense, like they were waiting for a bomb to drop. It was so strange and foreign. I used to beg my father to take us back to Texas, but he wouldn't listen. He kept saying that this was where we belong, that this was our 'homeland,' whatever that meant. 'Mah homeland is in Tex-as, Daddy,' I'd drawl.

"And this language, that was the worst. A ten-year-old Texan trying to learn both Arabic and Hebrew? You can imagine how that sounded."

"Almost as bad as a Floridian," Sarah commented.

"That's right. You came late also. That's why I think we have a lot in... "

Absalom stopped as a revolving security light from a distant building bathed Sarah's face in a warm blush. He felt a strange sensation in his chest as he gazed upon her.

"My goodness. I was briefed that you were beautiful. It seems that was quite an understatement."

"It's a curse, but I've learned to live with it," she said, only half joking.

"I can imagine it is in your profession," he said. "You wouldn't want to get shot down over enemy lines."

"I have enough problems dealing with our side."

"Anyway," he continued, regrouping. "The reason I wanted to speak with you is obvious. I'd like to enlist you in my cause."

She recoiled at hearing the word "cause." Matt had often spoken bitterly of her blind devotion to Israel, which he termed her "cause."

"Are you okay?" Absalom asked, sensing her uneasiness.

"Yes. It's nothing. Just a flash of memory. What exactly is your cause, Mr. Absalom?"

"Please, call me Jonathan. My cause? You've heard the speeches. It's simple. A strong Israel. We shouldn't have to suffer because of what happened. We should take advantage of our victory for the good of our people."

"How much advantage?"

"As much as we can," he said winking. "It's a tough, cruel world out there. We'll only have the upper hand for a short while. We must gain all we can now, while we're in a position of superiority."

"I have a problem with that."

"I kind of thought you would," he said, laughing softly. "Let me assure you... "

"Forgive me for being blunt, but I've heard the speeches," she said, interrupting. "It's a moot point. I'm a military officer. I can't take sides in political battles. You know that."

"I know. But you can resign. I can promise you a top position in my government. Anything you want."

Sarah felt her blood rise. If this had been Matt or anyone else, she'd be boiling. But she forced herself to remain composed.

"I'm one of the best fighter pilots in the world," she countered. "You want me to throw that away to become window dressing for a politician? No thanks!"

"I wouldn't expect you to be window dressing," Absalom responded in a calm, assured voice. "I'm fully aware of your skills and talents. I respect what you are more than you know. It's just that the military can be extremely limiting. Its function is to kill and destroy. I think you can use your abilities on a greater scale for the good of Israel. I think you can heal and build."

That pitch hit home a lot stronger than Sarah was willing to admit. Following the war, she had nightmares about the killing. She held herself personally accountable for the deaths of tens of thousands, possibly hundreds of thousands. It was a sanitized destruction accomplished from the emotional safety of the sky, but that didn't excuse it. In her nightmares, she was on the ground, watching as stadiums full of people were consumed by nuclear flash fires each time she pressed a button in her baby blue jet. Like everything else in her life, she hid her anxiety under a well-developed icy exterior. But the dreams made her doubt that she was cut out to be a soldier capable of inflicting death on such a massive scale.

"I can't get involved in a political campaign," Sarah repeated, her anger diffused by Absalom's compliments. "My job is to serve the government, the current government. You are basically trying to overthrow that government. You're doing it legally within the system, but that's what it amounts to. I may agree with some of your ideas, but I can't join you, Jonathan. It's impossible. Even if I wanted to."

"Because of the American?"

Sarah looked at him in surprise.

"I know about Matt Slade." He smiled. "You forget who I am. I think it was a raw deal. We weren't going to touch the guy. The people consider him a hero. But they made you believe his life was in danger so they could attach some puppet strings to your shoulders and dangle you around at their parties. Typical politics. You don't have to hold to that agreement. It was a sham. They played upon your emotions. I wouldn't do that."

"Sure you would."

"Yeah, you're probably right," he admitted, throwing up his hands in surrender. "I'm a politician too, and politics is a nasty, nasty business. You can't get away from that. But in here, Sarah, in here," he said, pounding his chest, "I'm a decent man. I try to keep that kind of thing to a minimum."

"At least you're honest."

"Sometimes, in a dark park overlooking a glittering city, a

lonely little homesick boy from Texas can be painfully honest."

"How much of that little boy is left inside the ambitious politician?"

"Far too much for my own good, I think. It makes me weak. Gives others the advantage."

"I don't think so. It may be your strength."

"You obviously don't know politics."

Sarah paused for a second, collecting her thoughts. Absalom was so different from what she had expected. She thought he would either give her a rah-rah speech and try to sweep her into his campaign on a wave of patriotism, or simply place his cards on the table and make her a generous offer that would be hard to refuse. The soft sell and appealing personality was disarming.

"Look, Jonathan, we can stay out here all night, and you couldn't change my mind. I don't know what I'll be tomorrow, but right now I'm a military officer, and I have to act that way. And whether I was deceived or not, I gave my word that they could play this heroine game with me for a while. So I'm blocked on two counts. I'm sorry, but the answer is still no. I can't get involved."

"I'm sorry to hear that," he said, motioning for her to walk back to his car. "I can't say it wasn't expected. They told me you'd be loyal. I'm disappointed but I admire you even more."

"It's certainly been nice meeting you," she said, extending her hand. "I'm sure we'll cross paths again. If you win... "

Sarah didn't have to complete the sentence. Absalom knew what she meant. Only in his mind, a mind inflamed by Sarah's intelligence and beauty, he took it much further. The thought sent shivers all over his body.

Inside the sleek automobile, Absalom's ever-present aide, Josh Silverman, was idling away the time chatting with the driver and reading a thriller. A fellow Harvard law graduate, Silverman, like most of Absalom's team, was an American transplant. Absalom's facial expressions and body language telegraphed that the late-night recruitment effort hadn't been a success.

"No luck?" Silverman asked.

"I want that woman," Absalom said, his voice firm and demanding.

"She'd be a big help, that's for sure. The people love her."

"No. I mean I want that woman. You should have seen her face out there. You should have seen her eyes sparkle when she got a little miffed. I've never seen a more gorgeous creature. I've given a thousand speeches in my life without choking on a single word. I've used women and discarded them like tissues. But out there in that park tonight, my knees were so weak I could hardly stand. I have to win this thing now, Josh. I have to take control of this little speck-of-desert-dust country. She's loyal to the government. I then, must be the government. Then she'll be loyal to me."

"Forgive me, Jon, but this campaign isn't about putting notches on your belt. It's a lot bigger than that."

"That's where you're wrong, Josh. That's why I'm the representative and you're the aide. This is about power. That's all politics is ever about. And power means crushing your enemies and getting what you want. And one of the things I want most is that woman."

"Women are everywhere."

"Not like this one. This one is special."

"Yeah, so were the last ten."

"I'm serious. I've never felt like this before."

"Wonderful. We choose the one park where Cupid's lurking around wearing a yarmulke. Well, let's try to keep this bit of midnight magic to ourselves, shall we?" Josh said, growing nervous over his boss's motives. "Publicly, let's stay focused on less carnal ideals."

"Of course, Josh. That's the way the game's played," Absalom answered, rubbing his hands together. "And no one plays it better than I do."

As the hardships in Israel continued, Jonathan Absalom's fervent speeches created a vocal uprising. The emergency election was instituted, and Absalom's "Save Israel Today!" party ran roughshod over the more dovish Prime Minister's Labor Party, winning a clear majority in the Knesset.

Absalom was quickly installed as Prime Minister by a vote of his party. His first act declared Israel to be in a state of war and wrested control from the Knesset. His second was to select a very special person to serve as his Chief of Staff.

This time, when he dangled the smooth, "Israel needs you to heal, not kill," bait, Sarah accepted. Absalom was the government, more so than any one person before him. The people had spoken, and they wanted to do things his way. As their freely elected leader, Sarah was bound by military honor to serve him.

However, that's where her loyalty ended.

A month after settling in to her new position, he called her into his stately office early one evening under the guise of going over the military budget. The lights were dim when she arrived. He offered her a glass of expensive French wine. She declined.

"Come on, we're celebrating," he said, pouring himself a tall drink. "I want to make a toast."

"To what?"

"To my victory."

"You've done that a hundred times already. It's time to stop celebrating and get to work so we can make good on some of your campaign promises."

"You're right. It is time to get down to business," he said merrily. Sarah could see that this wasn't his first glass—or bottle—of the evening. "Sarah, my sweet, I've tried to fight my feelings for you, but it isn't working."

"Try harder," she said, edging away from his desk. From her years in the military—and her life as a beautiful woman—she had learned the best way to deflect unwanted advances from a superior: be firm and direct so he got the message, but lace her response with humor so as not to bruise the man's ego or incite him to anger.

"I'm serious."

"So am I. You're married. And you're drunk. What you're thinking is out of the question."

"Why?"

"It's politically inappropriate and religiously immoral. How's that for a pair of reasons?"

"Unconvincing."

"That's because you're not thinking with your brain."

"That's not true. I admit there's a strong physical attraction, but you've moved me on every level a woman can reach a man. You're in here," he said, placing his hand over his heart.

"In there?" I thought that's where the 'decent man' resided. These aren't the schemes of a 'decent man.'"

"They are. Not schemes, but real feelings. Believe me. You... you're so incredibly beautiful, I can't help myself. I want you. I need you."

"You and every other man in Israel. Stand in line. Last time I checked, the end was somewhere in Jerusalem."

"I'm not every other man. I have line privileges."

"Jonathan, you have a lovely wife and three kids. You don't need this. You're talking an ugly scandal here. It will lower you in the eyes of the people, hamstring your leadership abilities, and throw the government and all of Israel into turmoil. I can't be a part of anything like that."

"Nonsense. No one has to know."

"Oh, you view me as your little mistress, huh? Is this the 'decent man' talking again? Well listen, I'm not anybody's mistress. I get better offers than that in the cafeteria downstairs!"

"That's not what I meant."

"Isn't it? Get this idea out of your head, Jonathan. It will never happen. I'm not that kind of woman. Hopefully, when you come to your senses, you won't be that kind of man."

"You're certainly feisty, aren't you?" he said.

"You haven't seen anything yet. You're lucky you didn't get pushy about it."

"A physical threat? It would be worth the pain just to feel your touch. Even if it's a slap."

"I don't slap."

That sobered the leader for a moment. She felt him staring at her, trying to determine if she really meant what she said.

"No, I bet you don't," he said, conceding defeat. "OK, General, I apologize. I don't think I can stop trying, though. Not the way I feel about you. These things a man can't control."

"That's a problem you men have. No control. And you think your tenacity is an aphrodisiac."

"That's because it works."

"Not with this soldier."

"If you want me to change my marital status… "

"That's the last thing I want. You go home, tell your wife you love her, hug your kids, and I'll forget we ever had this conversation."

Sarah turned and walked briskly out of his office. Absalom shook his head, chuckled, and took a drink from his glass.

Driving home, Sarah was surprised at how little Absalom's behavior bothered her. From the way he looked at her, she had known for weeks that it was coming. It always did. She had fended off so many advances in her life that they hardly fazed her anymore. Years of living in military barracks had not only hardened her, but given her a male perspective on relationships. From what she saw, men were governed by their primal instincts, some to the point of destroying everything else in their lives to satisfy their lusts. The only difference was that some men controlled it better than others.

In a sense, she was relieved that Absalom had finally made his play. The problem was, these things rarely ended with the first rebuff. She had little doubt that Absalom would continue to turn up the pressure. Sarah, however, was confident that she could handle it and not allow Absalom's adulterous intentions to interfere with her job. She could do a lot of good for her country in her position. If she had to put up with an occasional pass to accomplish her altruistic goals, it was a small price to pay.

Although she was unwilling to accept him as a lover, she remained loyal to Absalom as a leader. When he began taking control of the Middle East, country by country, she was convinced that it was the right thing to do to end centuries of war and hatred. She even climbed back into the cockpit and flew a few well-publicized missions against Jordan, Iran, and Iraq—countries that balked at being led by Jews.

She began to question him, however, when he started using harsh tactics to blackmail and bully European, Asian, and African leaders into handing him the reins of their countries. He accomplished this non-violently through his stranglehold on the world's oil supply, and more importantly, by withholding Israel's advanced technology in combating radiation poisoning. By riding the wave of nuclear fallout, Absalom was swallowing up one nation after another in rapid succession.

"Jonathan, how far do you plan to take this?" she asked one afternoon after he had taken a particularly hard stance in negotiations with Chinese leaders.

"All the way. As far as we can. Do you expect me to just give them what they want?"

"Yes. That would be the decent thing to do."

"This isn't about decency. This is about power. What do you think would happen if I just gave them the medical technology? They'd use it as a weapon. They'd use it to further suppress their people and empower themselves. They'd withold it from rebel groups, religious factions, or ethnic pockets they don't like in order to purge their country of dissidents. If I hand them the magic, I strengthen their corrupt government and sentence their people to another century of slavery. Do you want to be responsible for that?"

"I guess not."

"You guess right. And do you think it would end with the radiation medicine?"

"I don't know."

"Has it with any other country?"

"No."

"That's right. Next week these same little devious Chinese will be back here begging for oil. That's not medicine to save their suffering people; that's pure greed. They need the oil to fuel their military and keep their people under their thumbs. You want me to just give them that, too? Support their brutal reign with our oil, at our expense? No! We have the medicine. We have the oil. So we take over. It's the law of the jungle. And we'll be nicer. Everybody wins."

"Especially you."

"And you, too. Better us than those evil snakes."

"Then why do you squeeze them on the radiation cure? Why don't you wait until they come for the oil?"

"Haven't you learned anything? You just think I've gone mad with power? They come for the medicine, and I cut a coldhearted deal. I say 'give me your government or you can watch the flesh rot off your bones. I don't care. Take it or leave it.' You know what that does? That allows them to go home and save face. They have to make the sacrifice to save their people. I'm the bad guy, and they're the heroes. My approach stabilizes the transition. And it keeps them from using medicine to kill, not heal. Don't forget that.

"Next week, when they come for the oil, they'll just be the devious dictators they really are, trying to cajole me with talk of keeping their economic base afloat when all they really want is to maintain their strangling grasp around the throats of their beloved people. With the health threat removed, they'll be arrogant and unwilling to compromise. They're pigs. All these world leaders—Europe, Asia, Africa, everywhere—they're all greedy pigs. Believe me, either they give me control, or they can rot."

"And what about you, Jonathan? Some might argue that you've become the biggest pig of all."

"Impossible," he said with a smile. "Pork is forbidden."

"Seriously."

"Seriously, Sarah," he said, his voice smooth and persuasive. "It has to be done this way. If we had to deal with every tin-plated leader in every country, we wouldn't be able to save anybody. We don't have the time to wrestle with each country's politics. We need the power to go in there and provide the medicine and food now, before people start dying. We tried it your way in Germany, and look what happened. While they were reliving World War II, taking votes in their congress, and worrying about Jews taking control, a million people died agonizing deaths. Our doctors and soldiers were attacked and killed trying to save them. I'm not going to force our relief teams to go through that again. I must have complete control. This way, the relief effort will work efficiently, and no one, including our own doctors, will die.

"Look, Sarah, you know how I feel about you. I put up a lot of fronts for a lot of people, but you know the real me. Right now, the world needs to be united. When things settle down, I promise I'll give the countries back. We'll hold elections, and they can return to self rule. Many of these countries will be free for the first time. China, for one. We have a chance to convert that huge nation to democracy. No more students crushed by tanks. We can't pass up that opportunity, can we?"

"I guess not."

"So don't worry. I know I can be difficult, but remember that inside," he said, tapping his chest, "I'm a decent man."

The conversation with Absalom left Sarah dazed, just as so many others had. One minute he seemed like a power-crazed dictator intent on conquering the world as part of some unspoken personal master plan. The next, he was a clear-thinking, benevolent leader concerned with rescuing the sick, easing suffering, feeding the hungry, and improving the overall condition of the world. Because of the dichotomy, she had no idea who the real Jonathan Absalom was.

Two months later, Sarah clashed with Jonathan again over Great Britain. Absalom, no longer patient enough to allow the radiation cloud to clear the way, dispatched a premature request to take over the once-dominant island nation. Britain told him to drop dead. Like a petulant child with an overflowing toy box, instead of enjoying what he had, he craved what he didn't. Absalom wanted to launch an attack, but Sarah convinced him that America wouldn't stand for it. Such a military strike would be a disastrous public relations move in the eyes of the world.

"It would cause a rumbling inside the countries that are already under our wing," she advised. "Wait. Be patient. When the time is right, they'll fall in line like the others."

Absalom ignored her until she personally refused to fly with her fellow pilots on a planned British attack mission and threatened to go public with her reasons.

Three months later, as the nuclear cloud finally reached the British Isles, the clamoring from the suffering British people was such that they peacefully voted to join the United Continents, the name Absalom christened his growing empire.

With the United Kingdom under his belt, Absalom was ready for his final conquest, the most important of all.

THIRTEEN

Matt returned to America as an odd kind of hero. His courage and bravery during the foreign war was admirable, but as the aftermath of the Soviet-Israel confrontation loomed, his achievement was regarded as distant and impersonal and never really caught the public's imagination.

After the initial splash of publicity that greeted his arrival, the Medal of Honor recipient quietly went back to his job as an airline pilot, rejecting modest offers to write a book, go on a lecture tour, and enter local politics.

It wasn't that Matt was shy or unselfish. He remained low key for other reasons. Stories of the suffering in the Soviet Union and Europe were starting to receive widespread coverage, a factor that tarnished his shining medals. He remained uneasy about Israel's future behavior, and fearing that if the Jewish nation turned aggressive, whatever thin hero's cloak he wore would be stripped away.

He had already been branded a traitor once and had no desire to feel the sting of that accusation again. The best option, he concluded, was to quietly fade into the woodwork.

Only fading quietly into anything wasn't Matt's style. It was torture waiting for distant events to set the course of his life. And the toughest part was waiting alone.

Matt tried to ease his loneliness by turning to the spiritual. Even with Jill gone, his inner longing to become a Christian remained. Only now he didn't have her to guide him. He was confused about what to do. He went to a few churches, but the congregations were oddly dispirited and the preachers far less fervent than he remembered before the war. When he asked one pastor about making a personal commitment to Christ, he was brushed off.

"The path to heaven is to attend church regularly and give as much as you can afford in the offering plate," the man stated.

Although admittedly weak on the issue, Matt knew this didn't square with what Jill had taught him. After another minister said virtually the same thing, he gave up on church and attempted to find the answers for himself. He located one of Jill's Bibles and began to read.

Matt found the Old Testament interesting from a historical standpoint, especially the events surrounding Israel. But he was impatient for quick answers and information that he could directly apply to his life. He made it to Numbers before skipping to the index to search for familiar names and stories he recognized from Sunday school. That proved more fruitful. He enjoyed revisiting the Bible's more action-packed passages and love stories. The strong man Samson had trouble with a beauty named Delilah. David battled the giant Goliath. And then had his own problems with women, particularly a bathing beauty named Bathsheba. Daniel faced the lions. Jonah was swallowed by the great fish. The familiar accounts were comforting, and re-reading them as an adult gave them new meaning. But Matt was more entertained than enlightened. He still wasn't finding the answers he sought.

The answer, he concluded, had to be in the New Testament. He began reading it like a man searching for clues to a mystery. He poured through the four Gospels, surprised to learn that they repeated the same story of Christ's life on earth from four different perspectives. The accounts were fascinating, particularly the passages that quoted Jesus himself. He was astonished, however, to learn how short Jesus' time as the acknowledged Messiah actually was. He found it incredible that those three short years could have had such a lasting impact upon the world.

The reading slowed down after Jesus's death. Matt wondered

why the New Testament would be written so that the main character was killed off in the first section. Regardless, it was interesting to see how the disciples carried on, and how Jesus' teachings spread.

Hungering for some feedback, he couldn't wait to get to work the following day. He was flying a long red-eye route from Washington, D.C., to London, and Danny would be his co-pilot. That would give him ample time to discuss his thoughts with his friend.

Shortly before takeoff, a flight attendant entered the cockpit and announced that someone was going to take the jump seat, a smaller chair recessed between the pilot and co-pilot that flight examiners use to evaluate a pilot's performance. More often, the seat was used by off-duty pilots traveling on personal business or deadheading to their home city—and then only when the flight was full and no other seats were available. Usually, the captain had the power to OK a jump seat request.

Matt was annoyed that the attendant hadn't asked his permission. He was also disappointed that they'd have a third wheel that evening. He had wanted to talk with Danny in private.

"Who is it?" Matt asked. "I haven't given the OK."

"I don't know," she shrugged. "Some big shot from headquarters."

"Oh man, just what we need—some weasel from HQ looking over our shoulders all night," Danny moaned. "Do you think it's a spot examination?"

"Could be," Matt said. "Either way, it stinks."

Matt had just spit out the words when a large, older gentleman in a rumpled western suit entered the cockpit. The two pilots recognized him instantly. They looked at each other in amazement.

"What stinks?" the man asked in a deep, robust voice.

"Nothing, sir," Matt gulped. "We were just talking."

"Well, hope you boys don't mind the company. I've got a big meetin' in London tomorrow, and I nearly forgot about it."

"No, sir, we don't mind," Matt said. "It's an honor. We're glad to have you aboard. I think there are some seats open in first class, though. That might be more comfortable for you."

"First class? That's for sissies," the man snapped. "I like being in the pit. I used to fly some myself back in the old days."

"That's an understatement," Matt acknowledged.

The big man was James Welby, the world-renowned aviation pioneer and World War II hero from Oklahoma who founded the airline. Welby was a legendary Air Force test pilot from the early days of jet propulsion. He had spent time as an astronaut and circled the globe a few times before retiring from the military to start his own airline. A billionaire in his mid-eighties, he had turned over most of the day-to-day operation of the huge air carrier to his sons.

Matt wondered what meeting in London could be so pressing as to require the attendance of the Big Kahuna himself. He wondered, but kept his mouth shut.

Danny, petrified by Welby's presence, also kept quiet. Matt doubted the co-pilot could speak even if he tried.

After take off, Welby eased the tension by relating some stories about his days as a test pilot.

"Yeah, you boys today, the jet does all the work. This ain't no jet, it's a video machine. Mah grandson could probably fly it better than all of us. When I was flying, all we had was a big old propeller and a rubber band. I practically had to flap my arms to keep my tail from draggin' the ground. Don't know how I ever survived. Crashed three times. Busted myself up pretty good each time. Broke half the bones in my body. And believe me, boys, I feel every crack each mornin' when I roll outta bed!

"They left me for dead once in the Sonoran Desert down there in Arizona. This piece of junk Eli Absalom built stove up on me like a dove full of bird shot. Sank like a rock, skidded and burned to a crisp in sixty seconds. I was thrown clear or I woulda been toast. If it wasn't for a pack of Injuns, I'd have been buzzard bait.

"First thing I did when I got out of the hospital, I went to Absalom Enterprises, walked right into Eli's office, and laid a roundhouse right across his ugly mug. 'Don't you ever build a piece of flying cow manure like that again!' I told him.

"He looked at me, rubbin' his jaw, then said, 'how should I build them?' We spent the next three hours designing the G-100 fighter jet. Eli was OK. Gave me my start in business."

James Welby turned out to be a friendly, huggy bear of a man. Soon, even Danny felt comfortable enough to join the conversation.

"Is that the same Elias Absalom whose son is taking over half the planet?" Danny asked.

"That's him," Welby answered icily.

"So what's so all-fired important that you've got to be in London?" Matt asked. "Are we merging with British Air?"

"Naaah. Nothing like that. Actually, that's just a cowboy's ruse. I don't need to be in London. I don't even like London. Too cold and rainy and the people talk funny."

Matt looked at Danny. Pleasant as he was, if the Big Kahuna wasn't going to London, why was he there?

"So, what am I doin' here with you boys tonight? You probably think I'm a senile old coot who likes to tell stories to a captive audience."

"No sir," Danny said.

"So why are you here, Mr. Welby?" Matt asked.

"I'm here for you, Matt."

"For me?"

"I heard you were lookin' for some answers. Maybe I can help."

"You know what happened to my fiancée?"

"No, that's one I can't help you with. You'll have to figure that out yourself. But I can help you with your other search."

"What other search?"

"For the answer to what's eatin' at your soul."

Matt jerked. "How do you know about that?"

Welby smiled. "I have my sources. Tell me what you're feeling."

Matt had planned to tell Danny all about it that very same evening. He had been eager to tell Danny. Now, faced with explaining it to James Welby, he became nervous and tongue-tied.

"I don't know... I just... there's a longing inside me, an emptiness. I feel God reaching out to me, but I can't seem to find his hand. It's like I'm in a fog. I was going to come to grips with this before, with Jill. Then that disappearance thing happened, whatever it was, and she was gone. After that, the war started and I never had a chance to catch my breath, much less think about my soul. Nobody in Israel was talking about that kind of stuff, anyway. When I finally decided it was time to really get to know God, I didn't know what to do or say. And nobody I asked seemed to have the answer. So it's been frustrating."

"I know what you mean," Welby said, putting his hand on Matt's shoulder. "I went through just what you're going through. I lost some good people. My wife's gone. So are two of my daughters and a son-in-law. I don't know why some are gone and some are here, but it made me start thinking about God myself. I searched, like you have, for an answer. My parents were God-fearing people. I went to church regularly when I was younger. I knew a lot about the Bible, but I never felt it inside. It was like another course I was taking in school.

"As I continued my search, I kept thinking about Larry Spencer. He was in the Air Force with me, a gung-ho Christian type who kept trying to bring me closer to God. He was trying to turn my book knowledge into a real spiritual relationship. But I ignored him for the most part.

"I hadn't thought of Larry in decades. Then after what happened with my wife and girls, I couldn't stop thinking of him. I started remembering what he told me about feeling God inside, about praying like I was talking to my father, about living my life as if God was watching every step I took. I remembered what my parents had said, what my Sunday school teachers taught me about turning my life over to God. So I fell to my knees and thanked God for Larry and my parents, apologized for being so distant all those years, and put my life in God's hands. After I did that, that Texas-wide emptiness eased. But not completely until I followed up on the moment. I read my Bible, studied Jesus' teaching with a new heart—not as a schoolboy forced to learn, but as someone eagerly willing to be taught. I've tried to take the knowledge and apply it to my everyday life, to live the way God wants me to. When I began doing that, the emptiness began to fill."

"I'd like to do that. I'd like to fill my emptiness."

"Go ahead."

"Now?"

"Now's as good a time as any. Better actually. We're a little closer than everybody else." Welby grinned.

"What do I say?"

"You'll think of something."

"OK. Danny, take the controls. That's all right, isn't it sir?"

"I'll let it slide, considering," he said with a smile.

Matt clenched his hands and began to pray. As he did, he started to remember some things Jill had told him months before.

"Dear God, I need forgiveness. My life has been empty without your presence and your guidance. I've felt so lost and alone. Not just because Jill's gone, but because she was going to lead me to you. I believe that you sent your Son to die on the cross for my sins. I ask you to take the controls of my life, help me to grow in my faith, and use me to serve your will."

Matt opened his eyes and let out a sigh of relief.

"You think that was OK?" he asked.

"Do you think it was?" Welby answered.

Matt smiled the brightest smile of his life.

"Yes, I do, sir. I do!"

"Welcome aboard, Matthew," Mr. Welby said, shaking his hand.

Welby turned to Danny.

"How about you, son?"

Danny was stricken with fear. It was bad enough he had to go through this with Matt. Now his boss, the legendary James Welby, had put him on the spot. If he declined... well, there was no telling what Welby could do.

"Come on, Danny, you know your father always wanted to get

closer to God," Matt said. "Besides, you know more about the Bible than probably either one of us."

"Is that true, son?" Mr. Welby asked.

"My father was real religious. He used to make me go to church and Sunday school until I was eighteen and left home. We argued about the Bible all the time. He kept trying to convert me, and I kept shooting down his arguments. You know, smart aleck, know-it-all teenager stuff. I studied the Bible just so I could disprove it to him."

"Obviously, a lot sank in," Welby said.

"Maybe that's why Dad tolerated my arguments. He wanted me to remember, even if I didn't believe."

"I bet your Dad's missing. Just like Matt's Jill. Just like my wife and the girls."

Danny nodded, his eyes welling up with tears.

"It's high time you got right with God, son."

"Yeah, it's high time, Danny," Matt seconded.

Danny bowed his head, closed his eyes, and in an emotional voice, said a perfect conversion prayer as if he were reading it from a book.

Matt and Mr. Welby looked at him with surprise when he finished.

"I kinda already knew one," he said sheepishly. "My father used to type up prayers and post them on the inside of my door. There were a lot, covering a wide range of things, but the one I just said was my favorite."

"Why didn't you tell me?" Matt demanded.

"You never asked."

Welby threw his big hands in the air, then they all broke out in laughter.

"I'm real proud of you boys," Mr. Welby said. "This kind of commitment takes a lot of guts. You boys are something special. I'm going to the head. When I come back, I'll tell you the rest of the reason why I'm here."

"The rest of the reason?" Danny said after Welby left the cockpit.

"We'll find out soon enough," Matt predicted. "This has

already been some night."

"You can say that again."

"Did you mean it?" Matt asked.

"I don't know. It was under duress. I knew that's what Mr. Welby wanted. He's the boss. How was I going to say no?"

"So you didn't mean it."

"I didn't say that. I'm just saying I had no choice. But even so, I think I meant it."

"I hope you did. If you didn't, or if you're not sure, let it settle and we can talk about it again."

The two men were quiet for the next few minutes.

"He's something, isn't he?" Matt said.

"Mr. Welby? Yeah, great guy. He's one of us, only he had to take a tougher road."

"It's like a miracle he was here tonight."

"Not really. He was here for a reason. You."

"Why would he care about me?"

"You're an important guy. He must know your record. The war and all that. Plus, he probably knows about your government work, the stuff I don't even know about. I think he has plans for you."

"What plans?"

"I think we're going to find out when he comes back."

After another pause, Danny broke the silence.

"Do you feel any different?" he asked.

"Tremendously. But not like you mean. I've wanted to do this. I've needed to. I delayed too long. I feel... I don't know, relieved. At ease."

"I don't feel anything."

"You will. I feel safe. Like I'm flying with a net now."

The net is what the guys coming after us will be carrying, Danny thought.

Welby returned to the cockpit and took his seat.

"You boys been talking about me?"

"Just a little," Matt said. "We're certainly curious about what you said."

"Good. I couldn't tell you anything before I knew where you stood. Matt, I know your search for God is sincere, so I'm at ease with you. Danny there, I'm not so sure about. We had him in a wringer. Like with me and Larry Spencer, it may take a while for this night to sink in. But a man's gotta take a chance, so I'm going forward.

"There's a lot of strange things happenin' in the world these days. Hurricanes and earthquakes rippin' apart the land. Wars like we've never seen before. Starvation and sufferin' worse than ever. People turning up missing all over. A lot of bad stuff. But you know what worries me most? Eli's kid Jonathan. What he's doing over there in Israel and Europe and the rest of the world, something ain't right about it. They say he's bringing peace and unity, but I know that boy, and I never trusted him. I don't think his papa ever trusted him much either, though he wouldn't admit it.

"But even if I did trust him, I'd still be worried. You can't give a man that much power without it goin' to his head. And once it goes to his head, anythin' can happen."

"That's over there," Matt said. "We're safe here... aren't we?"

"Word is, he's comin' after us next."

"How?"

"Don't know yet, but you can bet your boots he's comin'. He's a Texan. Don't forget that. He might have spent half his childhood in Israel, but take my word, that boy's a Texan. He's not gonna be happy until he's in charge over here."

"What can we do?" Matt asked.

"Funny you should ask. I've already planted the seeds of resistance. The way I figure, it's got to be built around new Christians, people like you and me and maybe Danny. It's got to be new Christians, 'cause as far as I can tell, there aren't any old ones left anymore.

"When Eli's boy gets his hands on the rest of the pie, he's going to have to make some big changes. He's bitten off a lot more than any one man can chew. To keep it hanging together—and by 'it' I mean his world empire—he's got to streamline the operation. He's gonna try to mold everything into one pot of clay. Among other things, he's not going to tolerate religion. Religion is the biggest threat to his power. He has no obligation to Christianity at all. That'll be the first thing to go.

"Then all us Christians will be in a bind. So we got to prepare now. Maybe it won't happen. Maybe he won't be able to take control here. Maybe he won't eliminate religion. Maybe I'm just an old goat talkin' outta my hat. If so, then we can all breathe easier. But if I'm right—and my gut tells me I am—we're gonna need to link together to survive."

"How?" Matt asked.

"I'll give you the details later. Just wait until you're called."

Welby paused. "Oh, and there's one more thing."

"There's more?" Matt wondered out loud, emotionally drained by the events of the evening.

"Unfortunately. Now, this is gonna hit you where you live, Matthew. But it all seems to be hittin' you, so take this as just another sign that God's got you in the fire well. That lady of yours—not Jill, but the other one—she's up to her pretty little eyeballs in this with Eli's son. If you have any plans on being with her, or if you just care enough about her to care what happens to her soul, you'd better get her away from that guy, 'cause when God drops the final dime, anyone who was with Eli's son might have hell to pay, literally."

"What can I do?"

"Don't ask me! You're the hero type. You'll think of something. Oh, and one last thing. Just in case you're not quite motivated enough, he's in love with her, so watch your step."

"He's in love with her? How do you know all this?"

"I know. That's all. I have my sources. Now I'm beat, boys. Got up with the chickens this morning. I spotted one of those expensive double-sizers open in the rich people's section back there, so I think I'll turn in. I got a lotta work ahead of me if I'm going to lasso this kid of Irv's before he gets too big for his britches."

Welby slowly lifted his large body from the jump seat and disappeared into first class.

"He's right. We've got to save Sarah, Danny. Before it's too late," Matt said.

"What do you mean 'we'? I don't want any part of her, especially if she's in with that guy Absalom. I never liked her anyway."

"We've got to get to her," Matt repeated, ignoring Danny. We'll explain what Mr. Welby said. She'll understand."

"Are you kidding? She's Jewish. She'll think we've gone stark raving mad!"

"She'll understand," Matt said with conviction, trying to convince himself as much as his friend.

FOURTEEN

A fierce winter ice storm greeted the pilots as they prepared to land in London.

"Would you like to divert to Liverpool?" the tower radioed. "It's nasty down here. You're coming in double zero, RVR 500."

"Negative," Matt answered. "These people need to be in London. We'll sleigh ride it in."

"It's your boat, Captain. Be careful."

The harsh double zero weather—zero visibility in front and above, with a Runway Visual Range of 500 feet—was the least of Matt's worries. The possibility that Sarah could be part of some evil empire had eaten at him for hours. By comparison, landing a 163,000 pound Aerospatiale A320 Airbus in a slush pile was a minor annoyance.

"Maybe we should go to Liverpool," Danny suggested as the ice began to pound the windshield. "We can go see where the Beatles got their start."

"Never done a double zero, eh?" Matt said. "Piece of cake. Besides, Liverpool's fogged in. I checked earlier. The runway's shorter, and the storm's heading that way. We'd just have to circle back. Let's get this over with now."

Matt armed the auto brakes, double checked the anti-skid cycle, gave Danny a wink, and brought her in. Halfway down the frozen runway, a buzzer sounded, signaling an auto brake failure.

"Left or right?" Danny asked.

"We'll know in a second," Matt said, cool as the ice building up on the huge jet's wings.

The Airbus lurched to the left. Matt stomped on the right rudder pedal, causing the right brakes to lock up. He grasped the joy stick in both hands and held it firm. Matt felt like he was hauling all 163,000 pounds in his arms. The jet skidded to the right, shuddered, then straightened out.

"Whew!" Danny said, gasping in relief.

"Not so fast. Our tires are going to blow."

A series of explosions rocked the cockpit. Matt gave Danny another wink as more buzzers and alarms rang.

"And a brake well fire on top of it," Matt said, glancing at the controls. "Best big jet in the sky, and it's still predictable as rain. Get ready to release the emergency exit slides. And tell the FAs to keep the people calm."

The jet skidded to a halt inches from the end of the runway.

"What happened?" James Welby asked as he entered the cockpit.

"Double zero weather. Brake fire. Blown tires," Matt answered.

"Is that all?" the big man cracked. "I thought it was something really bad."

The exit slides inflated at the front and back ends of the Airbus, avoiding the Fourth of July light show around the landing gear. A fire truck, racing to the scene, skidded, banked sideways, and took out the entire front slide. Matt, observing the truck from the window, winced and shook his head.

"Divert all the passengers to the rear slide," he announced.

"Why?" Danny wondered.

"Keystone firemen."

Despite the drama of the landing, the exit was orderly—thanks to Matt's confident and calm directions over the intercom. After the jet emptied, Matt took his turn on the slide. At the bottom, he caught a small boy who had escaped from his mother in the snow and was trying to climb the rubber mountain.

"Hey, this isn't Disney World, little buddy," Matt said, handing the boy to his thoroughly rattled mother.

"That was fun!" the boy exclaimed.

Matt laughed. "It was, wasn't it?"

Danny found Matt packing in his hotel room later that evening. They weren't scheduled to fly again for another day, and the ice storm was still assaulting the city outside.

"Where do you think you're going?"

"Israel," Matt said without looking up.

"In this weather? In the middle of your schedule? You've got to bring the bus home tomorrow."

"No time."

"Wait a minute. You can't throw your career away over some crazy theory we discussed in a dark cockpit. What would Mr. Welby say?"

"This is more important."

"You have responsibilities to the airline and to the passengers. You can't abandon them. This is the kind of thing that has gotten you in trouble in the past. It nearly got you killed in Israel."

"I put what's important first."

"Leaving three hundred passengers stranded, many on personal business that to them is as important as yours, is not very Christian."

Matt stopped packing. He had been far too undisciplined his entire life, a habit that didn't square with his new faith.

"I've got to do something."

"No you don't. We have time. Let's see what happens. This guy Absalom might not be as bad as Mr. Welby thinks."

"Welby wouldn't be organizing a resistance if he wasn't sure."

"You don't know that. He said he might be wrong."

"He's not telling us everything."

"Even if he isn't, why us? Why do we have to be the heroes?"

"Because we might be the only Christians in the world right now."

Danny paused, allowing the implications of Matt's statement to sink in.

"That's mind-boggling," he said. "Arrogant, too. Especially for me. I'm hardly the model."

"Me either. But if we're all there is, it's a big responsibility."

"And throwing away your other responsibilities hardly sets a good example. It's a moot point, anyway. If Sarah believes in Absalom, there isn't a thing you can do about it."

"If there's a chance, I've got to take it. We're not just talking about her life. We're talking about her soul, for all eternity. What's missing a few flights compared to that?"

"There's no reason you have to miss any flights. Look at this." Danny handed Matt a copy of a British newspaper. "She's coming to us."

The headline on the tabloid read "Ab to Shoot for U.S. Helm." Matt read the first paragraph out loud: "'In an effort to unite the world, British Prime Minister and EuroAsia leader Jonathan Absalom has announced his intention to enter the upcoming United States Presidential race.'"

"This is incredible!" Matt exclaimed. "See, it's going to hit us next."

"Why isn't he just blackmailing us like he did all the other countries?" Danny wondered.

"We don't have a death cloud hovering overhead to weaken our resolve. Besides, he figures he can get what he wants through an election. He'll probably win."

"Read paragraph five," Danny suggested.

"'Absalom, an American citizen by birth, said at a news conference in Paris that the upcoming election offered an unprecedented opportunity to bring together his growing family of nations. As he spoke, his beautiful Chief of Staff, the Israeli war hero Sarah Gold, stood proudly at his side.'"

"What a joke," Matt huffed.

"Joke or not, Golden Sarah will be coming to America soon. You can talk to her there. That's better. They're not gonna be real happy about seeing you in Israel. Johnny Boy probably has a thing for her, just like Welby said. He's ruthless. I wouldn't mess with him on his own turf."

"You think he wants her?"

"He wants the entire world. Why make an exception with her?"

Danny had a point.

"You think she likes him?"

"He's a bit slimy, but you know what they say, 'Power is the best aphrodisiac.'"

"I've got to go to Israel," Matt said renewing his packing.

Danny closed the lid on Matt's suitcase.

"Not now. Wait until she comes to us. You'll accomplish nothing by getting yourself killed in Israel."

Sarah publicly played her part as Absalom's chief assistant, standing by his side as he gave inspiring "welcome aboard" speeches to nation after nation as his empire expanded. Privately, she continued to have misgivings about his character and the psychological effect of his unprecedented rise to power. The quest for the American presidency, to her, seemed like extreme overkill.

She had a number of questions she wanted to ask her boss, questions that needed to be posed in private to avoid receiving his pat, staged answers. That was a problem. She had avoided being alone with him since the late-night meeting in his office, and she wasn't looking forward to fending off any more advances.

With both his campaign staff and his top government operations personnel preparing to relocate to America for the duration of the election campaign, however, she forced herself to confront him. She lingered in her office after hours for nearly a week before the right opportunity presented itself.

"Sarah! What a surprise. Come in," he said as she stood in the doorway of his palatial office. "Have you changed... "

"This isn't about that, Jonathan. Please, let's not go through that again. Not tonight."

"OK," he said. "Just business. What's on your mind? You haven't been yourself lately."

"I'm worried about this. We're moving too fast. We can't control the nations we have right now. Why do you want to become the President of the United States?"

"Because it's there," he said, smiling.

"I'm serious."

"So am I. Sit down, Sarah."

She inched forward, searching the room for any sign that he had been drinking. His mood swings were directly related to how much alcohol was in his system. When sober, he was a brilliant, energetic leader who truly appeared to care about uniting the world into a peaceful family and improving the condition of the common man. When he drank, he transformed into a selfish, mean-spirited dictator who craved power like a drug and was controlled by his baser instincts.

This evening, she could see no evidence, either in the room or in his behavior, that he was intoxicated. Breathing a sigh of relief, she took a seat in front of his desk. Absalom stood and began pacing in the large office.

"Can't we slow down? You don't need America. I'm afraid... " she began.

"That it might be the domino that topples the empire?"

"Exactly."

"I understand. Sometimes I worry about that myself. Then I think about all we've accomplished. Most people thought that this wouldn't work. That uniting Europe, Asia, Africa, Great Britain, and the Middle East under one rule would be impossible. But it's working. You can't deny that. The relief efforts are going smoothly. We've stopped the suffering, starving, and dying everywhere but Russia. The scientists say that we'll be able to go there in a few more months. I'm not really looking forward to that. The reports from Russia have been horrible. But when the time comes, we've got to help those people, whoever is left, the best way we can.

"Outside of Russia, there are only a few small pockets of civil unrest in the remote areas of Africa and Asia. For the most part, the world is at peace."

"So we end up with the same question," Sarah said. "Why do we need America?"

"Because that's where Benny McGuirk lives."

"Who?"

"Benny McGuirk. The neighborhood bully back in Texas. He used to pick on me. Beat me up. When we played baseball, I'd usually supply the bats and balls because we were rich. Benny would take them from me and then turn around and not let me play. He said I wasn't good enough. He'd even take my glove. When I told my father, Dad would just buy me more. That's the way my father thought. He'd just buy his way out of problems.

"One day, I refused to let Benny take my glove. I tried to fight him, but he was too big. He beat me to a pulp. Then he said something I'll never forget: 'You're just a weak little rich boy. You'll never amount to anything.'

"So why America? That's where Benny lives. Benny doesn't care how many countries I rule in the rest of the world. All Benny knows is America. That's all that counts."

"It's a touching story, Jonathan, and I'm sure it had a deep effect upon you. But I still don't understand."

"This is for me, Sarah. I need this. America is my home. I've never felt comfortable in Israel. I know little about Europe, England, and Asia. Africa is totally foreign. So I'm ruling places I don't really care about. I'm governing people whose cultures and languages I don't understand. It's like a football player who plays in Canada instead of the NFL in America. Or a baseball player who plays in Japan instead of suiting up for the New York Yankees. It's not the same. You don't feel like you've really made it. I want to be President of a place I understand and care about. If I don't, I'll never feel successful.

"Hang with me on this one, Sarah. We're going to do it right this time. No coercion. I'm not forcing anyone to buckle under because I have what they need. This is an election. The American people will have the free will to vote for me or send me packing. That's important to me."

"And if you win, what then?"

"Then we'll run the whole show from America. And we can use the tremendous wealth and natural resources in the United States to balance things in the rest of the world. We'll bring the Third World nations up to speed, educate their children, even things out. And once everything settles down, we'll hold elections and the people can vote on whether they want to stay a part of the union or splinter off under their own rule."

"Will you be able to do that? Will you be able to let go?"

"I think so," he said smiling. "I might be eager to retire by then. This is hard work."

Sarah looked deeply into Absalom's eyes to determine if he was speaking from the heart or just trying out his latest line. She couldn't tell. When he spoke like this, she wanted to believe in everything he was trying to accomplish. And she had to admit, it would be fun to be part of a campaign for President. After all Absalom had done, it would be interesting to see how the American people viewed him.

"There's one other thing, Jonathan. I hesitate to bring it up, but you're in an unusually receptive mood tonight, so I'm going to give it a try... "

"My drinking?"

Sarah nodded.

"You think it's becoming a problem?"

"It causes a tremendous personality change. When you drink you become a different person. I don't know that other man. He frightens me. He frightens a lot of us. You have so much power at your fingertips. You can guide or destroy entire nations. You have to keep your mind straight."

"It's not that bad, Sarah. It just gives me courage when I feel overwhelmed. Don't worry, it's still me inside, either way. But if it bothers you, I'll cut back. OK?"

"Do it for yourself, not for me."

"If I did it for myself, I wouldn't stop. You, now you'd be worth it."

"Do it for you, Jon. Please. To accomplish your goals. When do we leave for the U.S.?" she asked, changing the subject.

"Next week," he said, flashing his million-dollar television smile. "We're going to win!"

After Sarah left, Absalom opened a lower drawer, pulled out a bottle of Scotch, and poured himself a large glass. He downed it in one gulp.

"You and me," he said, looking at the bottle. "No one is going to stop us. Not even her."

Jonathan Absalom tossed his hat into the Presidential ring a mere three months before the election. He met with immediate opposition as both the Democratic and Republican candidates turned their guns away from each other and on to him. None of it mattered. After decades of lackluster Presidents, the public found the handsome Harvard grad turned world leader irresistible. He quickly shot to the top of the polls.

Absalom's appeal was unmistakable. He offered Americans a *bona fide* celebrity to rally around. His appearance, charisma, and eloquent speech were intoxicating. Plus, he brought to the table an attribute that no other candidate could hope to match—guaranteed peaceful international relations. His campaign slogan, suggested by Sarah, was simple and devastatingly effective—"Peace on Earth, Goodwill Toward a United Humanity."

The campaign's symbol was equally appealing—three arms raised high—one black, one white, the third brown—woven around each other and ending in a large, green clenched fist. The green not only symbolized a United Earth; it brilliantly avoided the messy question of which color would end up on top.

His campaign speeches were equally compelling. Absalom described the earth as a dangerous Tower of Babel operating contrary to the laws of nature.

"The world's ethnic, cultural, and nationalistic divisions are building into a powder keg, leading to an explosion that will eradicate human life and plummet us back into the era of the dinosaurs. What happened in Israel and Russia is only the beginning. Our technological advances are far out-pacing our humanity. We are learning how to destroy ourselves before we understand why we shouldn't.

"When we imagine life on other planets, how do we perceive it? Do we envision angry worlds made up of hundreds of different peoples and cultures constantly at each others' throats? Or do we prefer to view our sister planets as populated by a single, peaceful race? In the world of science fiction, the most popular books, television shows, and movies give us this second view. Some writers have written about worlds where diverse species of humanoids live together on a planet torn by hatred, racism, war, and relentless strife. But we prefer the plots about planets where the people are united. Even our most imaginative creative minds don't want to perceive of other worlds as divided as our Earth.

"It's time we join together as one. It's time to put our nationalistic egos and jealousies aside. Time to stop calling ourselves Russians, Israelis, Arabs, Africans, Canadians, Mexicans, Japanese, Chinese, or Brits and become simply residents of our beautiful blue planet. It's time for a United Earth!"

Such speeches met with thunderous applause in a country weary of anger, hate, rampant crime, class divisions, and violent riots.

The more popular Absalom became, the more desperate Matt was to rescue Sarah. When he tried to reach her, she sent a message back that such a meeting "wouldn't be prudent at this time." She didn't elaborate. Matt and Danny began stalking her like assassins, eventually using Matt's American and Israeli military identifications to talk their way past the layers of security and duck into Sarah's hotel room in New Orleans.

Matt could hardly contain himself as he waited. He longed to cast his eyes upon her again and drink in her dark beauty. He ached to smell her perfume, hold her in his arms, kiss her lips—if only for a few seconds. Maybe she was unhappy. Maybe she would realize how much she missed him, and they'd leave together that very night. Maybe...

Matt's dreamy thoughts were interrupted by Sarah's arrival.

"You've got to get out of here, now!" she screamed.

"Nice to see you, too," Matt said. "Give us a few minutes."

"No. Just leave!"

"We're not leaving until you listen to us. We just want a couple of minutes."

"Please, Matt. Please! Your life could be in danger."

"So is yours. And more. Just listen."

Matt finally calmed her enough to give her his pitch. He gave her a quick version of his search for God, his commitment, and their belief that Absalom was going to lead the world to ruin. Then, two-thirds of the way through, he looked at Danny and saw an expression on his friend's face that brought him up short. He realized how disjointed—how absolutely insane—it all sounded.

Sarah was quiet for a moment after Matt finished. Then she rose to her feet.

"Do you believe this, Danny?"

The co-pilot just shrugged sheepishly.

"You two have completely lost your minds! This is a wonderful opportunity to end hunger and suffering and ethnic hatred all around the world. A united planet will be a peaceful, happy planet. But instead of seeing that, you two have come up with these wild stories of an evil empire. I don't need this."

"You've got to understand, Sarah... "

"I don't know what's happened to you Matt," she interrupted. "I know you've been through a lot with Jill and me, but you've got to get a grip on yourself. It sounds like you've joined a cult or something. I gave you your time. Now you have to leave. Please."

Matt, crushed by his inability to get through to her, allowed himself to be led to the door. When it opened, he looked squarely into the face of Jonathan Absalom.

"Sarah, what is this?" Absalom asked as he slipped into the room.

"Old friends. They were just leaving."

Absalom stared at Matt as if he were trying to figure out where he'd seen him before. Matt felt his blood rush. There was something creepy about Absalom, something off. The politician's eyes burned a bit too brightly.

When the recognition came, Matt saw Absalom's mouth and neck tighten for an instant before breaking into a phony smile.

"Matt Slade, of course," he said, extending his hand and ushering Matt and Danny back into the room. Matt felt an odd electric charge run up his arm as his flesh met Absalom's, but he didn't flinch. "The world owes you a great debt of gratitude. I guess I, like all the people of Israel, owe you my life."

"Just doing my job, sir."

"What brings you here?"

He glanced at Sarah. She appeared petrified.

"Visiting one of my old fighter pilot buddies. We were a close-knit group."

"That's right—you two flew together, didn't you?" Absalom said, obviously knowing more than he was letting on. "You two were the major heroes of the Freedom Confrontation. Sarah's gotten a lot more mileage out of it, though."

"She had the right last name."

"That she did," Absalom said with a laugh. "Hey, maybe you can help me with an endorsement. I assume you're pretty well-known here?"

"Not so much anymore. Fame is fleeting."

"So it is. But we could write something for you that'll bring it all back. My media people are pretty clever. You'd make a great subject. I'll even pay you. Think about it."

"I will, thanks."

"Well, I've got to go give another speech. This campaigning is more taxing than I thought. I have to run this world you saved, you know. Sarah, are you coming?"

"In a minute."

Absalom gave Sarah a brief chilling look, then pasted on his smile again.

"Get back to us if you want to do the spot," he said to Matt. "We'd sure like to have you aboard. We could do something together. Kind of an 'I saved it, now he's the man to run it' type of ad. It could be fun. Could be a boon for you, personally."

"I'll certainly consider it."

Absalom gave Sarah another piercing look, then left the room.

"That was smooth," Danny said, mopping his brow. "I nearly got scorched by all the tension in the room."

"You've really done it now, Matt," Sarah said icily.

"Why? What's going on between you two?"

"Nothing. But… "

"But he's not happy about it. Isn't he married?"

Sarah nodded.

"Where's his wife?"

"In Israel, with his children."

"Great. Are you his mistress?"

"How dare you... " she said, raising her hand to strike him.

Matt caught her wrist. "Still quick with your right, huh? The guy's a creep—can't you see it? Don't you see his eyes? He's possessed by something."

"He's a great leader. He'll be good for the world."

"This guy is going to be the worst disaster the world has ever seen. Mark my words. After he gets America, what next? What will be left to satiate his mad cravings?"

"Sarah," Danny said quietly. "Sarah will be next."

A dead silence fell over the room.

"Even that won't be enough," Matt finally said. "Remember what we told you here tonight. Watch for the signs. We'll always be here for you. You can get out at any time."

"I've got to go," Sarah said, this time with far less conviction.

"Remember what we've told you," Matt repeated as they walked to the door. "I know it sounds crazy, but keep your eyes open."

Matt and Danny walked silently through the crowded foyer and entered the elevator.

"She's scared," Danny said.

"I know."

"And I don't think it was because of what we said."

"I don't either."

"That was strange," Danny added, his body shaking from a sudden chill. "I remember her being cocky, bossy, and kind of arrogant—like the rest of us, only worse because she had to compensate for being a woman. I never saw her afraid of anything."

"I never have, either. She's ice."

"The guy must be hitting on her pretty hard. Did you catch those looks? Why doesn't she just quit and lose the creep?"

"Because she feels she can do more for her country, for the

world, if she stays. She's got that Jewish thing about suffering."

"Maybe, but it's eating at her. And she still loves you."

"How can you tell?"

"Her eyes. It's written all over her. And he lusts after her. Wants her bad. That's the dangerous part."

"Speaking of eyes, did you catch his?" Matt asked.

"Yeah, you noticed that, too? Looks like he's on intimate terms with a bottle. He's one frightening little dude. How does he hide that from the television cameras?"

"He's not angry when he's giving speeches. He was angry about something up there tonight."

"Yeah, you! He probably thinks you're the reason he's not scoring with the golden girl. I tell you, he'd take you out in a second. Are you going to do that tape for him?"

"Are you kidding? I'll do one for the other side first."

"So what are we going to do?"

"I don't know. Wait. Sarah's not ready yet. But I think she might be getting there. Let her boil in that tension a little longer. She might welcome us next time."

"Next time? Next time we'll be shot on sight!"

In the limo downstairs, Jonathan Absalom was waiting impatiently for his Chief of Staff, growing angrier by the minute. When she arrived, he lit into her.

"What were you doing with him?"

"He just came by unannounced."

"Don't lie to me! How did he get past security?"

"I don't know. They were already in my hotel room when I walked in."

"I don't believe that. You're lying!"

"He's a soldier. A good one. Plus he has the proper credentials. He probably just waved his military identifications. The guys probably recognized him. He's well-known in Israel. His face was everywhere for a while. The people see him as a hero."

"What about you?"

"That was the past. And it's none of your business."

"Everything about you is my business."

"Look, I told you the truth about him. He contacted me before, and I told him not to come. OK?"

"Do you still love him?"

"I haven't been able to love him for a long time. I don't want to talk about this anymore."

Absalom turned away in frustration. He stood on the verge of conquering the whole world, but he couldn't get through to this one woman, a woman he wanted more than anything else. His mood softened. He took her hand.

"I'm sorry. I'll tighten security. He won't be able to get to you again."

"I don't want him hurt."

"He won't be. He just won't be able to cause you any more anguish. I promise."

Sarah turned and looked out the window. She had achieved all her dreams, and then some. She was the second most powerful person in the world, by far the most powerful woman in history. And yet, she was miserable.

She missed Matt.

A month later, on November 3, Jonathan Absalom received 38 percent of the vote in a close, three-way election—enough to earn him the right to move into the White House and complete his goal of a united world under his leadership. He returned to Israel to wait out the lame duck period, then was sworn in as President before a tentative nation the following January.

A week after taking office, Absalom announced some sweeping changes designed to further unite his empire. The changes directly mirrored both his innovative leadership and the influence of the alcohol that was slowly taking control of his brain.

He outlined it all in a speech given from his world stage in Washington.

"We stand at the precipice of a new Earth, a united planet where ethnic, racial, cultural, and nationalistic boundaries will soon no longer exist. You chose me, country by country, to unite a fiercely divided world tearing apart at the seams. This is my mandate. In order to accomplish it, there will be some things that might initially seem hard to swallow, but only if you view them with your old, prideful, nationalistic minds. Open up. Expand. I ask each individual, black, white, and brown, to view themselves as a citizen of the Earth, and nothing more.

"From this day forward, there will no longer will be borders blocking people from enjoying any part of this beautiful planet. You are free to come and go as you please, anywhere and everywhere. No Customs. No immigration departments. No duties or tariffs. Just a free, United World.

"From this day forward, there will be one language spoken on the United Planet. This language will be English, for the simple reason that it is already the international language of business and is the second language of choice in virtually every country. I will immediately institute a five-year educational program to teach those who don't speak English the new Earth language. A world that speaks as one will be united as one.

"The military forces of the world will be melded into one unit under a central command, thus ending all possibility that war will rear its ugly head on this planet again. An army cannot fight itself. Instead, this United Army will serve as a powerful police force that will be used to eliminate the ravages of crime that infest this planet. Criminals, be warned—the decent citizens of the world are taking back our streets. You no longer have a place in this society, and punishment will be quick and harsh.

"Similarly, any country, race, or culture who, in their own greed and selfishness, chooses to reject their induction into the World Family will be dealt with as criminals. For this to work, we've all got to be in it together.

"Now, this next change is going to be one of the most unifying measures of all. For the good of the United Earth, we will all throw off the chains and shackles of the most divisive and hate-inducing aspect of life on earth today. This planet will no longer tolerate brutality, murder, or prejudice in the name of religion. From this day forward, we wipe the slate clean. All diverse religions will be combined into one faith—a religion of all peoples, far more enriching to the soul. The United Earth will worship God in the United Faith. A new book will be written that incorporates the best of all the world's religions and simplifies it into a highly satisfying worship experience. Muslim, Islam, Buddhist, Hindu—even my own childhood religion of Judaism—will all become one.

"You see, I too am going to relinquish my religious heritage, but I will give it up gladly for the good of the United Earth. We can no longer base our divided lives upon false prophets or self-proclaimed Messiahs. We must put our divisive beliefs aside and simply worship the God who created us all.

"Our new United Faith will be identified by a special symbol. All residents of the United Earth will receive a computer identification microchip implanted in their wrist. This 'Chip of Life' will number and identify each individual as a member in good standing of the United Earth and the United Faith. The Chip of Life will enable the recipient to hold a guaranteed job, purchase goods, travel, and transact business. Before receiving it, world citizens will swear an allegiance to the United Earth and relinquish their current religious affiliation. The 'Chip of Life' will be our passport to peace and prosperity, to unity and mutual acceptance.

"Our new world is offering to everyone a wonderful gift in the 'Chip of Life,'" Absalom said with a suave smile. "There's a great new world on the horizon. A world of Peace on Earth, and Goodwill Toward a United Humanity."

Matt and Danny sat stunned in their cockpit, listening to the thunderous applause that followed Absalom's address. They were midway through another trans-Atlantic flight, and Matt had piped the President's speech to the passengers as ordered.

"So much for our lives as Christians," Matt muttered.

"What do you mean?" Danny asked. "It sounds like the answer to all the world's problems."

Matt looked at his friend with a shocked expression. "Don't you understand what this means? If we don't renounce our

Christian faith and embrace this new religion, we won't be able to work, buy food, or travel. This 'Chip of Life,' as Absalom calls it, means death to anyone who won't accept it."

Danny shrugged. "I don't see that it's such a big deal—"

"You're not thinking of taking that chip, are you?" Matt interrupted. "That's what they do to dogs and cattle."

"Do we have a choice?"

"Sure."

"What? What choice? You just said, no chip, no job, no food, no life."

"Are you ready to denounce Christianity?"

"He's not really asking us to denounce it. We can still believe in God…"

"What God?"

"The same God. The Father. He's just asking us to forget the Son, sort of as a compromise. You can't wipe out Buddha and Mohammed and those guys without taking out Jesus. It's just politics."

"God the Father said the way to him is through his Son. That is the major principle of what we believe."

"No, the Son said the way to the Father was through him. That was Jesus talking. Maybe he was inflating his own value."

"That's a terrible thing to say."

"Maybe none of this will happen. Doesn't he have to pass it through Congress first?"

"He'll steamroll it through. A guy like Absalom doesn't have much use for Congress. Either he'll twist enough arms, or he'll declare a state of emergency and implement it under some forgotten clause in the War Powers Act like he did in France and England. He's a genius at finding those kind of loopholes. He could also threaten to shut off our oil supply, like he did in Germany. Just grind the whole country to a halt. That'll bring us to our knees real fast.

"He'll have his way, you watch," Matt continued. "What he just outlined is all going to happen. We've got to be ready for it. You're going to have to get off the fence and decide where you stand."

"I know where I stand," Danny insisted. "I just don't know if I have the strength to fight the whole world. This guy means business. We saw him up close, remember? You're right. He's not going to back off."

"The enemies of God never do. This is nothing new. Think about it. People have made sacrifices for their religion since the beginning of time. How many times before have governments tried to stamp out Christianity? Russia? China? Cuba? It never works. Never. Persecution only makes faith stronger. This is just another cycle."

"But this is our cycle. We'll be in there with the lions this time."

"So be it. At least we'll be dying for something, for a greater purpose. Do you really want to follow this maniac?"

"No."

"I'm not taking the chip, Danny. Whatever the consequences, I'm not going to do it. Because if we do, the real consequences will be a million times greater.

"How do you figure that?"

"We'll be forced to denounce our beliefs. I won't do that."

"Maybe it won't be that bad," Danny said. "Let's try to think positively. It's just a computer chip. This isn't the end of the world."

"No? I'm not taking the stupid chip. That means it's the end of my world."

FIFTEEN

As Matt predicted, United Earth President Jonathan Absalom easily got around the United States Congress. Citing the continuing crisis in Russia and the need for a massive, unified relief effort, he pushed a measure through the newly empowered United Nations—a body he controlled—that gave him the right to declare a "world emergency," for humanitarian reasons. The legislation, which he immediately enacted, enabled him to overrule individual congresses or parliaments whenever an issue involved multiple countries and benefitted the world as a whole.

After creating such a gaping loophole, he was able to institute his sweeping changes with a speed and ease that defied convention. His platform was couched in glowing, euphemistic language, sweetened by his personal charm, backed by his transcontinental political empire, and enforced under the thumb of the combined world military. The scattered pockets of rebellion that sprang up among religious zealots in the Muslim and Hindu countries were quickly and ruthlessly crushed giving Absalom an undercurrent of intolerance to go with his benevolent, fatherly image.

Surprisingly, there was little protest from Christians. The government quickly discovered that there wasn't the same bedrock foundation of belief among post-war churchgoers as there had been before. Thus, the switch from Jesus, Mary, and the saints and prophets of the New Testament to a single, homogenized god went smoother than expected. Cash-carrying government officials, promising large increases in tithing membership, were able to convince many pastors to organize mass inductions into the new United Church. These preachers offered transportation, counseling, and guidance to help persuade their congregations to denounce their faith in return for the Chip of Life.

Other more cooperative priests and pastors learned the injection technique and performed the "Gift of the Chip of Life" ceremony right in their churches. Basing the procedure on the popular rite of the Last Supper, the priests and pastors wielded injector guns, invited their flocks to come forward, and plugged in the chips in the same manner as they once doled out wine and wafers. In such a "holy" setting, congregations had little trouble denouncing Jesus—even as statues and paintings of the now-rejected Messiah peered down upon them from podiums, walls, and stained glass windows.

Despite the massive changes, the United Earth began to function smoothly. The success that followed Absalom's bold measures made the people respect him even more. His popularity, based strongly upon his personal appeal, continued to grow. Anyone who dared to challenge him, even in private conversation on the local street corner, risked not only harsh punishment from the joint military-police force, but the scorn of their own friends as well.

But not everyone was a believer.

Matt Slade managed to duck getting the chip for nearly three months. Citing the pressures of time and his busy international flight schedule, he and Danny put it off as long as possible. But the three-month "Welcome Home Period" was quickly coming to an end, and excuses were no longer tolerated. As the pressure mounted, Danny began to crack.

"I'm going in," the co-pilot announced during a layover in St. Louis. "They have an injection office, a Life Center, right across the street. The handwriting is on the wall. I've already been prevented from eating in restaurants and buying a soda at the local 7-Eleven. They have monitoring devices everywhere—they've sprung up like weeds. We can't escape them."

"We can, and we will," Matt argued in the plush hotel room.

"We've already made it this far. Don't throw in the towel now."

"We haven't made it anywhere. Next week, we become criminals. Blankenship at headquarters has been on me for weeks about getting the lousy chip. He held back my last paycheck. They've threatened to fire me three times already."

"I've been through it all, too. It's meaningless."

"It's going to be too hard. There's too much suffering confronting us. This was all your idea. You and Mr. Welby forced me to become a Christian. You got me into this mess. I just did it to appease you two."

"You don't mean that."

"I do. I thought I was serious at the time, but I've realized that I just did it for you, because of our friendship. Now the price is too high."

"I won't let you do it."

"Hey, you have no choice. It's my life," Danny said, growing increasingly agitated and bitter. "Besides, you just became a Christian for a woman. You're just afraid Jill will come back and realize you were conning her all along."

"That's not true!"

"Come on. I didn't get anything from Jill out of it, so it means nothing to me!"

Matt's face flushed with rage. He took a step forward and clenched his fist.

"Now you're going to beat me up? If you're so worried about my soul, how can you attack my body? What a hypocrite! You want to hurt me now? Then just leave me alone. Let me get the chip like everybody else. If your insane ramblings are correct, that will hurt me worse than anything you could do with your fists."

"What's happening to you, Danny?"

"Me? What's happening to you? I'm sick of your demented ramblings about evil empires, the resistance, searching for God, and all that other baloney. You're wrong. None of it is true. I read a story that explained exactly what happened to the missing. Some aliens took Jill and the others. They were scared off when they saw the advanced weapons we had during the war. In order to keep the aliens away, the world had to unite. That's what happened. Absalom knows it. He's not evil. He's our savior. Look what's happened since he's taken over. The world is calm. There's peace, and everyone's happy. We're united. Nobody has turned up missing. And even this new religion is working. Everyone believes now. Before, half the people believed nothing. This guy Absalom is a genius!"

"That's crazy. You don't believe that."

"Don't tell me what I believe. It's no less crazy than what you believe."

"You're just scared. Feeling pressured."

"You bet I'm scared! For good reason! In a few days we become hunted criminals. We'll be rounded up and executed. Don't you understand that?"

"I've faced execution before. I'm still here."

"Well, you won't be after next week. But I plan to be."

"Jesus will protect us." The words came out stilted, as if by rote, but Matt held his ground.

"Jesus? He couldn't even protect himself from being fired by Absalom! How is he going to protect us? I don't care what you say; I'm going. I'm getting the chip before it's too late."

"Don't do this, Danny."

"Don't do what? This life is all we have. There is no paradise. Heaven is nothing but a myth parents tell their children about to keep them from tearing up the house. Just like the North Pole Elves and angels, God and Santa Claus. They're all the same Fairy tales. If it makes you feel good to believe, then believe. But don't get yourself killed over it. That's stupid!"

"You're not thinking straight. You're afraid. Wait a couple of days."

"You're not listening to me. It didn't take. I didn't mean it when I gave my life to Jesus. I'm denouncing it right now. I have been for the last ten minutes. It's already too late. Even by your addled thinking, I'm already doomed. So what does it matter if I get the chip or not?"

"You're right," Matt agreed dejectedly. "If that's the way you feel, I can't help you."

"You're not well, Matt," Danny said with a resigned sigh. "You lost two women you loved, one right after the other, within the span of a couple weeks. Bam, bam, like two blows to the head. It was too fast. You'll recover eventually. You'll find another woman, one who is better than either of them. I just wish to God you could see that. Come with me. Let's just get the chip and get this nightmare over with."

"So the aliens won't eat us?"

"So our own government won't eat us."

"I can't go, Danny. I won't. You shouldn't either."

Danny came over and put an arm around Matt's shoulders. His eyes filled with tears.

"We've been through a lot together, buddy," Danny said. "You've been through even more. You still have time."

"So do you."

Danny smiled, gave a mock salute, and disappeared out the door. He didn't return for nearly three hours. Matt found him sitting in his hotel room, staring blankly out the window. His face was ashen and his movements were robotic.

"Was it that bad?"

Danny didn't respond. He appeared dazed.

"Danny?"

"I remember there was this big thunderstorm," he said softly, still peering out the window. "I was a kid, a little boy, three or four. I ran to my parents' bed, terrified. Dad said there was nothing to be afraid of. 'It's only God bowling with the angels,' he said. After that, I was never afraid of thunderstorms."

Danny sat in silence for another five minutes before speaking.

"After going through all the paperwork, I got in line at the Life Center. It's like getting a driver's license, only worse. They do it *en masse,* but each chip contains specific information about the owner, so you have to make sure you get your own chip. It was kind of busy because people procrastinate, you know, and we're getting near the end. This young lady was in front of me in line. She was cute, with a nice figure, so I started to talk to her. She was a nurse at a local hospital, and she wasn't too happy about it—stress and all. The closer I got to the Injection Technician, the more nervous I became. My senses started to blur. Sounds grew louder, but harder to distinguish. The nurse was talking, but I couldn't understand her anymore. My knees started feeling weak. I was dizzy.

"I don't know what happened to me. I didn't faint or fall, but I lost time somewhere. The next thing I knew, the nurse was showing me where they made the implant on her right wrist. They punch it in there between these two thin bones that stick out a little on your wrist," Danny said, showing Matt his left wrist and pointing with his right index finger. "Just wedge it in place there." The technicians use this nail gun-looking thing, which they load with your chip right before they fire. The gun has a head like one of those electric razors, with three swirls, two on top and one underneath. They lay your arm on a table, place the swirls on your wrist to brace the gun, then fire in the chip from the center of the swirls. It's driven in with this needle head, which retracts and is pulled back into the gun."

Danny shook his head, then continued. "When she was done, the nurse in front of me held up her wrist to show me the little red spot where the chip went in. 'It didn't hurt as bad as I thought,' she said. Only I didn't see the red spot. Instead, I saw the temporary indentations made by the brace. They don't last long, a minute or two, then quickly fade. The swirl pattern left by the brace looked like three intertwined fists.

"Well, that did it. I was in a state of near-panic to begin with, and those symbols of Absalom's campaign threw me over the edge. I felt like they were swastikas and this was Nazi Germany. I just ran out of there to get some air. I walked around and around the block, trying to compose myself and go back inside, but every time I got near the door, I just froze."

"So you didn't get the chip?"

Danny shook his head.

"What are you going to do?"

"I don't know. Try again. Die. One of those."

"You won't die. We're going to be OK. I know it. I don't

know how or why, but we're going to survive this."

"I don't think so," Danny said, staring out the window again. "I barely survived today."

Matt had been trying to get through to Sarah since the day of the President's speech. He left coded messages for her to call "Pocahontas" at various locations. Either she was ignoring him, or by the time she received the message, he was flying somewhere else.

She finally returned his call late one night.

"You can't keep calling me like this," she said. "You're making things bad for me."

"Have you gotten the chip?"

"No. I've been too busy. But I'll get it before the deadline."

"Don't! If you do, you're sentencing your soul... "

"I don't want to hear that. Not on this phone."

"Danny tried, and he couldn't go through with it. He said the impression the machine leaves looks like three fists."

"So?"

"Don't you understand? That was Absalom's campaign symbol."

"I know. I designed it. So what?"

"It scared Danny to death. He said they reminded him of swastikas."

"That's nonsense. It symbolized a united world. We're bringing peace, not prejudice. I've got to go, Matthew. Please, just do as they say."

"I'm not going to get it. I can't. It's spiritual suicide!"

"Do as they say, Matthew. Don't risk your life again over something so foolish."

The following evening, Sarah came home, kicked off her shoes, and collapsed onto the soft sofa of her Washington townhouse. It was snowing outside, and the ten-mile trip from the White House had been slower than usual. Running the world was not as much fun as she imagined. The workload was tremendous, the travel exhausting, and the President had started pressuring her again for a physical relationship.

She was so tired she didn't notice the intruder until he was a few feet away. Fear instantly cleared her head. Dressed in white and wearing a motorcycle helmet, he motioned for her to sit in one of her dining room chairs. After she obeyed, he removed his helmet.

"Matthew!" she said with enormous relief.

"I was all set to wear black, but this snowstorm threw me for a loop. You know how hard it is to find white pants on short notice?"

Before she had a chance to respond, he came closer and gave her a passionate kiss. She went along initially, letting all the loneliness of being away from the man she loved pulse through her body into her lips. Halfway through the kiss, however, she returned to her senses and pulled away.

"What are you doing here? Why this charade?"

"You haven't kissed me that way in a long time, Sarah," Matt said, touched by her response.

"Forget that. Answer my questions!"

"I need to talk to you. I wanted your undivided attention." He grabbed her right hand, turned it over and searched her wrist for the telltale red dot. It wasn't there.

"Thank God," he whispered.

"Matthew, you've gone too far this time. You can't break into a person's home—especially mine. It's a capital offense in twenty different countries!"

"None of that matters anymore. I'm not taking the chip. How many times can they kill me?"

"Once is enough. Why did you have to sneak in here?"

"I didn't think you'd let me in if I knocked."

"You're right!"

"I was going to kidnap you. But I decided that I couldn't risk the lives of the others. So I've got to do it here."

"What others? Do what?"

"If you just listen to me for a few minutes, I'll never bother you again. No more crazy stunts, nothing. We'll end it right here. OK?"

"You promise?"

"I promise."

Sarah looked directly into his eyes. "The only reason I want you to go away is for your own safety. You know that, don't you Matt? It's more dangerous for you now than it was in Israel. I'm doing this because I care about you," she said softly.

"I know. And I have to do this because I love you."

Matt retrieved a small New Testament from his back pocket.

"In our recent and past conversations, you've revealed a disquieting gap in your religious education."

He flipped through the pages and began reading from the account of the death and resurrection of Christ from the Book of Mark. He then skipped over to John 3, verses 3 and 16. He followed by explaining how he surrendered his life to Christ under the guidance of James Welby, how he had matured since then, and how much it had meant to him to grow in his faith.

When he finished, he closed the book and looked at her.

"That wasn't so painful, was it?"

"I can see this is very important to you," Sarah said, "and I respect that. But do you really think I wasn't aware of what you read? That's our Bible, our history you're reading from. My people studied it and rejected it a thousand years ago. What makes you think I'll accept it now?"

"Because you have eyes. And ears. And half a brain when you clear away all the egotistical fog this power trip has filled you with. You know what's going on with Absalom. You're part of it."

"What is going on, Matt? I don't understand you."

"I love you, Sarah. I always have, and probably always will. I can't change how I feel. But I understand something now. For the first time, I know why you left me five years ago. You had a cause that was more powerful than our love. You asked me to understand and accept it, but I was too immature and foolish, and I had nothing like that in my life to relate to. I made you choose me or Israel. It's a decision I've always regretted."

Sarah's eyes misted as Matt continued. She had never cried before, and wouldn't this time either. But she had a difficult time holding her emotions in check.

"Now we've come full circle," he said quietly. "Your 'Cause' has been fulfilled in ways you never even dreamed. Only it's grown into a monster, mutated and spread like cancer. You're not doing this for Israel anymore. You're not saving people and making the world better for humankind; you're registering us like cattle, telling us what God to worship, killing our spirit, and depriving us of basic freedoms. If you weren't so close to it, you'd see it the way I do.

"You see where I am now?" Matt continued. "I'm where you were five years ago. I have a Cause, and it's as simple and stripped to the bone as yours once was. I'm not taking that chip because I can't turn my back on God, on Jesus."

"Even if you're wrong?"

"I'm not wrong."

"And what is your Cause?"

"Initially, just to survive. That will be tough enough. Just to eat and drink and make it through a day in this brave new slave world. After that, to establish an underground to help others like me survive. I know it's hard for you to believe, but there are many, many others, all over the world. People are reading the Bible and waking up. People like me and Danny who had this stuff pounded into our heads for years and rejected it. Danny can quote Scripture, chapter and verse, and yet at this very moment, he continues to wrestle with his own conscience. There are thousands, maybe even millions like him around the world. We're confused and unsure, but we have one thing in common. We're all remembering. And we're remembering something so vivid that we are physically and emotionally unable to denounce a belief many of us don't even swear to yet. That's bizarre, but it's happening. The consequences are extreme. Our lives are on the line. Yet people all over are refusing to submit.

"These are people who had relatives who were Christians and may have had only one or two conversations with them. Some people just recall a pitch from someone who knocked on their door, or they heard a street preacher arguing with teenagers on a corner. Some recall flipping through a cable channel late at night and hearing one of those television evangelists warning about the end times and tearfully begging people to be saved. Others, in foreign countries, listened to a missionary or read a tract handed to them by a friendly American. There are hundreds of other ways, but the message got through. Even among those who rejected it, it got through.

"So that's my world now. It's not pretty and it's not going to be easy. I may not survive a week, but I'm going to try. And as crazy as this sounds, I want you to come with me. I need you."

Sarah reached out her hand and touched his face.

"You've grown up so much, Matthew. I've never seen you like this. You've finally matured and shed that wild, destructive streak of yours. I probably love you more now than I ever have. But what you ask, that's a tough one. You want me to go from the top of the mountain to the very bottom. That's too steep a drop."

"Not to save your soul."

"Can't I help you more by staying in the position I have?"

"I don't think so. You're too close to the fire. You can help us by joining us."

"Can you stay here with me tonight? We'll talk. Let me think."

"I don't think so," Matt said, "There's so much I've got to do before the door slams shut. We need supplies to set up safe houses and establish networks. There's so much work to do."

"You still have time. Stay with me."

"I'll stay for a while. If it gets you to join me, I'll stay for a few hours. Until the storm clears."

A knock at the door interrupted them.

"Go hide in the laundry room," Sarah whispered, her eyes filled with fear. "It's probably someone from the government."

Sarah ran to the window as Matt ducked into the small utility room. She looked out through the snow and saw the President's blue limousine out front, surrounded by Secret Service cars. She ran back to the kitchen.

"It's Absalom!" she whispered to Matt. "Half his security force is outside. Don't come out for anything, no matter what happens. Don't even breath."

She went back to the door and opened it.

"What took you so long?" the United Earth President said as he staggered through the doorway. He had been drinking and was still carrying a bottle of champagne in his hand. "I had a little celebration after the Joint Bozos of Staff meeting and looked around and couldn't find you."

"I was tired and wanted to get home before the roads clogged."

"Smart thinking," he slurred. "You're always so smart. That's why I love you."

He leaned forward to kiss her, but she backed away. He stopped and held his hands apart. His eyes burned as never before.

"I've conquered every country in the world. I've subdued every religion on the planet, but still you reject me. Do you know how that makes me feel? Do you realize how angry that makes me? I have everything. I'm worshiped as a god by millions, and you … you make me feel like nothing! I won't have it any more."

"We've been over this before, Jonathan. You're drunk. Go home to your wife."

"Not this time," he said, taking off his jacket and loosening his tie.

"What do you think you're doing?"

"What I should have done months ago," he said, unbuttoning his shirt. "I'm having you, right here, right now, tonight, whether you like it or not. If I can take a hundred nations by force, I can take one woman!"

"You'd violate me by force? And you say you love me?" Sarah backed away.

"You shouldn't have rejected me."

"If you try to do this, you undo everything you've accomplished. This will be the beginning of the end for you."

Absalom lurched forward, grabbing hold of Sarah and trying

to force himself upon her. She put her arms to her chest and whipped them outward, breaking his hold. She then turned and flipped him to the floor. He landed with a thud.

"Not bad," he said with a fiendish laugh. "I forgot that you're a little war hero. But you're going to have to do better than that."

He rose unsteadily to his feet and grabbed for her. She ducked under his arms and reared up like a cat, slashing her fingernails across his face. He recoiled in pain, then charged forward, his hands reaching for her throat. Sarah sidestepped him, swung her right foot, and cut his legs out from under him, dropping him backward to the floor. As he fell, his head crashed against an end table, knocking him dizzy and causing blood to gush from a gash. He writhed in pain, then shot up like a demon.

"I won't have this!" he screamed. He raced toward her again. She used his momentum to throw him into the wall. He smashed against it, then dropped hard to the floor. Shaking his head, he slowly lifted himself up, and staggered to the door, beaten and battered.

When he was gone, Matt raced to Sarah's side.

"Are you OK?"

"I'm fine," she said, trembling and falling into his arms. The implications of what she had done began to sink in.

"It sounded like you gave him a good thrashing."

"He'll be hurting tomorrow."

"I wanted to come out, but I thought you could handle him. I'm sorry, but I just remembered what happened before, during the war and... "

"You don't have to apologize," she said, calming down. "You did exactly what I asked. You let me fight my own battle. You never did that before. You really have changed."

Another knock sounded at the door, a hard, angry rap.

"He probably wants to apologize. Go back inside," Sarah said. Matt disappeared into the next room.

When she opened the door, she was shocked to see the

President, battered and bloody but crazed with determination, standing with three of his security agents. He pushed her back and the four of them entered the room.

"Take her!" Absalom screamed.

"Matt!" she cried.

Matt came roaring into den. Fueled by fury, he quickly disabled the agent holding Sarah with a kick to his kidney. He put a choke hold on the second agent, slammed his head into the wall, and knocked him cold. Sarah snatched a pistol from the belt of the third agent and cracked him over the head, rendering him unconscious.

President Absalom stood stunned as the violent drama unfolded in blinding speed.

"Where the hell did *he* come from?" he slurred. Realizing the trouble he was in, the President rushed for the door. Matt caught him. Before Sarah could stop him, Matt unleashed a crushing blow to Absalom's jaw, shattering it and knocking him out.

"Why did you do that?" Sarah screamed.

"He deserved it."

"He's the President!"

"He's a common rapist. A criminal. How can you defend him?"

"You should have let him to leave. The embarrassment alone would have stopped him."

"He wasn't going to leave. He was just going outside to get more of his men. Then we would have had to fight off ten of them instead of four."

Sarah sank to the couch. "What are we going to do?"

Matt stood over the President's prone body. "We can end this nightmare right here." He pulled a weapon from the holster of one of the unconscious security agents.

"No!" Sarah shouted, jumping up. "You can't kill the President of the world. Then you'll be nothing more than an assassin."

"I'll never have an opportunity like this again. We can change history."

"Is this your Cause, Matt? To be a killer? That isn't the Christian way. You're supposed to turn the other cheek, not murder a political leader!"

Matt pointed the gun at the President's head.

"Don't do it, Matt. That's not the way it happens in that book you read me. Show me where it says, 'And then Matt Slade shoots the Beast in the head.' He's got to live out his destiny. You've got to let him."

Matt continued to point the gun at Absalom's head.

"I'm with you now," Sarah said in a soft, warm voice. "I have no choice. Not after tonight. So we'll survive on our wits and operate this underground, together. I'll even try to learn about your faith. But I won't be able to do any of this if you kill him. We'll never get out of this house alive. There are fifty men outside. Think, Matt. Think. We can be together now. Let's just get out of here."

Matt pulled the gun away, then dropped it to the floor.

"Get your things and let's go," he said. "I parked the motorcycle out back."

Sarah packed quickly, then she and Matt slipped out the back door and down the stairs to Matt's Honda. Although there were a half-dozen Secret Service agents covering the back exit, they weren't yet aware of what had happened inside. They recognized Sarah and allowed her to travel with Matt through their midst.

As she wrapped her arms around him, Sarah knew she was riding into a terribly uncertain future. Even so, she felt strangely happy. Nothing, not her Cause or his, would ever separate them again.

SIXTEEN

The snow from the unseasonable March storm made the roads so slick and treacherous that Matt and Sarah had to make their getaway from the most powerful force ever to rule the Earth at a snail-like twenty miles per hour. It didn't matter. The weather was so blinding that they might have been able to ride through the heart of Absalom's entire army without being noticed.

The dazzling holiday scenery added the final touch of irony to Sarah's escape. Absalom had ordered government offices to display colored lights in a show of unity for his master plan and requested that the public do the same. It was a brilliant public relations stroke on multiple levels. Using Christmas lights to celebrate political events would dilute their effect as a reminder of the birth of a no-longer-tolerated deity. Come December, Absalom didn't want three hundred million people to climb into their attics, look longingly at the lights, and realize, many for the first time, what they actually represented.

In addition, by dressing his harsh, totalitarian decrees in joyful Christmas colors, he could better deceive the gullible public into thinking that they were sipping eggnog instead of swallowing bitter poison.

Thus Matt and Sarah made their leisurely escape through a late season winter wonderland that provided a strikingly beautiful cover.

Matt guessed that Absalom would think they had holed up somewhere in the city until the weather cleared. The instant the blizzard passed, he would order the military to throw a net of roadblocks around the capital. So, instead of hiding in the apartment of a fellow pilot based in Washington, as was his initial plan, Matt decided to ride the storm out of Washington.

He told Sarah to hang on, and he headed the Honda south, away from the storm. A safe house was already established in Wilmington, North Carolina—part of a growing network of havens and hideouts that James Welby had been busy preparing in anticipation of Absalom's actions. Matt and his prized recruit could stay there until they decided what to do next.

The snow eased to a sprinkle in Virginia and melted away completely in North Carolina. They pulled into the safe house shortly after midnight. Matt advised Sarah to keep her helmet on until they were inside.

At the door, Sarah noticed that before Matt said a word, he crossed his wrists at his waist, and then raised his right fist in an arch to his head. The owner of the modest brick house, a man named Harold who operated an auto repair shop, warmed instantly upon seeing the strange signals. He welcomed them inside.

Half a dozen people were camped in the living room of the home. A dozen more were sleeping in the surrounding three bedrooms. Matt stood in the center of the room and introduced himself to those who remained awake. Then he motioned for Sarah to remove her helmet. An audible gasp filled the room.

"It's her!" a young woman screeched. She and others backed away from Sarah as if she were a rabid dog. Sarah was stunned by the reaction.

"See how a girl gets a reputation," Matt whispered.

"Listen up," he said to the group as more people, hearing the commotion, began to awaken and filter in from the bedrooms. "I know it may be difficult to believe right now, but Sarah Gold has joined us. Despite her former position with the government...," he said, taking her right hand and raising it before the crowd, "she remains clean. With her knowledge of the government, not only here but all over the world, her value to us is immeasurable. In a few days, possibly even by tomorrow morning, you and the rest of the world will know why she's joined us—why she had to join us, and why she can never go back. The first wave of stories will be lies, but the truth will come out. I ask that tonight you trust me as a fellow Christian, give us shelter, and celebrate this great victory for our Cause."

"Is she a Christian?" another woman asked.

"Not yet. She's Israeli. That makes it tough. But she will be."

"Can she speak for herself?" someone else asked. Sarah was about to answer when Matt interrupted.

"She has experienced a terrible trauma tonight. We both did, as you can see from our bruises. I'd prefer that she get some sleep before she gets the bare light and rubber hose treatment."

"I'm OK," Sarah said. The sound of her familiar voice frightened the crowd further. Many backed away again.

"I'm not sure that any of us are ready," Matt said.

"It's just… that *voice*," the first woman said. "We've heard it so many times before on television and radio. It was the voice of the, of the… "

"Enemy," Matt said, completing her sentence.

"That's right," the others chorused.

"Well, it's obviously not the voice of the enemy any longer. It's the voice of our friend. You'll get used to it," Matt gently explained.

"How do you feel about this?" someone asked Sarah directly.

"It's all happened so fast. I don't understand any of it. I don't understand half of what you're saying, the codes and symbols you're using. I'm confused, exhausted, and afraid. Matt will tell you I've never felt this way before, but I've never been in trouble like this before."

"What trouble?" someone asked.

"We'll discuss that tomorrow," Matt interrupted. "Please let us get some rest."

"OK, that's enough," Harold cut in. "You all know Matt Slade, what he's done for us so far, and what he will continue to do. If he trusts this woman, whom you've probably guessed means more to him than just another recruit, then that's good enough for me. We welcome them and extend the hand of friendship."

Harold crossed his wrists. The others followed suit. Matt crossed his and thanked them. Harold led Matt and Sarah to a small office in the back, handed them some blankets and pillows, and left them alone.

Sarah quietly made their beds, deep in thought. When they were both in bed for the night, she began her questions.

"Matt, who are these people?"

"Babies."

"Babies?"

"Baby Christians."

"Meaning?"

"Long before any of this began, Christians were displaying little fish symbols on their cars. You probably saw it a hundred times. Funny thing is, no one remembers what it was based on. Some say it comes from Jesus' invitation to his disciples to become 'fishers of men.' Others vaguely recall that the symbols were displayed in memory of Jesus feeding the 5,000 from a couple of fish and a few loaves of bread. I've heard another person say it comes from the skeleton of the sailcat, a tiny fish whose bones form a crucifix. Whatever it meant, it's now the symbol of our movement."

"That's what the crossed wrists mean?"

"That's it. Forming the sign of the Fish. We're babies, remember. We had to keep it simple." Matt laughed.

Sarah rolled over and touched his arm. He could feel her hand trembling.

"Matthew, what's going to happen to me?"

"You're going to join us and lead again."

"Oh, you've got it all worked out."

"To the T."

"But I mean... you know. He's not going to accept this. He's in love with me."

"Not anymore."

"How do you know?"

"You don't sexually brutalize the woman you love. He's sick. There's no love in the man."

"He won't stop. He'll hunt me down."

"So what? He's going to hunt all of us."

"But I might make it worse for these people."

"No one can make it worse. Get some sleep. We've got a big day ahead of us."

Sarah lay quietly for a while, unable to sleep.

"Matthew, can we win?"

"We're not here to win," he whispered, half asleep. "We're here to survive. To keep the movement alive. That's our victory."

The next morning, when Matt and Sarah came out of the office, they were greeted with hearty applause. The reaction startled them.

"It's all over the news," a young man said. "Your attempt to kill the President and overthrow the government. They say it's because Sarah was power hungry, but we know better."

"That's not true," Matt said. "That's not what happened. We're not assassins."

"But... "

"I told you the first story would be lies. That's the spin they put on it."

Matt and Sarah walked over and looked at the television. Their photographs were displayed on the screen as the newsman told the audience about the alleged coup attempt. The government was requesting that anyone who saw either Matt or Sarah should immediately call the police.

Matt shut off the television and turned to the group, now numbering nearly thirty.

"I visited Sarah last night to convince her not to take the chip and try to get her to join us. While I was there, the President came in. He was drunk, and he tried to rape her. She fought him off, but he came back with three Secret Service agents. They all tried to attack her. We stopped them and escaped. That's what happened."

The group sat in stunned silence.

"The pig!" a woman finally said, breaking the tension. "He's worse than we thought!"

"Are you all right?" another asked as the women gathered around Sarah to comfort her. "It must have been awful."

"I'm OK, thanks to Matt."

"Praise God," others said. "Praise Jesus for saving Sarah."

Matt left Sarah inside with the women and wandered out to the back yard with some of the men, including the homeowner.

"Whatever story people believe, yours or Absalom's, you two have become our symbolic leaders," Harold said. "This is just what we need. Someone to rally around. Travel will be hard, but the underground will embrace you like royalty."

"I think we should get the true story out," Matt said. "The media remains free for now. We can use the attention to tell the world about the underground. Not so the government can stop us, but to let the world know that we exist, that not everyone is taking the chip."

Matt returned inside and motioned for Sarah. They spoke privately.

"Do you know any reporters? Someone who can recognize your voice and know it's you?"

"Many."

"What about the New York *Times*?"

"There's a man there, Peter Jackson, who's interviewed me four or five times."

"Call him," Matt said, ushering her into a bedroom where there was a phone.

"And say what?"

"Tell the truth. Tell him what happened. Then I'll tell him that we've got you and will protect you."

"Why?"

"To let the world know we exist. And to let the world know what Absalom is really like."

"They may not print it. They may not be able to."

"The government doesn't control the media."

"No. They've supported Absalom so far, so there wasn't a need. But... "

"Go ahead. Make the call. It will probably be the last story written by the free press."

Sarah's interview appeared on the front page of the New York *Times* the next morning. The White House denied her accusations, but because it was an exclusive interview, the *Times* gave her side a lot of play. There were accompanying features on the backgrounds of both Matt and Sarah, and another story about the existence of a Christian underground and how it was now sheltering the former Chief of Staff.

The sensational story spread like wildfire across the world. As war heroes, Sarah and Matt made credible witnesses. Sarah had been a popular figure as Absalom's right hand. Because of her great beauty, the story of the attempted rape was plausible. An ill-conceived attempt by Absalom to counter it proved to be a disaster. He rushed in front of the cameras before the scratches, swelling, and bruises on his face had healed. He spoke in mumbled tones through a jaw wired shut. His muted grunts and swollen face acted to confirm the account Sarah had given of the skirmish in her home, right down to the three scratches on his left cheek. The public knew that assassins shoot a President. They don't engage in a cat fight and then let him go.

Absalom's sorry performance was especially shocking outside America. For the first time, the people of the world saw a man who wasn't in control of his emotions. He was alternately enraged, flustered, and insecure. He stuttered through his clenched jaw, contradicted himself, and stumbled over hard-to-understand words. Most of all, he looked guilty. Women across the United Earth were convinced that he had indeed tried to rape his beautiful Chief of Staff and had been clawed across the face in the process.

While the news of the attempted rape consumed the first wave of reports, the story of the Christian underground had the deeper effect. With a few days still to go before the computer chip identification system went into effect, those who had rejected it were thrilled to learn that not only were there thousands of others like them, but there was an organized movement to help them survive. Similarly, new Christians, who thought they stood naked and alone, were overjoyed to discover that they weren't.

Others, hundreds of thousands of others, who were haunted by an inner voice imploring them to turn to Jesus, were given the courage to do so. In the first week following Sarah's story, nearly a million people around the world either linked up with the existing safe houses or formed their own networks, complete with communication avenues and travel routes.

The Christian rebellion spread so fast and with such fervor that Jonathan Absalom and his United Earth Military could do nothing to stop it. The more reports there were of safe houses being discovered and Christians burned out and executed, the more people gave their lives to Christ.

As Matt predicted, Sarah's interview started a domino effect that signaled the end of the free press. Newspapers universally printed virulent reviews of Absalom's appalling post-rape performance. The story was followed by polls revealing that a majority of the public believed Sarah. The underdog appeal of the grassroots Christian movement fighting the Goliath world government reversed the anti-Christian bias of the liberal media. Follow-up stories on the Christian underground remained mostly sympathetic, painting the baby believers in heroic terms.

Then, two weeks after Sarah's interview, Absalom issued an edict to censor the media. This was met with howls of protest from newspapers and television stations that refused to comply. Eventually, the military took control.

The war against the free press further tarnished Absalom's image and was widely ineffective. Smaller newspapers, television stations, and radio outlets outside the major cities and media markets continued to print the news independently until they were discovered and shut down. Private computer networks and fax technology picked up the slack. The public itself became its own news force.

Absalom, increasingly frustrated by the strength of the rebellion, continued to perform badly in his attempts to counter it. As long as Matt and Sarah remained free, his rage and frustration were evident.

During a European Economic Summit meeting at the Capitol, Absalom embarrassed everyone by opening with a question about the status of the hunt for Sarah. Josh Silverman, his longtime aide, was forced to call a recess. Silverman maneuvered the leader into an adjacent conference room.

"Look, you've started every meeting the past month, regardless of the topic, with the same question. You've interrogated the Chinese, the Thais, the Koreans, people who don't know anything about this... "

"I want them to know," Absalom interrupted. "She may be hiding in their country!"

"They don't care. They have bigger concerns than your love life. The people are starting to think you're coming unglued over this. It's making everybody nervous. And it's sending out bad signals. Since you've been fixated on finding Sarah, there have been uprisings in five different countries. They've sensed a weakening at the top, and it's given them the courage to try and break away. This isn't what we need."

"Those were small, distant nations. We crushed them."

"We shouldn't be spending our time crushing little countries. You were entrusted with this power to unite the world and bring peace. You've got to get a grip on yourself or the major countries are going to start pulling away."

"I just need her back, Josh," Absalom said, squeezing the back of a chair in his hands. "I never realized how much I loved her until she was gone. It's hard for me to function without her. I go to bed thinking of her. I keep wanting to dial her number to ask her a question. I can still smell her perfume in the room. I've got to get her back!"

"We're trying, Jon," Josh sighed. "It may take a while. But we'll get her. In the meantime, we need you back on deck steering the ship. The whole world depends on you. It's critical that you pull yourself together."

"You're right, you're right," Absalom said. He adjusted his tie and brushed his hair, steeling his resolve in order to reconvene the meeting. "Let's go fix Europe's problems. We'll open the markets between Europe and China and drop all duties. That will stimulate growth in both areas. We've got to get these people thinking as one, not as separate nations."

"Now you're talking, boss."

Despite Silverman's steady hand, Absalom's renewed emphasis on running his empire was only temporary. He remained obsessed with finding Sarah. He placed a price on their heads that rose from a million dollars to more than a hundred million—all to no effect. The absurdly high bounty merely convinced everyone that Absalom was deranged. Many felt the only reason he wanted Sarah captured was so that he could try to rape her again.

As a result, the more he hunted the former Scorpion pilots, the more popular they became. The WANTED posters of Matt and Sarah that the United Earth government plastered on virtually every building around the world became collector's items that built their legend further.

Sarah emerged as a heroine among the Christians, yet she balked at becoming one. Matt left the issue alone, allowing her to adjust to the pressure she was under and the constant hardships they endured on the road. Instead of pushing her, he gave her time to soak in the kindness, unquenchable spirit, and courage of the people they encountered as they traveled the safe house circuit. By the beginning of their third month on the run, she was ready.

"I'm a fraud," she said to Matt as they huddled in the basement of a safe house in Iowa. "These people look up to us. They welcome us. They support me and believe me instead of the President. Yet I've been unwilling to join them in their most sacred decision."

"It takes time," Matt said. "Your upbringing, your belief system was so different."

"Why didn't you ever ask me why I refused to receive the chip?"

"I was just happy you didn't."

"They tried to get me to take it a few times, but I always came up with excuses. I didn't even know why myself. I would just feel real funny, flushed with fear, then make some excuse. Part of it was that stuff you and Danny told me. I didn't let you know, but that scared the life out of me. Another part was that something inside told me it was wrong. Not from a political sense, but from a spiritual sense. And this wasn't because of the stuff you read to me that night. It was just inside me."

"Many people have reported the same feelings, the same paralyzing fear, when they went in to get the chip. Just like Danny."

"A third reason was that I knew you'd never take it. And if I did, I'd be losing you forever. I know you think that I left you before for my Cause, and you probably think I abandoned you again when I made the deal to save your life, but each time, deep in my heart, I knew it was only temporary. I knew we would be together again. Even when I heard about Jill, I still felt we'd end up together. But when they came at me with that chip gun, I flashed back to every wonderful moment we ever had. And that gun, the one you say leaves the fist imprints, was going to shatter our bond forever. I couldn't allow that to happen."

"What would you have done, then?"

"I don't know. Stalled. Quit. Run. I had a lot of pull with Absalom, so maybe I could have gone without it."

"I'm flattered, but I like your other reason better. The innate sense that it was wrong. That was Jesus calling to you."

Sarah didn't answer. Matt thought she had fallen asleep and was about to doze off himself when he heard her voice, soft and tender like he'd never heard it before.

"I've seen him, Matt," she said. "I see Jesus in these people's faces when they greet us. I see him as they labor, not for themselves, but for the movement. I see him most of all in their lack of fear. A hundred million dollars to turn us in—can you imagine that? Someone could be as rich as a king, yet no one has betrayed us. Some of these people are starving, and no one has betrayed us. It's a miracle.

"There's no rational reason this... this crazy rebellion should be happening. Absalom's plan for a numbered, registered society should have worked. There was virtually no objection to it when it was announced. The people came willingly to the Life Centers. We had no idea how many were refusing. We didn't even have a concept of why."

"Because you can't kill an idea," Matt said.

"It's more than an idea. It's something these people have inside them. There was such a strong belief in Israel. That country has survived for decades on faith, just as the Christians are surviving now. But there was always something missing. We were waiting for our Messiah, but history was spinning ahead. Things were happening that were supposed to happen after the Messiah came. Now I see that these people—these kind, gentle people who are helping us—have already found him.

"I'm tired of waiting, Matthew. I'm tired of living a lie. Most of all, I'm tired of turning my back on a Savior that came from my own people. Isn't that crazy? We reject him, our own brother, while the rest of the world accepts."

"And now you want to accept, after virtually everyone else has rejected him? When accepting him could cost you your life?"

"Yes. It's time."

Sarah got to her knees on the faded blanket. Matt knelt down beside her and placed his arm around her shoulders. In a strong, steady voice, Sarah surrendered her life to God and accepted Christ as her Savior. Tears began to fall from her eyes as the power of the moment took hold.

Finally, she's crying, Matt thought, knowing that her rare display of emotion sealed the conviction in her heart.

Sarah awoke the next morning with a new spirit directing her ever-present fierce determination. She outlined plans for how the rebels could grow in strength and number without being detected, and how they could establish farms, food services, transportation, banking, communication, medicine, and even their own security force, all right under the government's nose. She knew Absalom paid attention to the heavily populated East and West coasts and ignored the Northwest. She knew which roads, highways, ports, and shipping routes the government monitored, and which they deemed insignificant.

The day after she truly became one of them, Sarah wrote the blueprint for the construction of the entire Christian underground.

By the second day, she had something entirely different on her mind.

"If we're going to be sneaking around together, we should be married. We've been setting a pretty poor example."

"Name the time."

"One hour. There's a former Methodist minister among the group here. He's going to renew his calling and will start by marrying us under the oak tree in the back yard."

"You've got a date."

An hour later, Matt, Sarah, and the minister, all dressed in jeans and down coats, stood under the giant oak and said their vows in front of two dozen beaming and teary-eyed Christian rebels.

"We should have done this years ago," Sarah chided after they kissed.

Matt was about to protest, then realized her joke.

Finally bonded, the once star-crossed lovers spent their honeymoon outlining Sarah's plan to a roomful of baby Christians gathered together in a farm house in Iowa.

"Are you happy, Matt?" she asked as they snuggled together in a sleeping bag in the barn later than evening.

"Very much so, Sarah."

"Really? You seem a little down. You don't have any regrets?"

"About you? Never."

"Then what is it? Spill your guts, Slade."

"Ever since we met I've wanted to spend my life with you. But it was never like this. Never in a barn in Idaho... "

"Iowa."

"Yeah, Iowa. Wherever we are. On a mattress of cold hay in Iowa on the run from the government, the Earth's Most Wanted, poster children numbers one and two."

"Who's one?"

"You."

"Is that why you're upset. Because I'm number one?"

"No, silly," he said, poking her in the ribs. "That's hardly an honor. I just wanted to be able to love and cherish you in a house full of little Matts and Sarahs and let the world go away."

"We'll have that," she said.

"You think so?"

"I know so. We're on the outside now. One day we'll be on the inside. That's how politics works."

"This is different."

"How so, fly-boy?"

"It's so... so personal. So big. No one has ever had to fight such a powerful enemy."

"The bigger they are, the harder they fall."

"Come on, be serious."

"I am. All through history, people with a cause have defeated bigger, stronger forces. They were victorious because of what was in their hearts. That's why we'll prevail."

"You think?"

"I think. Besides, what does it say in that Bible of yours? Maybe I should break into your house and read it to you."

"That was pretty crazy, wasn't it?"

"Uh-huh. But it worked. It worked so well that I remember the ending you've apparently forgotten."

"What ending?"

"The very end, where it says who wins."

Matt smiled as he caught on.

"So stop worrying and kiss me," Sarah ordered.

Matt kissed her, then pulled back

"But what if... "

"No more talking," she said, putting his finger to his lips. "We've waited a long, long time for this night. Just kiss me."

Matt and Sarah spent the rest of the year traveling from one safe house to another, wearing disguises, never staying longer than a few days, but always remaining long enough to plant the seeds of Sarah's master plan. They received counseling from the Christian leader over short-wave radio, but they didn't visit with him in person because Matt feared it would devastate the movement if they were all captured at once.

Instead, the newlyweds acted as decoys, drawing the bulk of the government's attention as they traveled through the underground—giving inspirational speeches to private gatherings, shaking hands, and offering updates on the activities of Christians in other areas. From this grassroots perspective, they watched as the movement slowly took hold. What began as isolated pockets of frightened believers huddled together in safe houses sprouted into an entire resistance network, linked together, at Sarah's direction, by modems, personal computers, and obscure satellite television channels.

The code to the government's wrist identification system was eventually broken by Christian computer hackers in California. Data was pumped in to allow people to pass the chip checkpoints by punching in a number and a password. These people told the operators their chip had become defective, or the implant had become infected, and they were waiting for a new one. Using this method judiciously, the rebels were able to get past checkpoints and purchase supplies.

As a backup, the names and phone numbers of sympathizers among those who had received the chip were detailed in constantly updated lists that covered virtually every city. The sympathizers, while risky to trust, were tapped to purchase weapons, ammunition, computer supplies, and other materials that were guarded under tighter security.

Midway through the second year, a secret headquarters was established on a remote ranch in Montana. A smaller, interconnected branch center was built 250 miles away to enable Matt and Sarah to come in from the cold while still keeping their distance. A war room was constructed in Welby's headquarters that consisted of a communications center with an internationally-linked computer and satellite system. At designated times from their separate locations, Welby, Matt, and Sarah made announcements, gave pep talks, and broadcast critical survival information to followers all over the world—giving the Christians a tremendous sense of unity.

In conjunction, an emergency rescue network was created to bring supplies to groups straining under government scrutiny.

A month later, just as Matt and Sarah were getting used to sleeping in the same bed for more than two nights in a row, a technological breakthrough threatened to splinter their own ranks. A counterfeit chip was developed by the movement's main computer branch in California. The potential use of these chips caused an immediate rift among various groups of Christians. Many believed that getting any chip, real or not, was a form of blasphemy. Others argued that it wasn't the technology that was the problem, it was the oath and denunciation of God before the implementation that constituted the blasphemy. The issue was eventually presented to Welby to decide. He, in turn, consulted Matt and Sarah.

Matt was anti-chip, pointing out that the symbol of the schools was the crossed wrists, and the way Christians introduced themselves to each other was by displaying a "clean" wrist, free of the small red dot that identified those implanted with the chip.

"If you display Absalom's brand, whether it's his or ours, it's still his mark. How do we justify that? And how will we be able to tell who is with us and who isn't?"

Sarah countered with the oath argument. She felt that a wrist with a "Christian Chip" remained clean, and that they could devise another secret code or symbol to identify supporters.

The argument became moot when an informer led authorities on a raid of seven safe houses in New York. All those with unmarked wrists were shot. Seventy-eight baby Christians died that night, pushing the argument in Sarah's favor.

After that, the movement expanded even more rapidly. The fake computer chips enabled the Christians to emerge from the underground and filter back into society.

Still, many remained uneasy.

"It was better when we were all together in our groups," Matt told Sarah at their permanent hideout late one evening.

"We had to evolve out of that," Sarah countered. "We were sitting ducks gathered together in the safe house. Look at how many died because of it. And it was getting worse. You have to remember that, as we grow, so do the forces against us. Before, when one person was discovered, the whole group was destroyed. This way everyone is scattered around. Our people have infiltrated the enemy camp. If a major offensive is launched, we'll be able to counter-attack from the inside. This move is critical to our survival. It's also the inevitable progression of our Cause if we are to become victorious."

"I can't argue with you," Matt said. "I just have a bad feeling about this."

SEVENTEEN

"This is like driving a Model T," Matt joked as he took the controls of a six-passenger, Lear jet someone had donated to the Cause.

"It's Air Force One-quarter," Sarah joked, strapping herself in.

"More like Air Force One-tenth. But it'll do. It beats walking. And we've done a lot of that lately."

"I thought you enjoyed those nightly walks around the ranch. You said it makes you feel free."

"It does. And I do."

"So stop griping!" she quipped.

Matt and Sarah were flying from Montana to Miami to huddle with leaders of the major South American groups. The Christians on the other side of the equator were having the same heated debates regarding the counterfeit chips that had previously divided the Americans. But their situation was more difficult to solve because the persecution in South America wasn't as aggressive, and the deadline for implementation of the chip identification system kept getting pushed back. The United Earth representatives had encountered major problems in forcing the rural population to comply. Those who knew nothing about computers were not eagerly rushing in to have a large, bulky gun shoot a foreign object into their bodies.

The lack of enforcement in rural South America, as Sarah predicted, was attributed to Absalom's policy of numbering and registering "civilized" people in developed nations first. She suspected that the President would eventually lose interest in trying to register and chip the masses in foreign ghettos or Third World nations. Absalom referred to them as "stone-age barbarians" who had "no impact" upon his rule.

Knowing this, Sarah had suggested that she and Matt hide out in Brazil, Africa, or Asia until things cooled down. Matt vetoed the idea, saying they would stick out in those countries and make easy targets for bounty hunters. In contrast, they could blend in better in America, move around easier, and most importantly, have a hand in building and shaping the rebellion.

The scheduled South American conference was especially appealing to Matt because it gave him a chance to go home. He hadn't been to Miami since the war. In fact, he had specifically avoided the hurricane-ravaged city because of the bad memories it harbored. Instead, he bunked with pilot friends around the country while planting the seeds of the rebellion.

Now, happily married and relatively secure after surviving a year on the run, Matt was confident that he could face the ghosts of his past.

"Is Mr. Welby OK?" Sarah asked.

"Yeah. I talked to some of the others. They said he's just getting up in years. He's worked so hard getting this movement going, he's wearing himself out. Plus, Absalom has put a bounty on his head, too. His son said he wants to turn over more of the responsibilities to his lieutenants, including us."

"Why did he select us for this meeting?"

"He was going to go himself before he got sick. It was a last minute thing. He knows we're from the area, so he probably thinks we'll know our way around better and be safer. I am looking forward to it. I think I'll try to find Danny if we have some free time."

"What happened to him?"

"I'm not sure." Matt frowned. "I lost track after you came aboard and we went on the run. I've seen his name occasionally on the list of supporters in Miami. He seems to bounce in and out of the movement, as if he's still not sure where he stands. Same old Danny."

"You think it's safe to contact him?"

"It should be. Danny's mixed up, but he's harmless. Mr. Welby advised me not to contact him until he makes up his mind. That's one of the reasons I haven't called or tried to track him."

"If Welby said that, maybe we should keep our distance."

"Maybe that would be the smartest thing to do, but I'm having problems with it," Matt said. "Danny needs guidance. If he can see how we've grown as Christians, how we've survived despite being enemies of the government, it might inspire him to make a real commitment. I also want him to see how it's changed you. If he sees that you're happier on the run than you were when you were a big shot government official, it will have a powerful effect upon him."

Sarah squeezed Matt's hand and smiled.

"I still think it's risky, but if you feel led to contact him, we can give it a try."

To get to Miami, Matt, Sarah, and the three security officers with them were flying a zig-zag pattern across the sky. The intricate, computer calculated route was designed to avoid the snoopy radar of major airport towers or military bases. An unregistered, uncharted private jet buzzing across the sky at night would be certain to attract attention.

"Uh oh, we've got company," Matt said, frustrated that their precise planning had hit a snag. He pushed the throttle to increase his speed, but the Lear jet was no match for the approaching shadow. "Looks like Air Force. Maybe an old F-18. What is it doing out here?"

"I'm sure we're about to find out," Sarah said, turning up the volume of the radio.

"This is U.S. Air Force Captain David Honeycut. Please identify yourself."

"Honeycut," Matt said to Sarah. "You ever heard of this guy?"

"No. Must be a kid."

"Are we getting that old?"

"What are you going to do, Matthew?" Sarah said, an edge of fear in her voice.

"What I always do. Wing it."

"Captain Honeycut. This is Colonel Roger Peterson, U.S. Air Force Reserves. I'm on a private charter to Jacksonville."

"State your air code, sir."

"Air code?" Matt asked Sarah. "What's that?"

"Something new the government instituted. We got problems."

"Hey Captain, I've got it somewhere. Don't make me fish for it."

"State your air code, sir."

"These new punks, no respect," Matt said off the air. "Where are you based, son?"

"Please state your air code, Colonel."

Matt shrugged.

"Tell you the truth, son. I misplaced it. This was a last-minute thing."

"Please follow me down."

"Oh come on. Is that necessary? I'm on a tight schedule."

"Please follow me down."

"If we go down, we're dead," Sarah said, stating the obvious.

"Don't worry. We're not going down," Matt assured, glancing down at his screen. "These rookies usually fly in pairs... There it is, his buddy."

"What's the situation?" the second fighter radioed.

"Private aircraft refuses to give air code," Captain Honeycut explained. "Says he's an Air Force Colonel."

"Did you punch it in?"

"Yes sir. The name checks. Colonel Roger Peterson. But he still refuses to give the code."

"Colonel Peterson, what is the problem, sir?"

"I forgot it," Matt answered. "Can't you boys cut me some slack? I've got some oil tycoon types who need to get to Jacksonville, pronto. I'm going to have a lot of egg on my face if I have to go down and go through a load of red tape."

"You've got to give a code, Colonel. You know that. We're going to have to take you down. Please follow."

Sarah scribbled a note and handed it to Matt. He brightened.

"OK, boys, listen up. I'm going to tell you something, and tell you once. If you don't want to end up flying rusty cargo buckets the rest of your career, you'd better do exactly as I say. Code 667532. EM. FRBO. Say nothing, and get off my tail!"

Inside their cockpits, the two young pilots punched in the code. They were shocked to see their screens flash the top secret identification that came back—*Jonathan Absalom. Emergency Mission. Full Radio Blackout.*"

"Roger. Yes sir," Captain Honeycut acknowledged with a gulp.

The pilots peeled away and scattered like mice into the black night.

"Nice trick," Matt said, sighing in relief. "How long were you going to wait before you pulled that little rabbit out of your hat?"

"It just came to me," Sarah said, surprised herself. "I overheard it once while in the cockpit of Air Force One. The numbers flashed in my head. I didn't even know if they were correct."

"Praise God for flashing numbers. Let's try to get our own code in the future. If they weren't so green, they'd have challenged us."

"We'll work on it. By the way, who's Peterson?"

"An old friend. I knew he was in the reserves. I thought it would fly. Normally it would have, but things are tightening up."

"It's a new world."

After that scare, they made it to Miami without further incident. Matt touched down on a private air strip, and they were taken by car to a small, empty safe house on Flagler Street in the heart of Little Havana. Matt wanted to go for a drive to the beach, but Sarah was nervous about being recognized at checkpoints and talked him out of it. Feeling trapped, he picked up the phone. When Sarah emerged from the bathroom, she was surprised to hear him giving out their address.

"Who's that?"

"Danny."

"Are you sure he's OK? I still have my doubts."

"Yeah, he's OK. I was there when he refused the chip, remember? We've been friends since I was a kid. Aside from everything else we discussed, I just need someone to talk to. I'm crawling the walls."

Twenty minutes later, a series of patterned knocks sounded at the door. Matt opened it. Danny entered with a beaming smile and a vigorous embrace.

"You two look sensational!"

"Life on the run appeals to us," Matt joked.

"It must! So how have you been?"

"Great. We got married."

"Married! To each other?"

"No, we each married someone else," Sarah cracked.

"I never thought I'd see the day. So how's married life, Matt?"

"It's not the way I envisioned it, but then nothing is anymore."

"Yeah. Rough scene with the Pres, Sarah. You guys should have killed that goon when you had the chance."

"I wanted to," Matt said.

"I'll bet you did. So what are you doing here?"

"A conference with the South American leaders. They're having problems with the counterfeit chips. Same as us last year."

"When?"

"Tomorrow morning."

"Where?"

Sarah raised her eyebrows at Danny's inquiries.

"I don't know yet. Got to keep these things secret. How about you? I heard you're still flying for the airlines. How'd you manage that?"

"I'm not sure. The chip system is a little sloppy. I think because I put all the paperwork in that day, it was registered in the computer that I got it. I just said it was defective and I was waiting for a new one. Same thing you guys did later when the hackers got wise. By the time someone—that jerk Blankenship to be exact—got suspicious, the counterfeits were available. I was one of the first to try it out. Works like a charm," Danny explained, tapping his right wrist. "I even made Captain."

"Congratulations," Matt said. "That's amazing."

"It certainly is," Sarah seconded, a trace of doubt in her voice.

"You guys want to go out, get something to eat? Bet you haven't had black beans and rice in years."

"That'd be great!" Matt said. "I'm dying to have... " He looked at Sarah. She shook her head. "Guess not. Too risky. Especially in this neighborhood. Someone might recognize me from the past."

"From the past? How about from the 'wanted' posters I've seen all over the planet?"

"That too." Matt laughed.

For the next hour, the three caught up on old times. Matt and Sarah slipped in their testimony about how happy they were since they committed their lives to God and had the opportunity to study Jesus' teachings and grow as Christians. As Matt predicted, Danny was extremely interested in Sarah's transformation, peppering her with questions about turning away from Judaism, her spiritual growth since making the commitment, and most of all, her decision to abandon her powerful government position and cushy existence for a much harsher life on the run.

"I realize now how empty that life was," Sarah explained. "I was acting out of a twisted sense of patriotism and loyalty, at first to a single country, then later to a misguided ideal about uniting the world under one benevolent hand. In reality, we were uniting it like oxen under a single whip. Now the goals are so much greater, and so much more fulfilling. Christianity is facing its toughest challenge ever, and it's up to people like us to keep it going. It's as if we've been personally charged with keeping the memory of Jesus alive. We've been re-educating people about his teachings and his great sacrifice. You can't imagine how rewarding this is. What I did before doesn't even come close."

Danny was silent for a moment. Matt could tell he was moved by Sarah's comments. He appeared confused, torn over what to do.

"I guess you're just working for a better boss, now," he quipped, clumsily making a joke to break the tension.

"That's for sure," Matt agreed.

"I'd like to talk to you some more about this," Danny said. "It's one thing to talk about God, but to really see it take hold in someone's life, like it has with you two, that's impressive. I'll drop by tomorrow after the meeting. Give me a call."

"OK. Great to see you," Matt said, putting his arm around his friend and showing him to the door.

After he left, Sarah and Matt walked out on the porch to enjoy the night air. They could hear the muted strains of lively salsa music drifting in from a distant party.

"You sure you trust him?" Sarah asked.

"We've had to trust a whole lot of people, Sarah—virtually all of them strangers. If we can't trust our friends, who can we trust?"

"His story is way off. To go that long without the chip? The counterfeits weren't available for nearly a year. I can't see him lasting that long in an airline job where he was constantly being checked."

"I thought of that. He's probably got a real chip. Broke down after the deadline and went in again. He's listed as a sympathizer on some lists, which would support my theory. But we've trusted other sympathizers."

"He's lying, and that scares me. You think we should change houses?"

"No. If he was going to sell us out, they'd already be here. Besides, what you said really affected him. That was worth the risk right there. We gave it our best shot. Now it's up to him to once and for all choose his way."

Five miles down Flagler Street, Danny pulled into the far end of the parking lot of a Cuban grocery store. A tall, thin man in a dark suit emerged from the shadows and entered Danny's vehicle.

"Did you plant the transmitter?" the man demanded.

"In her purse. They're going to some kind of big meeting tomorrow with Christians from South America."

"Good. That's when the transmitter will activate. We'll probably grab them there."

"You promised that nothing will happen to Matt. You'll let him go. Right?"

"That was the deal. Absalom doesn't want Slade. He just wants the woman."

"You're not going to hurt her? She's a lot different than she used to be."

"He just wants to talk to her. Try to convince her to come back to him. He'll probably let her go afterward. Don't worry."

"When will you let my mother and sister go?"

"Tomorrow. After we capture the woman."

"If you've hurt them... "

"They're fine. This is just business. Government business. There's no need to harm your family as long as you perform."

"Was there a need to kidnap them?"

"It worked, didn't it?"

"What if Matt hadn't called me?"

"He would have, eventually. What are you so upset about? You'll get your money. Enough for ten kings. You can buy your mother and sister matching mansions."

"I don't want your blood money. I just want my family back."

"You'll get them back, and the money. That's the way we want it. It helps ease our guilt," the man said with a sarcastic laugh. "We'll meet here tomorrow night at ten. We'll have your mom, your sister, and a big fat government check. Don't be late."

The man left the car and disappeared into the night.

Danny lowered his head onto the steering wheel and cried.

"Dear God, forgive me."

The next morning, a car arrived and took Matt and Sarah to a palatial home owned by a South American recording artist. It had recently been rebuilt at Gables by the Sea, an exclusive suburb of Coral Gables. Waiting inside were thirty representatives from South America. After introductions, they got right to work.

The debate over the counterfeit chips was hot. Matt and Sarah, frustrated in their attempts to heal the division, began to outline how they faced the issue in America and what had resulted. Just as they were beginning to make some headway, a security officer came running into the room.

"We've got an army of police and government agents on the way!"

"How close?" Matt asked.

"Half a mile, and closing fast."

"Danny!" Sarah said, her eyes wide with fear and fury. "Danny!"

"Is that boat out back operational?" Matt asked.

Someone nodded.

"OK, you guys scatter," Matt ordered, addressing the frightened delegates. "Take off your suits and filter through the neighborhood. Find some homes under construction and blend in as workers. They're looking for me and Sarah, so you should be OK."

With that, Matt and Sarah dashed outside, hopped into the twenty-foot ski boat, and cranked it up. They roared out of the channel toward the ocean.

Matt, sensing danger, cut the engines as they hung a sharp right and approached the mouth of the channel. Bobbing in the water in front of them were five massive Coast Guard cutters, each one packed with soldiers pointing rifles.

"Kill your engine and wait to be boarded," a voice ordered over a loudspeaker.

"Can we go back?" Sarah wondered.

"Negative. We're trapped," Matt answered, nodding to the wall of armed soldiers and police officers that had sprung up like magic and were now lining the canal banks behind them. "They must have been hiding there all along. We played right into their hands."

Matt and Sarah were handcuffed in the ski boat and escorted back to the house, running the gauntlet of stoic soldiers and police lining the banks. Hundreds more surrounded the two-story, Mediterranean-style home. The house was empty. Despite the massive show of force, the South American representatives had apparently escaped.

Matt was taken in a car and whisked straight to the airport, where he was immediately flown to Washington. Sarah was on the same jet, but the two were kept in separate sections.

During the flight, Matt recalled the afternoon Danny went in to be chipped. He remembered Danny showing him his wrist. Suddenly the entire scene flashed through his mind. He cringed and buried his face in his hands. Danny had tapped his left wrist, not his right.

There was no cute nurse in line with Danny that afternoon. The triple fist impression that shook him so much had been on his own right wrist.

In Washington, Jonathan Absalom opened his daily briefing by hanging his head and lifelessly asking the same question he had asked at every meeting for the past two years. This time, there was no answer. He looked up and saw the smiling faces of his chief aides.

"You got her?"

"We got her. Slade too," an aide announced.

"Where?" Absalom demanded, leaping from his seat.

"Miami. This morning. They're on the way."

"How?"

"Slade's friend, Danny Simpson. We knew they'd get together one day."

"Good. Kill the guy."

"Slade?"

"No, not yet. Simpson. Don't pay the rat a dime. He sold out his best friend. I hate finks."

"Our people had his mother and sister."

"It doesn't matter. Sarah and Slade are far more valuable than his family. He's still a rat. Let them go, but get rid of him."

The aides looked uneasily at one another. A CIA representative nodded for a cohort to pick up a phone and issue the death order.

"When's she arriving?" Absalom demanded, unable to contain his excitement.

"Within the hour."

"Bring her here, to the White House. Take Slade to the CIA building for interrogation. What's on the agenda today?"

"We have an uprising in... "

"Forget that," Absalom said, waving the problems away. "Cancel everything for the rest of the day."

"But...."

"I want her here as soon as she arrives, got that?"

The aides nodded in unison. Absalom dashed out of the meeting room and headed back to his bedroom. He combed his hair, put on cologne, then, like a nervous schoolboy, changed his suit twice. He went back to the Oval Office to wait.

Time dragged as he paced the room. He checked for updates every two minutes, getting more agitated by the moment. Finally, there was a knock at the office door.

"Come in."

Four men burst into the room, dragging Sarah with them. They practically threw her inside. Her hair was disheveled and her eyes darted like a frightened animal. Absalom was stunned by her wild appearance. Even so, she still looked beautiful.

"Please, wait outside," he said to his men.

"I don't think that's wise. She's a trained sold... "

"Wait outside," the President ordered.

The men reluctantly left.

"Sarah, you're looking, ah, interesting."

She glared at him.

"I've missed you. More than I imagined. I'd like to start over."

She stared at him incredulously.

"You're all I've thought about for the past two years. I love you. I know that now. We belong together. Like it was before."

"After what you tried to do to me? Never!"

"I'm sorry for that. You don't know how much I've regretted it. I lost a great deal of popularity. My approval rating dropped like a stone. It fueled this crazy underground thing of yours, and that's really been a pain. There have been rebellions around the world, all because of that night. Believe me, Sarah, it has caused me great anguish. I've been punished dearly for my terrible mistake."

"Not dearly enough."

Absalom approached. Sarah backed away.

"I want you to reconsider. I'll divorce my wife. We can get married. How's that? Wasn't that the problem before? My marriage?"

"No."

"Then what? Just name it. Anything in the world can be yours. You want to rule a country? A continent? How about Europe? You can have all of Europe—and the Middle East, too. Let Israel swallow the whole region. Wouldn't you like that?"

"You tried to rape me! How can I ever forget that?"

"You were never raped."

"I would have been. And now you want to marry me?"

"I was drunk. Angry. You hurt me. I've never been beaten up like that. I wasn't thinking straight. Please forgive me. I love you, Sarah. I need you. It's not the same without you."

"I can forgive you, Jonathan, but I can never be your wife. I can never work for you again. I'm a Christian now... "

"Don't say that. Don't tell me that."

"I'm telling you. I'm a Christian. I can never accept the chip."

"You don't have to. You can even keep your religion. Just denounce it publicly, and you can do whatever you want in private."

"I can't do that. Not to God. Not to myself. Not to the others."

"Please," he said, trying to embrace her. "I need you."

She pushed him away. "No!"

"Stop this now!" he demanded, his blood rising.

"You stop it. You said I can have anything I want. Well here's what I want. Let me go. Let Matt go. If you really love me, that's what you'll do."

"That's the one thing you can't have. As for your friend, he will have to be punished like the others."

"He's not my friend," Sarah said angrily. "He's my husband! And if you kill him, you'll have to kill me."

Sarah regretted revealing that she had married the rebel leader the minute the words left her mouth.

"He's your *husband?*" Absalom said weakly, collapsing into a chair. "You married our enemy? Oh, Sarah, why?"

"Because I love him. I always have. And if you hurt him, I'll hate you forever."

"It's too late," he said, speaking in an odd, tortured voice. "Too late for that. Too late for everything. You've been defiled. Defiled in the flesh and in the spirit. You gave your precious body to a swine. You dirtied your soul with a false religion. My dear Sarah, I'm so sorry. I'm so sorry I have to do this. I wish there was another way."

"You're insane, Jonathan. You need help. Can't you see it? We can help you. Join with us. Let God heal you."

Absalom pressed a button, signaling the agents to come into the room.

"Take her away. Take her to the tank with Slade. I never want to see her again!"

In the basement of the CIA building, Matt Slade was being viciously interrogated. By Absalom's orders, he was stripped to his boxer shorts, tied to a ceiling pipe, and questioned about the rebels. Of specific interest was the location of the still-secret Montana headquarters. When Matt refused to answer, he was whipped and beaten.

The process began slowly because nobody in the CIA had a bullwhip. When Absalom issued the strange order, an agent had to scour the Yellow Pages to find a country western store in the Capital that sold them. When one was finally purchased, no one knew how to use it. Matt was slashed across the legs, buttocks, arms and head before the agents got the hang of this forgotten method of torture.

"Nice shot," Matt cracked through clenched teeth as the latest off-target blow sailed up around his shoulders.

"We should have just given him electric shock treatment," the chief agent said, turning his face away. "It's more effective and less ugly. We're ripping this guy apart."

"Yeah, and the guy's a war hero," another agent added. "I never thought I'd see the day when we'd torture one of our own Medal of Honor guys like this."

"Times have changed."

An hour of the brutal and frequently botched Old West-style interrogation left Matt bleeding, battered, and nearly unconscious. His ripped flesh caused so much pain that his nervous system was on the verge of collapse. Just as the agents were about to quit, Absalom rushed into the room, his eyes burning insanely.

"He looks too good!" the President ranted, grabbing the whip off a nearby table. "I'll show you how to thrash a prisoner!"

The President's first effort missed completely. His second was a foot wide. The third struck Matt too far in from the end, doing no damage. The fourth hit the pipe and wrapped around it. When Absalom tried to yank it free, he fell to the floor. Seething with rage and frustration, the President rose and threw the dangling handle of the whip at Matt, missing again. He ran toward the pilot and faced him.

"She was mine!" he screamed, punching Matt in the body. "Mine," he repeated, stretching up on his toes to crash a right across Matt's jaw. The agents turned their heads in shame and embarrassment as the President continued to pummel the defenseless pilot.

"Can't we stop this?" a veteran agent asked his boss.

"Who's going to risk it? You?"

The sounds and sights in the room faded as Matt passed into unconsciousness. The pain disappeared. In his dream, Matt found himself walking alone at night on a quiet beach. Still aware of what he had just been through, he touched his chest, face, and back, searching for blood. It was gone.

He saw a figure in the distance, looking out onto the water. As he approached, he could see it was a woman, wearing a flowing wedding dress, her face covered by a long veil. When he reached her, she turned to face him, then slowly raised her hands to lift the veil.

"Jill!" he shouted, embracing her with all his strength. "You've come back! Thank God."

When he looked at her again, the sadness in her eyes told him that wasn't the case.

"You haven't come back?"

She shook her head.

"Have I died? Is this heaven?"

"No, sweetie. You chose this setting because you remember how nice it was the last time we were walking along a beach at night. Do you remember?"

"After the hurricane. The waves were so big they scared you."

"They did. But it was still nice. It was one of the last times we were together."

Matt was overwhelmed with emotion. "I don't know what this is, but we're together now. I'm going to take advantage of it while I can."

"We don't have much time. Your circumstances don't allow for it."

"What circum..." Matt began. Then he realized that he must be close to death. "Oh." He stepped back and looked at her in the wedding dress. "Are we going to get married?"

"No," she said, smiling. "You never saw me in this dress. That moment was taken from you, so the longing remains in your mind. What do you think?"

"You look beautiful. Wonderful. Better than I imagined during all those lonely nights wondering what happened to you. I was so afraid it was something terrible. That you were being hurt ... "

Jill's eyes welled with tears.

"I wasn't. That's behind us, Matt. You must hang on now. I know it's bad. I know you're in a lot of pain, but you're going to make it through this and go on. And it's important that you continue. You still have so much to accomplish."

"Can't we accomplish it together?"

"I'm on the other side," she said, shaking her head again. "Besides, you have another."

Matt hung his head. "I'm so sorry about that. You have to understand. I didn't think you were coming back..."

"You don't need to explain," she said. "You don't have to feel guilty. This is the way it was intended to be. Sarah is strong in ways I'm not. She was right for this, for what she has to do. What you have to do. She has the knowledge to help the children. Don't despair, Matt. I still love you."

"I've never stopped caring about you. You know that."

"I know."

"Why couldn't we have been together? Why did all this happen to us?"

"It just did. And we should be proud. My purpose was to plant the seed in you. Then you were to bring her into the fold. We almost lost her in the sky. We almost lost you in Israel. But it worked out."

"Can we walk?" Matt asked.

Jill shook her head. "You've got to go back."

"Now?"

She nodded.

"Hang on, Matt," she said, slowly backing away. "I'm so proud of you. I'm proud to have been a small part of it."

"Will I see you again?" Matt asked, stretching out his hand. It was too late. The dream was over.

EIGHTEEN

The pain returned with such an agonizing onslaught that Matt thought he had been sucked through the sand and sent straight into hell. When he opened his swollen eyes, he was again staring into the demented, snarling face of the President. Spit flew from insane leader's twisted mouth as he continued to flail at Matt, cursing and screaming insults.

Absalom pounded away until he grew so exhausted that he could no longer lift his arms to strike his defenseless victim. Drenched in sweat and reeking of stale alcohol, he bent over to catch his breath. Recovering, he peered up demonically, shouted a final slur, clutched his heaving chest, and staggered out of the room.

Matt managed a smile as warm blood dripped into his eyes and fell in puddles to the floor.

At the Washington Monument, curious tourists and onlookers were drawn by workers hammering two wooden posts into the ground in front of the pale monolith. A platform with the United Earth Presidential seal—the three intertwining arms—stood to the right of the posts, its podium covered with microphones. Two building-sized video screens were planted on each side of the monument. Twenty-five television camera crews were busy setting up in front. The grounds around the monument were covered with television trucks with tall towers and sprawling satellite dishes. Military jeeps and armored trucks bordered the media vehicles.

The commotion continued to draw crowds to the area as the news spread that something big was about to happen. The posts, podium, and crowd shots were broadcast live on television, bringing in tens of thousands more as the afternoon progressed.

By six P.M., more than 100,000 people were gathered on the lawn. The crowd hummed with anticipation as they stared at the twin posts on the elevated hill. The setting sun cast a quarter-mile shadow off the towering monument, creating a line of darkness that split the huge crowd like a staff of death.

Suddenly Jonathan Absalom appeared unannounced at the podium. The crowd hushed as one. The United Earth President's hair was combed and sprayed. He was dressed in an expensive suit and bore little resemblance to the unkempt, raving maniac at Matt's throat just hours before.

"I have a wonderful announcement to make today," he opened. "After a long and courageous hunt, the violent leaders of the anti-United Earth underground have been captured."

Absalom turned and stretched his hand toward a white van parked near the monument.

"There!" he sounded. "Behold."

The crowd buzzed as Sarah was dragged out by four men, taken to the post closest to the President, and tied to it with ropes around her waist, hips, and feet.

"And there!" the President said, pointing to a second van on the other side. The crowd gasped as Matt Slade was dragged shirtless and unconscious to the other post, where he was lashed to it in a similar fashion. The crowd moaned and recoiled at the sight of his blood-encrusted, horribly mutilated body.

Sarah screamed in agony when she saw her beaten husband, a long, anguished cry that silenced the throng and echoed to the back rows of the mob. The scream also hit an emotional cord with the billions watching around the world on television.

The cameras closed in on Matt's maimed face and body. The twin video screens enabled the live crowd to witness what the worldwide television audience saw. The people were repulsed and angered by the obvious torture that had been inflicted upon the highly decorated soldier. As the cameras pulled back again, their anger turned to horror as the crowd realized that the President planned to publicly execute the two former military heroes—including the woman everyone suspected had rejected his advances. The mob on the lawn began to murmur their disgust.

An alert Secret Service agent picked up on the unrest. At his signal, a company of heavily armed soldiers poured out of trucks parked on both sides of the unruly crowd and formed a barrier in front of them.

Absalom, blinded by his vengeance, was oblivious both to the ugly mood of the crowd and to the nightmarish public relations disaster he was about to unleash. He walked over to Sarah.

"Don't make me do this to you," he pleaded. "If you renounce Christianity and agree to follow me, I'll let your husband live."

Sarah's eyes flushed defiance and exhilaration.

"No," she said. "I am a child of God."

The sound of his wife's voice cut through Matt's mental darkness and helped him regain consciousness. He lifted his head, looked out over the throng, and began to lift his blood-streaked right arm. He clenched his fist and strained mightily to raise it in a tortured half circle over his head. Each movement was amplified dramatically by the oversized shadow, projected on the wall of the monument by the television lights.

As the crowd watched, Matt lifted his left arm and crossed it at the wrists in the same semi-circle, forming the symbol of the Christian movement. The shadow cast by his arms spread fifty feet up the monument wall.

On the other side, as the crowd continued to watch in stunned silence, Sarah similarly lifted her right arm, then her left, and crossed them at the wrists to form the symbol. Her shadow was projected with equal size and clarity on the monument wall.

Slowly, arms began to rise in the crowd. The television cameras spun on their tripods to capture the dramatic, spontaneous reaction of the people. Row by row, in an awesome wave, arms lifted and crossed until most of the throng were standing with their crossed arms held high.

Absalom turned and looked out over the crowd. The worshipful looks in their faces filled his demented soul with rage.

"Glory to God in the Highest," someone shouted from the center of the crowd. The proclamation was repeated by a faint voice from the far back and echoed by a woman off to the left. Soon, the entire crowd took up the chant. "Glory to God! *Glory to God!*"

Absalom remained unmoved. He turned and ordered the soldiers to fire on Matt and Sarah. Instead, two thirds of the young men and women dropped their weapons and vanished into the crowd.

The remaining soldiers raised their weapons and took aim. As they waited for Absalom to drop his own uplifted arm, the crowd surged forward, engulfing the remaining soldiers, and wrenching their weapons from their hands.

An older man emerged from the crowd and slowly walked up to Absalom. He pulled a large knife from a sheath on his hip.

"I can't allow you to hurt any more of God's children," James Welby said as Absalom backed away. "If your daddy could see you today, he'd hang his head in shame."

Welby took another step forward, turned sharply to his right, and cut the ropes binding Sarah to the post. He then walked over to Matt.

"I thought Eli's boy might do something stupid like this in public," Welby said, slicing through Matt's bindings and freeing the pilot. "We were countin' on it."

"I'm glad he did," Matt said weakly, stretching his battered arms.

"You look terrible," Welby said with a smile as he inspected Matt's bruised face.

"Thanks. If I'd have known I was going to be on worldwide television, I'd have fixed myself up better."

Matt nearly collapsed in Sarah's arms. With her strength supporting him, he approached Absalom.

"You can join us, Jonathan," he said. "You can be forgiven... "

"Shoot them! Shoot them!" Absalom shouted at the soldiers. None responded.

"Looks like you lost this one," Matt said.

"This isn't over!" Absalom screamed, shaking his fist first at them, and then upward at God. "I'm still the leader of the whole world."

Matt kissed Sarah and struggled to stand on his own. As Welby followed, they moved past the disarmed soldiers and stopped in front of the now cheering throng.

"I'll get you yet," Absalom yelled, falling to his knees, his voice hoarse with rage and frustration. "There's no place in my world for you to hide!"

Welby shook his head sadly and put his arm around both Matt and Sarah. The crowd began to part, forming a narrow passageway as far as the eye could see. The three stepped into the river of grass as the protective path closed behind them.

"You can't hide," Absalom cried out again. "This isn't over."

More fiction from Servant Publications

Bloodlines
by John Jenkins and Mark Weaver

In this action-packed novel, a young couple, Mark and Katie MacDonald, discover the answer to the question, "Whence comes evil?"

Heirs to a family legacy, a beautiful home, and a troubling history, Mark and Katie are soon caught up in mysterious and life-threatening events. The remarkable discovery of Sam MacDonald's Civil War journals beckons Mark and Katie to trace the MacDonald line back to one of the darkest hours of American history. Here they realize both their roots and their calling. And like Sam, they are propelled into spiritual warfare and a bloody battle for the nation's soul.

Why is their adversary hell-bent on their destruction? Mark and Katie contend with powers who delight in shedding innocent blood and drawing bloodlines throughout history.

But Mark and Katie are also heirs of another bloodline, one that flows from their Master. And they have unseen allies who help them in their battle to put life over death.

Whence comes evil? Sam faced the darkness. But will Mark and Katie find the strength to do battle, both for themselves and the generations to follow? *$10.99*